megan squires

Cover art by Cassy Roop of Pink Ink Designs
Editing by Kerry Genova with Indie Solutions,
www.murphyrae.net
Interior Design by Jovana Shirley, Unforeseen Editing,
www.unforeseenediting.com

ALSO BY MEGAN SQUIRES

Demanding Ransom
The Rules of Regret
Draw Me In
Love Like Crazy

*To my readers who have stuck with me
this past year and a half.
Thank you for letting me pick up right where we left off.*

Part One

November 2004

One

Mallory

"I couldn't remember if he wanted cerulean or cobalt, so he's gonna have his pick of the blues."

Nana laughed into the receiver, a hearty, warm sound that reminded me of the apple pies she baked at the first sign of fall when the leaves gave up their green for rustier shades. How someone could make a noise almost edible must've been a talent reserved solely for grandmothers, I figured, and Nana had certainly perfected her recipe.

I slipped the crinkled plastic bag into my backpack and slid my shoulders into the armholes, leveling out the uneven weight digging against my shoulder blades. With my schoolbooks already in the bag, it didn't leave much room, but a promise was a promise and I wasn't about to let him down. Not today. Not any day.

"Can you tell Tommy I'm on my way back?"

"Of course," Nana said. "Be careful out there, Mallory. The roads are slick and you know all the crazies come out after dark. I worry about you. I always worry … like it's my job."

"No need, Nana. It's only four thirty, I'm on a bike, and you should be enjoying retirement. These are your golden years. Live it up. Get a country club membership or a new manicure or maybe buy yourself something sparkly." I chuckled into the phone pressed to my cheek as I unlocked my vintage Schwinn from the lamppost outside B Street Art Supplies. The chain clanged against the frame with a metallic clinking. I hopped onto the bike. The seat was cold on my jeans and I shivered under the discomfort and then pedaled quickly down the sidewalk to try to draw some warmth to my muscles. I felt that addictive and invigorating burn in my quads as I raced over the pavement. Picking up speed, the wind burned my face and bit my roughened and chapped lips, dry from winter's unforgiving chill. It was freezing, but I loved this. Being out in the frigid elements only made the warm harbor of shelter that much cozier. Juxtapositions were beautiful when they were in their most extreme. "See you in a jiffy, Nana!"

With a toss of my phone into the wicker basket attached to the handlebars, I pushed up to stand against the pedals and sped through town, my legs and mind having memorized every turn, every intersection and stop like an intricately choreographed routine. It was only ten minutes before I rounded the last corner, my tires gripping what little salty pavement remained exposed, and I pulled into the driveway of our modest three-bedroom home, the one I took my first steps in, and where I would likely take my last. I couldn't imagine ever being anywhere else and I couldn't imagine any other location for this life of ours. It was a good place and it was a good life. I figured I'd stay here as long as I could.

I saw Nana's silhouette dance against the orange glow through the kitchen window, the one draped with the embroidered white linen she'd sewn for its covering. Her hazy figure disappeared the moment she spotted me trekking up the walkway. She was at the door with a smile and a hug ready for the taking and I dove into her open and readied embrace, my snow dusted jacket pressed firmly to her large chest, thawing me upon contact. Before I could fully snuggle in, she held me out at arm's length, surveying head to toe with a keen eye. Clumps of melting slush fell to my feet, puddled dots of half-water, half-ice.

"Made it home unscathed, looks like," she said, nearly satisfied though not completely. As though checking every inch for a blemish, even looking behind my ears, she ultimately released me from her grip with a satisfied sigh. "Go wash up for dinner." She twisted her hands in her red and white checkered apron. "Pot roast and sweet potatoes. Your favorite."

"Is he downstairs?" I asked as I fished the store bag from my backpack before dropping my school things to the hallway bench. "His room?"

"In the study today." Nana held her hands together through the cotton fabric. "Better light in there, you know."

The den was at the easternmost side of the house, which meant he'd been there since morning, the only time of day when light—ethereal in nature—streamed in abundance through the large arched bay window. When I was a little girl, I'd curl up on the window seat and watch the dust float like glitter suspended miraculously in air. I'd collect Mason jars full of it, never knowing I was storing away mites and allergens, only figuring I'd captured my own little bit of magic in that precious glass bottle. That room and what he created within it was magic to me. To everyone, really. Surely that would permeate the air, too.

With quick strides, I jogged down the hallway. I hadn't shed my boots at the door and I now left dirty puddles in my wake, but I was too excited to worry about that. I'd clean it up later if Nana didn't get to it first, which I knew she would. She had a real thing for cleanliness.

The door was slightly ajar, and though he wouldn't likely answer, I still offered the courtesy of knocking.

"I couldn't remember," I said, toeing open the door to allow me through after a respectable pause. With a paint tube in each hand, I held up the two shades of blue I'd purchased from the store. I flicked them back and forth like the swing of a pendulum. "Which one had you run out of?"

Though the overhead lights were off—in reality probably never switched on—the last dregs of daylight funneled into the window, giving my eyes just enough assistance so I could see today's artistic expression. And, like always, it was a breathtaking one. My heart stuttered and my throat instantly lumped up, a ball of emotion lodged within it.

"Wow," I whispered as I made my way to the canvas propped on his easel in the center of the room. Today's masterpiece. "You've outdone yourself with this one."

It was abstract—like the good majority of his paintings—but this was different from the others. Where he usually preferred precise lines dissecting the colors, mood, and flow of his work, this painting blurred any boundary between shades and tones. All distinction was gone. It was swirling and twisting, absolute confusion articulated on the canvas with his brushes and oils.

It felt like it could be his self-portrait.

"I love this."

His deep brown eyes hadn't strayed from their fixated and focused gaze on his work. When I spoke, though, I could see the way his right eyelid twitched upward, a slight hint of movement, a glimmer of adjustment, like the grabbing focus of a camera lens. His body language, though sometimes reserved to the flutter of eyelids, was something I'd become in tune with over the last six years. I could read the recognition in them—the hellos and goodbyes, the please stay or please go's. I spoke his language fluently.

"Tommy, this is phenomenal," I told him, awe infiltrating my tone. "Is this one for the café or for keeps?"

One blink.

We'd be giving this away.

I knew I shouldn't be saddened by it—that there was no way we could keep all of his paintings without renting out a decent-sized storage unit to house them—but this is one I'd love to have. I felt him in the colors; I saw him in the strokes.

For some reason beyond any logic I could come up with, part of me thought that maybe if I studied this particular work hard enough, maybe I could break that barrier. I knew there was a piece of every artist held within their artwork, and I was sure my dad was in his somewhere. In *there* somewhere.

I looked to him, noticing that the damp cloth draped around his neck was in need of changing. With gingerly steps, so as not to startle, I crossed the room and took the fabric between my fingers, swiping his chin clean as I swept his graying hair from his eyes.

I'm sure my dad is in there somewhere, I thought to myself again as I stared down at him, at the same tired eyes his mother wore earlier, at the drawn expression and lazy downturn of his mouth.

I offered a small smile, the biggest one my heart was capable of manufacturing and switched my gaze over to the painting. He was in those colors. He was in the textures. He was in the paint. My dad was in there. Of course he was. He had to be.

"I love it," I said again, because if artists were embedded in a piece of their work, then it almost felt like a piece of me was saying *I love you* rather than *it*, and it felt genuine and right and long overdue. "I *love* it," I emphasized once more, giving his shoulders the slightest of squeezes.

Then I saw his reply, four sporadic blinks in return, but I pieced them together in my head and in my heart.

And I knew that he loved me back.

Two

Heath

"Grilled cheese, slathered in mayo and toasted on one side only. Pickle and barbecue chips. Strawberry lemonade. No ice."

I shot a glance over to Dom as I dumped the black plastic tub onto the Formica counter. The bucket was loaded with dirty dishes encrusted and caked with uneaten food, and my forearms killed from hauling it around the diner for the past hour. I flexed my hands and then balled them into fists to relieve some of the pressure, and it helped, only a little, though. It probably meant I should get back in the gym. I was turning into a serious weakling.

"How do you even know her order?"

Dom flicked his greasy hair back with a swift jerk of his head. He'd been asked by Sal to wear a hairnet, but there was no way Dom would be caught dead in one. Apparently, he preferred to risk his job over following health codes. "Because she's weird as hell. Orders the same thing every single Tuesday. Hard to forget crazy like that."

He was right, she was a little different, but I wouldn't go so far as to call her weird. Quirky, maybe. Quirky was harmless.

I looked at her as discretely as possible, but even if I were full-on gawking, I didn't think she'd notice. She was engrossed in the laminated menu in front of her and had ear buds tucked deep into her ears, her red hair curled around them. Why she would need a menu was beyond me since Dom said she was a regular with a "usual," but she appeared so lost in thought I didn't think anyone could break through it. A gargantuan jacket swallowed her whole, and she hadn't taken off the rainbow-striped mittens from her hands. She looked like she was prepared for the blizzard of the century, but the diner was a comfortably warm eighty degrees. Maybe it was from working my ass off for the past four hours, but I definitely had sweat collecting on my brow.

"She's kinda cute," I offered with a noncommittal shrug and emptied my dishes into the sink to make room so I could go back to bussing. When I looked back to her, her mouth outlined whatever words echoed from her headphones, and she swayed a bit in a seated dance on her barstool, her eyelids slipping shut, totally lost and content. It was adorable and I felt the smile sneak onto my lips.

"You need your eyes checked, Bro."

"Whatever," was all the comeback I had.

Dom was right about her order, and the way she ate it wasn't any less bizarre. It was one bite of grilled cheese, two tiny nibbles of pickle, one long swallow of lemonade followed by three chips. I felt like a stalker that I was even aware of the science to it, but I couldn't help but watch. She'd bit off her knit gloves with her teeth, one finger at a time, and arranged them on the counter so they were positioned one above the other, the fingers fitted together like a jigsaw puzzle. Then she picked up her sandwich, careful to flip it over so she couldn't see the grill-lined underbelly, which left only the mayonnaise-coated side. Which was totally gross, but something about it didn't seem gross because I was enamored by the detailed thought and meticulous purpose behind everything she did.

At some point in the evening, things picked up and I actually had to do my job. That meant I wasn't free to study this strange girl's even stranger eating habits any longer. I supposed that was probably a good thing because I'd developed an unhealthy interest in the way she prepared and consumed her dinner. Dom said she was a regular customer. That would mean all my Tuesdays would be shot to hell from here on out if I remained this transfixed on her. My schedule had recently changed and now I only worked Tuesday, Thursday, and Friday. I needed to focus during more than two-thirds of my shifts. My paycheck depended on it.

The Blue Duck Diner shut down at ten every night— eleven on weekends—but Sal, my boss, always instructed me to leave early. I had school in the morning and apparently there were child labor laws, all which worked to my benefit since I had one more year until adulthood. It meant I didn't have to stay and close up. I left that dirty work to guys like Dom who were already eighteen and didn't have school or curfew or laws protecting them from working a little too hard for a few too many hours.

The diner had one of those vintage Mickey Mouse clocks where his arms and hands would spin around his body like a contortionist, and when he twisted impossibly to the ten o'clock position, I clocked out, giving a wave and a holler to my coworkers as I shouldered the door open, slipping my beanie onto my head. The diner's bell chimed and I was greeted with a blast of icy air that felt like a cheese grater against my skin. It had been snowing with a vengeance for the last three weeks. At first, everyone got excited by that initial snowflake. How quickly we forgot that those downy white flutters quickly turned into black sludge that collected against the curbs and wedged cars in driveways as ice barricades. Winter was angry this year, and I was ready for Mother Nature to stop with the PMS.

My family's apartment was three blocks down from my work. Dad had offered me his car, but I figured waiting for it to warm up, along with scraping the sheet of ice from the windshield, would amount to work that didn't outweigh the benefit of temporary shelter. Instead, I just pulled my wool scarf tighter to my neck and jammed my hands into my pockets. I kept my arms flush to my sides in an effort to trap the heat to my body, but what resulted was a waddle that made me look like a penguin.

Which would've been fine had I been alone, without any witnesses.

But I wasn't alone. Grilled cheese girl was there.

Well, not really *there*, but up ahead peddling clumsily on her bike. She looked like she'd just gotten her training wheels removed. The only thing that seemed less uncertain than walking on an ice-coated sidewalk was *biking* on an ice-coated sidewalk. While the tread of my shoes slipped against the pavement, her tires wobbled in an uncoordinated way and it made me hold my breath tightly in my lungs. That hurt. Crazy bad. Everything hurt when you were freezing from the outside in. It was like I was watching a circus performer on a unicycle, waiting for one false move, one slip or fall.

It occurred to me that I'd been waiting for that false move all night. I had to admit, it was mildly refreshing to see her a little out of control like this. Her meal at the diner had been so controlled that it made me wonder about her. It made me question whether every aspect of her life was as methodically planned and executed. I couldn't imagine living like that. It would feel like a trap, a sort of prison, I supposed, and that seemed awful.

Seeing her weave and slide back and forth on the walkway made me smile.

Maybe that made me sick, but I didn't care. It was just my natural response to her.

And apparently my other natural response was to jog as briskly as I could to match her pace. I suddenly found myself gaining speed, my boots pounding the pavement, legs racing to catch up. And then, as the red *DON'T WALK* hand flashed on the light in the intersection, I was right at her side.

And she was on the ground.

I hadn't meant to startle her, but I guess when I said, "Hi,"—or more accurately screamed it—something about the act pushed her completely off her bicycle and onto the icy ground. She'd turned into an upside down turtle wearing a ridiculously large parka.

Words came out louder when you breathed heavier. Like all that extra air added volume, too. So I'd screamed at her. I felt horrible. And awkward. Why had I felt the need to run up to her? And why did I shout out my hello? God, I was terrible at this whole life thing. And now she was on the ground, her bike a crumpled metal heap on top of her body. Hurriedly, I bent down to lift the bicycle from her. I set it to the side and then offered my hand, not sure how else to repair this.

She looked up. "Holy crap, you're cute."

Well, that wasn't what I was expecting.

"Actually, I'm Heath," I said. And I winked at her. I freaking winked, like the idiot I was. I slipped my hand further into the gap between us and I waited for her to take hold, but maybe she didn't like to hold hands with idiots. That would be reasonable of her. For a split second, my insides spasmed as I wondered whether she'd take my hand or not. Why I was nervous, I had no clue, but I felt it buzz throughout my body. It was a sensation that I both loved and hated. Like being electrocuted. Maybe not quite like that, because that probably wasn't enjoyable, but there was definitely a current sweeping and tingling through my body.

"I'm Mallory. Mallory Alcott." Her eyes met mine. Each lash was tipped in white snow and it looked like glitter. "And Heath, has anyone ever told you that you're super adorable?"

"My mom, but she's obligated to think so because she shares half my DNA."

Apparently that was funny. Mallory laughed, a belly deep one, and sort of tossed her head back. It exposed her long, pale neck, which normally I wouldn't find to be a particularly hot body part, but considering it was the dead of winter and every other inch of her was covered, I found it completely hot. My stomach took a nosedive.

"Well, Heath, your mom is correct. Those dimples don't even look real. They're like manmade or something."

"Manmade dimples?"

At this point, Mallory finally took my hand. I never really had a favorite season, but I knew it wasn't winter. Winter had it out for me with its massive coats and gloves and scarves. It was hard to be intimate with so many layers between. Even still, it did feel strangely intimate as I drew her hand toward me. She rose her feet, then bent down to retrieve her pink and white bike from the sidewalk.

"Yes, manmade dimples. Hey, I figure if every other body part can be manufactured, dimples probably can, too. Yours should be the prototype."

Man, this girl was something else. I didn't know what to make of her, but I knew I wanted her to keep talking. It was freezing out—probably below—and we were the only ones on the streets. Everyone else sought shelter because that's what you did when it was dark and snowing and a school night in November.

I wasn't about to go anywhere.

"You have nice hair," I stammered.

"Ah, Heath." She slugged me on the shoulder and it was so startling that I had to plant my feet to avoid swiveling. "You don't owe me anything. I give compliments freely. I learned long ago that you should always say what you're thinking because you never know when the gift of words will be taken from you."

Though she didn't appear any older than me, I knew with that lone assertion that she'd lived much, much more life in those limited years.

And suddenly I found myself wanting to know exactly how she'd spent each and every one.

Three

Mallory

My heart had a voice, and she'd been yammering on and on all night. Tugging at my thoughts and infiltrating my dreams. She was quite the chatterbox. Twice I'd woken up with a racing pulse, my chest tight, and stomach feeling hollow and weightless like that first dip on a roller coaster. By the third interruption, I decided to get up. Sleep was not going to be had.

As I tiptoed down the hall, I saw an intermittent light flickering through Nana's door, which was cracked open a few inches, keeping her very much a part of the home as opposed to the somber room with the door locked shut at the end of the hall downstairs. Murmuring voices and canned laughter trilled in predictable measures from Grandma's quarters. She'd probably fallen asleep with the television on again. Grandmas did that. But Grandmas were also once mothers, and that mother's intuition—the one that wakes at the slightest creak, the faintest call—was still strong within her.

"Mal, sweetheart? Is that you?"

I stretched my slipper-clad foot across the threshold and slowly entered her room, the door creaking open. It smelled like vanilla in there and I took a deep, full breath. At the same time, Nana reached for the remote and clicked the TV off with one hand while flicking her nightstand lamp on with the other.

"Can't sleep?"

"Not even a little bit."

"Not even a *little* bit, huh?" She patted her hand on the downy white comforter that cloaked her. "That's no good. No good at all."

I loved how the conversation could've been identical to ones we'd had ten or more years earlier when she had darker hair and I had crooked teeth and a smattering of freckles that now, at the age of sixteen, had started to fade in intensity. We were different people on the outside then, but time didn't change the inside nearly as much. There was a warm familiarity to our midnight banter. Just like I did years ago, with a running start, I sprinted across the hardwood and vaulted onto her bed. The thud I made upon landing was jarring. I wasn't quite that slight, petite little girl any longer. I'd grown into my gangly limbs and big, buckteeth.

"Just narrowly missed them." Nana smiled.

I laughed. "Those boogiemen practically had me by the ankles!"

"How dare they!"

I adored Nana. She was my favorite person ever. I often wondered had she not been my grandmother, if I'd still have the same affinity for her. I figured I would. Everyone else seemed to love her just as much. She was a favorite among her choir friends. A star at bunko. Her banana nut muffins were to die for and she had fantastic old lady style with her almost lavender hair and matching pastel eye shadow. Age had been predictable with her, turning her into what appeared to be your typical elderly woman upon first cursory glance. But that spirit within her, that was unlike any other.

A spitfire. A dynamo. Even—admittedly—a cougar.

Nana was just plain awesome. Simple as that.

And she was my best friend. Naturally, she'd be the first person I'd tell about Heath. In her all-knowing ways, she beat me to the punch. "Spill the beans."

"Beans?"

"Beans." Her crinkled blue eyes went wide as she punctuated her words. "*Boys*. There are only two things that can keep you up at night. Indigestion and infatuation. I'm assuming it's not the former. So it must be the latter. *Boys*." Stretching into the space between us, she took hold of my hands. I could feel the thin texture of her skin, the way it seemed almost like crepe paper, frail and delicate. "Spill."

"It is a boy. I've seen him at the Blue Duck before."

"Ah." Nana nodded. "A waiter?"

"Busser, I think."

"That's good. The bussers are the ones who do the real work. Loading dishes and wiping down tables. A man who can clean is a keeper in my book. So is the cook. But a boy who just delivers the food and neither makes it nor cleans it up? He's only a middleman. Worth nothin' if you ask me."

I'd never thought of it that way, but there was much to life that I hadn't experienced through the same lens as Nana. At least not yet. She had fifty plus years on me.

"We ended up at the same stoplight on our way home. And I actually ended up on the ground."

"He pushed you, that little dickens—"

"No, no, Nana." I chuckled. "Not at all. He just took me by surprise."

"It's no surprise that he'd be interested in you. You've grown into quite the beautiful lady with a good head on your shoulders to boot. A real stunner."

It was a sweet thing to say, but like Heath's mom, Nana was obligated to say it. But maybe truth canceled out obligation. Some things were just plain true, whether you were obligated to acknowledge them or not. I smiled at Nana's compliment, hoping that was the case here.

"I'm not sure what to do."

"Well," Nana began. Her hand gripped a little tighter onto mine. I could feel the thick acrylic on her nails press into my palms. "You're going to call him."

"Call him? Isn't that his job?"

"Please, Mal. This is the twenty-first century. If you see something you want, you gotta take the bull by the horns. No sense waiting on a man to give you permission to do so. You liked what you saw, I gather?"

My stomach did that fluttering thing again. Just the thought of those dimples sent my heart into overdrive. "Yes. And his personality wasn't too terrible, either."

"All good things. So make your move. No sense in wasting anyone's time with the runaround. Much too old for games like that."

She always made me laugh with her unfiltered tenacity. "Maybe you are, but *I'm* not too old for them. Isn't that exactly what the teenage years are for?"

With a tsk-tsk, Nana shook her head. Then she lifted a bony finger and waggled it directly in my face, her head still swiveling, eyes now like beads. "The teenage years are about setting and creating patterns for your adult ones. If you wish to play the monotonous and boring game of love for the rest of your life, by all means, please start now." Nana's index finger found my nose and bopped it playfully. A slow grin spread onto her face, and it deepened the laugh lines she wore so well. "But if you want to live a genuine life, one filled with truth—true love, true heartache, true emotion—you have to go after what it is that you truly want."

20

I stopped by the diner on Wednesday on my way home from the paint store. Tommy was in need of chartreuse that day, and he was lucky because I'd snagged the last tube of it in his favorite brand, no less. I'd watched him paint later that night, something he occasionally let me do. I was always careful not to interrupt. Sometimes I wasn't sure if he knew I was there, but that was fine with me. I felt grateful to be a part of his creative process, even if only as an onlooker. It was a role I certainly knew how to fulfill with him.

Heath wasn't there when I'd slowed my bike down and passed by the restaurant. I'd craned my neck sideways to gain a better view through the frost-coated windows, but I saw some other young kid with the black tub, clearing the table closest to the entrance. Though Heath was the one I'd hoped to find, I sighed, brimming with relief that I didn't have to profess my interest today. I knew Nana was wise and that her long life had given her permission to speak into mine, but it still scared me to think of asking Heath out. If that's even what I'd planned to do. I wasn't sure what I'd do. I didn't have a plan, actually.

And apparently Heath didn't either, at least not a full one, because when he showed up on my porch Thursday afternoon, that was as far as his plan took him. Just to my doorstep, not a step further. His plan didn't involve words because there were none to accompany his knock that was just the right mix of hesitant and eager. All he had readied was the drop of his jaw, and his mouth popped open like he was waiting to catch flies with it.

"Heath!" I was the one doing the shouting this time. "What are you doing here?"

He wore a navy pea coat and he buried his hands deep into the pockets of it, practically down to his knees. His jeans looked two-toned, water creeping up the bottom third and leaving them darker than their original hue. He had boots on, which was a wise thing considering the snow hadn't let up much, and it was clear he'd trudged a long way to get here. If he was trying to play the game that Nana warned about, he'd failed. I'd found him out.

"You walked here?"

There were those dimples. "Two miles. Uphill, both ways." He snagged the wool beanie from his head and balled it up in one hand, then sort of flicked it against the other like you would a rolled up newspaper or magazine. I hadn't seen his hair before, as it had been tucked under a hat in the same way it was today. I don't know why I was surprised to see the soft blond curls that fell to his jawline. It shouldn't have surprised me at all. It fit what little I knew of him perfectly.

"Dimples *and* golden curls? God, Heath! You're like a mother's dream child. Sugar and spice and everything nice, dimples and curls—" I started to sing.

"Because she's a *girl*," he continued. "You calling me a girl?" His eyes were huge. "And you didn't even get the lyrics right. It's *ribbons and curls*."

"My mistake." I was grateful he'd said it all through a laugh because when put that way, it didn't have the sounds of a compliment at all. Not even a backhanded one. Why I'd started singing nursery rhymes to this boy was beyond me. "Sometimes I say stupid things." I still gripped the edge of the door in my hand. I pushed it forward and back as I rocked on my heels. My voice quivered.

"Sometimes I do stupid things, like show up randomly on a stranger's doorstep."

"Hey, I do that, too!" I smacked my hand solidly to the oak door. The sudden percussion made him jump and I felt bad about it. This was going about as well as I'd expected. "Only I show up at their place of work."

Heath had his head angled down, like he was studying his feet or finally realizing how soaked his pant legs were, and when I said that, his head popped right up and his gray gaze slammed into mine. "*So* much less creepy."

"But *so* much less successful. You weren't there, and I am here." My mouth couldn't stop smiling. With the temperatures the way they were, it felt as if it could freeze this way, this grin permanently adhered to my face. "It's actually much smarter to show up at my house. The odds are higher that I'd be here. Of the two of us, you are the smarter creep."

"I suppose I'll take it."

"How'd you even know where I lived?" I knew things like the Internet existed and addresses weren't secrets, but I wanted him to say. His turn to spill the beans.

"Class directory." He didn't know what to do with his hands and his poor beanie paid the consequences of that. It twisted back in forth in his grip as a mangled dishrag.

"Get out!" I slammed a palm on the door again, and the same reaction from Heath ensued. "We go to the same school?"

"Yep. Same grade even."

"No freaking way!" I let go of the door to push Heath square in the shoulders, and this time he was ready. He didn't budge but braced against my hands. I didn't know if it accentuated his already broad shoulders, but they felt incredible under my palms, even with that cumbersome jacket between them. "Heath, how on earth are we not a thing already?"

His eyes had been held open widely before that, but when I said it, they relaxed, smiling almost in that way only eyes could do. The dimples that pricked firmly into reddened cheeks gave me the answer I hoped to hear.

"Not sure, but give it time. I'm working on it." Even his chuckle was adorable. I wanted to squeeze him, but for once, I refrained.

"I'll work on it, too." I nodded. "I figure we'll have a higher success rate if we're both working on it."

"I like that idea." He stopped strangling his beanie. I could see his Adam's apple pull up and down in a tight swallow. "Can I take you out for dinner sometime? Any place but the diner?"

My hands were still on him. They felt comfortable there, and right. "How about you stay here for dinner tonight? You know, since you walked all this way uphill in the snow."

He offered a full grin. I wanted to memorize it, it was that good.

"I'd like that, Mallory."

"Me, too."

"But hey," he said. His left eyebrow cocked upward. "From now on, let me do the asking, okay?"

I slid my hands down from his shoulders. The snow that collected on his jacket sleeves made my palms slick and I swiped them against the front of my jeans.

"I suppose. It's just that my grandma gave me some advice to be bold and go for it. I'm learning how to do that, I guess."

"But I'm learning how to be a gentleman, and part of that involves you giving me the opportunity to be one."

My throat felt constricted. My pulse rammed in my neck, my fingers, my toes. I looked into Heath's light eyes and could feel my lungs burn with the breath I'd trapped in.

"Will you let me do that?" he asked. His head dipped down to search out my expression. He wasn't a whole lot taller than me. Just the right amount where I imagined my head could fit perfectly into the crook of his neck. Where my cheek would push to the warm skin on his collarbone.

I nodded my reply.

"Good." His full lips spread apart and he beamed. "So then, Mallory, would you like to join me for dinner at your house, with your family, and your food tonight?"

That breath I'd been holding, it flew out of my mouth, transformed into a burst of laughter. I nodded again. "I'd love to."

"Me too," Heath said. Our gaze held and neither one of us blinked and it was that moment where you felt as though you could fly or soar or jump and never land. I was weightless and giddy and completely mesmerized by this kid in front of me. "By the way, my last name is McBride. Just so you know. Now I'm not a total stranger."

Heath McBride. I really, really liked the sound of that.

Four

Heath

Mallory was an anomaly.

There was no rhyme or reason to the way she ate her dinner tonight, which, for most people, wouldn't be an issue. But I'd fully expected our mealtime to mimic the way she ate her particular order at Blue Duck last Tuesday, and it didn't. Not even a little bit.

Tonight left me crazy confused.

We'd eaten mashed potatoes with turkey and peas, and I kid you not, she'd mashed the entire thing together like a stew. As in, had turkey and potato and peas all on her fork at one time, consumed in one bite. And she drank water with ice. *Ice.* There went my theory that she was British. I'd heard once that they didn't put ice in their drinks. But Mallory clearly did tonight, and she clearly hadn't on Tuesday.

Tuesdays were different for some reason. A reason I really wanted to uncover.

We ate at the formal dining table with her grandmother, a woman she introduced only as Nana, and a man she called Tommy. I couldn't figure out the relationship with Tommy. He looked to be right in the middle between Mallory and Nana age-wise, but the fact that Mallory addressed him by his name made me think he probably wasn't her father. Or if he was, there was some story there.

Tommy was a man of few words. None, actually. I didn't know whether he was born the way he was or if some event in life had led to it, but he didn't speak, hardly interacted, and needed assistance to eat his food and get around the house, a job that Mallory seemed happy to help with. I hadn't been around many people like Tommy, and it was strange because *he* didn't make me uncomfortable at all, but instead I became uncomfortable with myself. Like I was suddenly aware of how easily I lifted my own utensils to my mouth and how effortlessly I could speak or engage in conversation. Somehow the things that I never thought about, I was thinking about. And I felt guilty over it.

But as I watched Mallory—how she readied and held out the fork for Tommy, bringing it up to his mouth all while maintaining eye contact and conversation with me—it made me realize there shouldn't be anything uncomfortable about it at all. I wanted to say it was human nature to feel sorry for those who were different from you in any way, but I wasn't sure that was the case. For Mallory, it was human nature to jab Tommy when he'd turned his nose up at his last bite of peas. Or when he'd burped aloud after a huge swallow of root beer like any man would and she'd scowled at him in reprimand.

For Mallory, it was human nature to treat Tommy as she would any other human.

That humbled me completely.

And it made me think she was the most awesome girl in the entire world.

After we'd eaten, we cleaned up the dishes, Mallory washing and me drying. Every time she would hand me a plate, I'd purposefully brush my fingers to hers. I wanted her to feel it, to know what I was doing—how I was trying to touch her—but she was so wrapped up in whatever it was that she was talking about, I doubted she noticed. Which was fine because I really wasn't paying attention to what she way saying, either. Instead, I found myself fixated on the *way* she said things. There was so much life in her voice. That was the only way to explain it. Every word she spoke was filled to the top with passion. Her whole body wore it. Her eyes would do this thing where they would round like silver dollars. Pure innocence. And she'd bounce up and down on her toes, not rising all the way, just a little bounce, like she was preparing to jump, revving up. And her smile. God, her smile. It was breathtaking. She had teeth that were probably a little too big for her face, but they looked just right on her.

"Heath." She paused, mid wash. Her hand found the faucet handle and pulled it down so the water shut off and the room quieted as the water dripped and trickled down the drain of the porcelain sink. "Why haven't we had any classes together?"

"I moved here last year. My dad got a position at the hospital. I lived in California before that."

"California!" I didn't think it was possible, but her eyes widened even more. "No way! So you're a surfer, huh?"

"Hardly." I took the plate from her hand and drew the towel over it, not sure it was doing anything anymore. It was sodden and damp, but I didn't want to ask for another one. I just wanted to keep her talking. Keep her in this moment.

"California seems to be as coastal as it gets."

"Not all of California is the beach. We used to live in NorCal. On a ranch. With horses."

"Horses?" she said breathily. "That's incredible!"

I never really thought it was incredible, mostly just a lot of work since my parents were always gone *at* work, but Mallory's reaction grew an instant appreciation for my time at the ranch. It almost felt like I should rush home to thank my parents for the childhood they'd given me, the one I'd taken for granted. I couldn't understand how a few words from Mallory could make me suddenly appreciative of my upbringing, but she did that. She was magic.

"Do you like horses?" It was such a lame thing to ask, but I knew I couldn't say anything nearly as interesting as what Mallory could. It wasn't like she was spouting off some intellectual ramblings or philosophical questions, but she was awe-inspiring still.

"I don't have much experience with them, but I'm sure I'd love them."

She was bursting. People burst with joy or gladness, but Mallory burst with life. Everything about her was magnified.

"I'll take you riding someday."

Her hand caught mine as she handed off the last plate. It was deliberate and welcome and I gave it a squeeze as she said, "I would *love* that."

I was sure she would. I had a feeling Mallory Alcott loved everything.

By the time we'd finished tidying up the kitchen, it was well past dark. I'd said that I was fine to walk home, but Mallory and her grandmother wouldn't allow it. The "crazies" came out at sundown, Nana had said. I wasn't sure who these crazies were, exactly, but she seemed to think the safest way to avoid them was in a car. That you needed the protection of metal and steel, and her 1976 powder blue Buick Regal evidently offered just that.

That vehicle was a tank. There were only two doors and they made me feel bad about myself as I struggled to open them. They were so damn heavy. I'd crawled into the backseat of the musty car, surprised when Mallory followed immediately behind. I was more surprised when she took the middle seat. It was intentional and so bold to sit right next to me, our thighs pressed solidly together.

I wondered if all girls were like this here. It hadn't been that way back at home in California. Game playing seemed to go with the territory. The chase. The retreat and then more chasing. There was no chase here, no game. Everything Mallory did meant something. Like she was telling me she liked me too, with not so many words.

And it didn't feel desperate or too soon. Hell, I'd known tons of guys at my last school who hooked up with girls without even knowing their names.

I knew Mallory's name.

I let that simple fact give me permission to start falling for her.

In reality, to continue falling.

Five

Heath

"You're home awfully late again." Hattie didn't look up from her phone. It illuminated her face, and when whoever she was texting replied, I could see the reflection of that, too. Her fingers flew across the little keyboard that was flipped out on the device.

It was eleven, but it was Friday, and that was my curfew. Hattie, my older sister, was nineteen. Her curfew wasn't until midnight, but apparently she didn't have any place better to be than on our couch texting her friends rather than hanging out with them.

"Yup," was my reply.

"You ever gonna introduce this mystery girl to us? You've been hanging out for weeks now." Again, no eye contact. It made me think of all the times I'd had my face glued to my phone. How I'd walk down the street with my fingers on the keypad. I never looked up. There must've been so much I missed. That night when I met Mallory should've been like that, but my battery had died halfway into my shift. Stupid thing never held a charge. I wondered if I would've walked right by her if it hadn't. If I ever would've noticed her.

"Come on, Heathcliff. Do we get to meet her?" Hattie asked again.

"Maybe."

I sauntered to the kitchen and yanked on the refrigerator door. Mom worked nights as a pediatric nurse in the ICU at Stanton Hospital and dad was an ER surgeon there. He'd been on call tonight, and based on the fact that he was nowhere to be seen, I guessed he'd gotten that call to come in. Even with their loaded schedules, though, they always made sure we were taken care of. The Tupperware filled with leftover lasagna made me smile. The Post-It note that read, "For you, Cliffy," made me laugh. Both things made me feel loved.

Our family didn't spend a lot of time together, but I didn't think the quantity of time was necessarily what it took to know how someone felt. The moments we had together meant something. I was good at loving intensely. Mom and Dad had shown me how to do that. Hattie? Not so much, but I knew these were the years where we weren't supposed to get along. Someday we'd be older with families and our own kids would play and grow up together the same way we'd grown up with our cousins back in California. Even still, I did love her, and I figured she loved me. The fact that she was asking to meet Mallory was a small and subtle sign of that, whether she'd ever admit to it or not.

"Mom made cookies." Hattie flicked her head toward the stove, fingers still tapping out a reply. "Peanut butter."

"Awesome."

I forked the lasagna and ate the entire bowl of leftovers in about four bites. Mom's cookies weren't warm any longer, but they were the underdone kind where the middles remained all gooey and the outsides were just the right amount of crumble. I slipped two into a Ziploc bag and took them with me to my room. My backpack was on my unmade bed and I opened it to throw the cookies in, right next to my calculus and chemistry books. I planned to give them to Mallory tomorrow at school. I didn't know if she liked peanut butter, but my guess was that she probably loved it.

In fact, I wondered if there was anything she didn't love.

I had to find out, so I grabbed my phone and punched her number into it. Plus, I really just wanted to hear her adorable voice.

"Heath!" She answered on the second ring. "How the heck are you?"

We'd been together twenty minutes earlier. I loved that she still asked the question, as though something had changed between then and now. Something *had* changed, entirely altering my mood: I wasn't with her anymore.

"I'm hanging in there. You?"

"I was better when you were here." Honesty. Everything she said was always truthful, regardless of whether it made her vulnerable or not. People were usually vulnerable with those they felt safe around. I took it as a compliment that she could open up so easily to me. "I had a lot of fun with you tonight. As always."

"Me too." Though she couldn't see me, I still felt self-conscious as I tugged my hoodie over my head and undid my belt, one hand still on the phone. My jeans dropped to the floor and I stepped out of them. I kicked them to the side and walked over to my bed, ready to get in.

"What are you up to?"

I laughed. What would her reaction be if I told her I was just lounging around in my boxers? I knew I'd get a genuine response, but I didn't want to embarrass her. She was too pure and so good and over the weeks we'd been dating, that had only become clearer.

"Just getting ready for bed." It was a safe reply. My heart suddenly jolted, wondering if she was doing the same. "You?"

"I'm already in bed." Her voice was soft and quiet. This was where the phone wasn't enough. I wanted to be there with her. The thought of holding her, the covers wrapped around us, made me sweat.

We hadn't really done anything in the three short weeks we'd known each other. Maybe that was because we spent all our time at her house with her grandmother and Tommy, who I'd found out was actually her dad. Hanging out with relatives was often a buzzkill, but in our case, I actually enjoyed their company.

I just enjoyed Mallory's company more.

We'd brushed hands and fingers and sat so closely next to one another that we could feel the rhythm of our breathing in the way our bodies pulled up and down against our touching shoulders. But I hadn't made that move to grab her hand and keep it in mine. I'd wanted to. I'd wanted to do that and more. But something about Mallory made me want to protect her, too. Made me want to take my time with her.

She had all the qualities of a girl you'd fall in love with, and I knew if I didn't go slowly, all our firsts would rush together. I wouldn't be able to help myself.

So I put it all off.

"What are you wearing?" The words fell out, mostly as a joke, but I didn't know if she'd interpret it as one.

"Heath!"

"Hey, it's an innocent enough question." I wanted her to pick up on the flirt in my voice. We could have a lot of fun with this.

"I'm wearing pink polka dot footsie pajamas."

"You are not."

"Sure I am. The kind with the flap and the buttons on the back. You?"

"I'm in my superman undies."

Mallory was in full hysterics. The way her laughter echoed through the phone would've made anyone else hold the device out from their ear to avoid the blare, but I didn't. I pressed it between my cheek and my shoulder as I slid down under my comforter.

"I bet that's something." She giggled, which was followed by a pause. I knew we were both picturing the descriptions we'd given one another. It made me wish she'd given me a little more to work with, but I had a good imagination. Even under all the layers—the thick wool sweaters and jackets and scarves—I could tell Mallory had an incredible body. There were girls that flaunted what they had, even in the dead of winter. She didn't do that. That made her hot as hell.

"Oh, it's something, all right."

Silence again, but it wasn't awkward. Hesitant, maybe. The ceiling fan above me ticked softly with each rotation. The circulating air curled a corner of my Sum 41 poster and it made a papery rustling. Even over those background noises, I could hear her shallow breathing. Could sense the rise and fall of her chest.

"Mallory." I hadn't meant to say her name, to have it escape on a breath.

"Heath."

I swallowed audibly. "When I kiss you, what's it going to be like?"

Maybe it was the sound of the heater kicking on, but I swore I heard a little gasp through the phone. "When?"

"Yes." Some of my confidence returned. I smiled to myself. "When I kiss you. Because it's a when."

"I don't know what it will be like." Her voice was small. "I've never been kissed before."

Of course she hadn't. I wanted to laugh, not at all to make fun of her, but just from the fact that all the pieces of Mallory fit together so completely. Everything made sense, which was unexpected, even though it shouldn't be.

"I'll tell you how it will go, then."

"Okay."

She liked this, I could sense it. If she hadn't, she'd let me know, because Mallory wasn't one to shy away from her feelings. She'd say for me to knock it off or that I was making her uncomfortable. I appreciated that about her, that she didn't let anyone get away with doing something she didn't want them to. So I assumed that meant she wanted to kiss me, too. I went with it.

"First, I'm going to make sure I've put on a lot of ChapStick ahead of time because this awful weather is terrible on the lips. No one wants to kiss that."

"I might want to kiss that."

I stuttered, not expecting her to interject. "Maybe, but only because you don't know any better. Sandpaper lips are no fun. Trust me."

"All right." She laughed. "I do."

And she did trust me, so I kept going. "I'm going to look you right in those light green eyes of yours. You'll recognize how it feels because it's the same look I give you every time I'm with you. That look where I'm wondering how on earth a girl like you literally fell into my life, and why you've let me stay around. My stomach is going to feel like it's both on fire and not even there at all, and yours will too." My breath quickened and I made sure that my words didn't try to match the pace. I deliberately slowed everything down. "I'll move a little closer …"

"Uh, huh."

"Not all the way, just enough where I can still look at you. You'll be able to feel my breath on your mouth. It will be warm and minty because I'll have brushed my teeth before coming over."

"I don't think I would care if you didn't."

"Still," I teased. "I will. Only the best for you."

"Aquafresh, then."

"Okay." I chuckled at her suggestion. "Okay. I can arrange that. Anyway, I'll move in and lift my palm to the back of your neck. My hand will probably be shaking, but you won't mind. My other hand will cradle your jaw and I'll pull you a little closer. Then I'll close my eyes." I couldn't believe I was doing this, and how turned on I was getting in just describing a kiss. I knew there were plenty of websites I could visit or things I could look up to get the job done a little quicker, but this was doing enough for me. As much as I should do with Mallory, I figured. "You'll take that as your cue to close your eyes, too."

"I am."

God, that girl made me smile. The thought of her—even if she was wearing those ridiculous pajamas she talked about—taking in every word I said, doing it along with me, was too much. She was too much.

"All right," I said. "Then my lips will meet yours. Soft at first. Just the bottom one. I'll lean in so our chests touch. You'll be able to feel my heart, how it thuds and pounds. Yours will do the same. You'll bring your hands around my waist and encircle your arms around me, too. I'll run my fingers through your hair and guide you with my hand on the back of your neck. It will be slow and you'll suddenly be able to feel it in every inch of your body. The way your toes tingle. How your legs are weightless. That flutter deep in your stomach. The pulse in your wrist. The sweat on your brow."

I needed to thank Mrs. Ritcher, my sophomore English teacher, for that section on poetry and prose. Clearly I had learned a thing or two from that unit. By the sounds of Mallory on the other line, I figured she was also grateful for the A+ I'd pulled out of that class.

"I feel it."

So did I. I felt every bit of what I was saying as though it was happening right here, right now. I wondered if they had those 1-900 number jobs for guys, too, or if phone sex was just a thing girls got paid to do. Either way, it wasn't like I'd experience this reaction with anyone else. It was just Mallory. Only her.

"It wouldn't last too long because I'd leave you wanting more. Just long enough to where those butterflies started to go away, but not before they all left completely. I'd take a step back and I wouldn't open my eyes until we were no longer touching. Then I'd flash you my dimples," I said. "And you'd most likely faint due to my mad skills."

It was absolutely quiet on the line. Radio silence.

I waited a moment. It felt like she wasn't even there anymore. Then I would be an idiot, having spent all this time describing a kiss to no one at all. Had Hattie heard me through the door, she'd never let me live it down. Maybe this wasn't such a good idea.

"Good God, Heath."

"Yeah?"

"That was the best first kiss ever, and it didn't even happen!"

I snorted. "I suppose that's one way to word it."

"Hmmm." The sound she made sounded contented, so warm and full.

"Hmmm." I tried to echo back, but my murmur was frustrated and gargled. But I was frustrated, so it fit.

"Heath?" she continued. "Was the real reason you called tonight to try to seduce me and get me all hot and bothered? Or did you have other motives?"

"The seducing was totally impromptu." I rolled onto my side and wedged the phone against my shoulder. My hair was long and probably in need of a trim, but the girls seemed to like it. At least Mallory did, and hers was the only opinion I cared about lately. I pulled a band off my nightstand and wound it around my hair at the base of my neck. "I actually called to ask you if there is anything you don't like."

"Anything I don't like?"

"Yeah." I nodded though she couldn't see. "You seem to have a love for everything, Mallory. It's contagious. But it made me wonder if there are things you don't like, too. You can't like everything."

"Of course there are things I don't like."

"Like what?"

The heater shut off and it was quiet again, except for the fan and the poster fluttering and my heart that I could hear as though it beat in my ears instead of my chest like it had gotten its location all wrong.

"I don't like that I have to wait until tomorrow to experience that first kiss. That's something I don't like … at all."

I smiled. "Me neither."

"Oh," she shot out like she had one last thing to say before hanging up. "I also don't care for peanut butter. But that's about it."

Six

Mallory

The last three weeks with Heath had been phenomenal. I knew people said puppy love wasn't authentic, how we fell desperately fast and hard, and rebounded just as quickly. I saw it happen all over school. One day there would be a power couple that appeared so solid, so perfect for one another, and then next moment they'd be broken up, their eyes already fixed on someone new.

That must've been the game Nana spoke of. Like pinballs, they'd crash into one relationship, then bounce over to the next. I figured their only real wish was to hope to score in the process.

It wasn't so with Heath. The more time we spent together, the more I became aware of all the hours in the day when we weren't together—all the minutes where I wasn't learning more about him, wasn't falling for the mere sound of his voice or the way he'd bite the pad of his thumb when lost in thought. How he'd flick his hair from his eyes with a subtle toss of his head. I'd discovered these adorable inflections and rises in tone.

I wanted to know everything there was to know about Heath.

It was the stage where he was new and exciting. When you met someone for the first time, it was like one of those presents wrapped in layers and layers of paper. Every layer taken off left another gift to uncover.

It seemed like there was no end to Heath's layers.

Like the fact that he was able to make me feel like I'd had my first kiss without even kissing me. Part of me wanted to be angry, worried that once we finally did kiss, that it wouldn't live up. How could it? What he'd described was so impossibly perfect that I was certain it couldn't be recreated. I'd fumble, I was sure of it. It would be slobbery and clumsy and unnatural. There was no way to do what he described without it being second rate.

But then I thought about my dad's paintings. When he'd first started, he'd used other artist's work for inspiration. His physical therapist had suggested he try his hand at painting shortly after the first stroke that happened when I was just ten. He said it would help with his movement. The way the brush would glide over the canvas would help him learn control again. It would be good for his muscles, and it would be good for his mind.

Nana had set up a place for him to paint in the den. She'd purchased three easels, and twice as many canvases. One day she'd been gone all afternoon and when she returned, she had at least a dozen books in her possession. I'd watched as she tore them apart, not in anger, but with excitement to her motions. Rip, rip, rip. Then she spread them across the floor like a quilt made of other artists' work. There was Starry Night and Ophelia and The Persistence of Memory. Finally, she'd taken a step back, one arm across her chest, the other propped up and held to her chin.

She'd studied him. When his gaze lingered on one painting for any length of time, she'd nod her head excitedly. "Yes! Yes! I agree." Then she'd slap it on the blank white wall.

There were at least twenty taped up. The rest she'd shoved aside.

And then she left him to do his work.

Not one turned out quite like the original. In fact, had you been asked to match them up with the pieces that influenced them, I doubted you'd be able to. But they were beautiful nonetheless. Dad had put his own spin on them, his signature. It didn't need to be exactly like the original for it to be beautiful.

Heath and I didn't need to be exactly like our expectations for us to be beautiful, either. Some things were best when you didn't expect anything to begin with.

I'd put myself to bed that night with that lingering thought and it was like I was opening up and entirely new door. One Heath and I could walk through together.

Or maybe a window.

Because at two in the morning, I jolted awake to the tinny sound of a rock hitting the gutter. His aim was off, which was a good thing, because had he been more accurate, my window would be sporting a fresh crack in it, fractured from the stone. That I would have to explain to Nana. But a dented rain gutter? That was probably a nonissue. No one paid any attention to gutters.

My feet flew over the cold and worn hardwood. I was at the window before I had time to think about what I was wearing or what I looked like or how it was the dead of night and boys most definitely weren't allowed in my house—much less my room—at this hour.

I just couldn't wait to get to him.

The window took a bit of jiggling to pry open. When I finally managed it free, I was met with darkness, not even the moon's glow to greet me. Cloud cover draped across the stars like a film. I scanned the yard, but my eyes wouldn't adjust. Blinking did nothing and squinting helped, but minimally. I'd hoped I wasn't dreaming it, some Romeo and Juliet inspired wish. Of course I'd wanted to find him outside my window. Every girl wanted that.

The night air blasted into my room. The curtains billowed around me like sheer cotton waves and I leaned my upper body out the window. Goosebumps rose over my flesh, pebbling every inch, eliciting a shudder from deep within me.

"Mallory." It was one of those shouts masked as a whisper. The same intensity, just not the volume. "Mal, you awake?"

"Heath?"

"I'm coming up."

I had no idea how he'd manage it, but I backed away from the window to allow him the room to make his grand entrance. Like he was Spiderman, Heath scaled the outside wall, pulling himself up the rusted drainpipe and using the gutter to grip onto with his hands hooked over it. With a crazy amount of upper body strength, he hoisted himself onto the slope of the second story roof. His boots slid against the frosty shingles. I threw a hand out to grab him, and he righted himself before spilling unceremoniously into my room.

"Heath." I tiptoed back to the window and lowered it shut. "Heath, what are you doing here?"

I had to ask it, but I knew. He was here for me. The thought that someone couldn't wait another minute— couldn't use the escape of sleep to fast-forward them to morning—was incredible. To be wanted in that way. Sure I had people in my life who were excited to see me. Nana always greeted me each morning with a kiss pressed to my temple. Dad would smile with his eyes in the way that only he could. I had friends at school who genuinely seemed to care about me. But this with Heath? This need that almost bordered on desperation made me feel like I served a purpose other than just being someone's granddaughter or daughter or friend.

I felt desired. He was the first boy to ever make me feel that way.

What I knew of love led me to believe I would never be able to forget him because of it.

It took a moment for Heath to regain his composure once he'd landed inside my room. He dusted off his pants, swatting his thighs with his hands to shake off the remnants of snow. Then that beanie came off his head with a jerk and he shoved it into his back pocket. He had a navy sweatshirt on and he pulled on the drawstrings of the hood, tugging them back and forth until they matched in length. This was him being nervous, I figured. Some people stammered. Others paced. Heath fidgeted.

"Hey." His shoulders sunk in relaxation with the word.

"Hey."

Even though I hadn't paid any attention to my wardrobe—or lack of—that didn't mean Heath didn't notice. His gaze dropped to my bare legs, to the oversized t-shirt that I wore like a dress. I could feel his gaze on me like it was physical.

"Wow."

I didn't know how to respond to that. I didn't want to be that girl who just stood there blushing, but there was no way around it. My cheeks were red and hot.

"You lied to me."

"Lied?"

"Those most certainly are *not* footsie pajamas."

"Well, I'm thinking you're not actually wearing Superman skivvies, either."

He gave me a lopsided smirk with a wink to accentuate it. "You will never know, now, will you?"

Flirting was not an art form I was adept in. I'm sure I'd had the opportunity, but it went unnoticed if it was ever there. Over the years, there had been a few guys I'd had crushes on. It never got past the puffy hearts drawn on binders with plus signs between names. Only a few close friends knew about the boys I'd liked. But now I was standing in front of a boy I liked very much, and I had a feeling he was well aware just how much.

I went to the nightstand to flip on the bedside lamp. Sharp white illuminated the room, and it cast long, jagged shadows like the light struggled and clawed to reach across the walls. Heath took one step toward me, out from the dark.

"So," he murmured in a hushed tone. He dragged his hand over his scalp. "I've never done this before."

"Snuck into a girl's room?"

"Liked someone as much as I like you. This quickly." One more step. "It kinda scares me."

"I'm scared, too."

Another step and we were standing right in front of each other. If I wanted to, I could reach out and press my hands to his chest or his hips or slip the errant curl that fell across his cheekbone back behind his ear. I didn't do those things. I stood still, unmoving. My choppy breath shook out of me and my fingers trembled as if I'd had ten cups of coffee. It couldn't have been noticeable to anyone else, but to me if felt like I was flailing. It made remaining still difficult.

"I don't want you to be scared of me, Mallory."

"I'm not scared of you. I'm scared of being this young and feeling this much. I'm scared that if I'm experiencing all of this now, I'll never experience it again, you know?"

"Not sure I do."

"You're setting the standard, Heath. Any other guy to come into my life from this moment forward will never live up."

Taking me by surprise, he grabbed on to my hand. "I don't want any other guys to come into your life." He lifted my hand to his lips and moved his mouth onto my knuckles. It was warm and his lips were soft and full. "I know that's selfish and probably unrealistic, but I'm not looking at this as some high school romance. What's the point of being in a relationship if you're not hopeful it will last?"

"To have fun, I guess. Be kids."

He brought my hand down from his lips but kept our fingers woven. His thumb traced circles over my skin. "I'm all for having fun," he said. "Believe me. Fun is good. But this is our beginning, Mallory. Why think about an end?"

That's when I kissed him.

Reactions came in all different forms. You jumped out of your skin when watching a horror movie. You burst out laughing at something funny. You cried when emotion overtook you.

And you kissed someone when you were absolutely falling for them.

At first he startled, drawing back when my mouth slammed boldly onto his. It wasn't the play-by-play like he'd described, and that was fine. I didn't take my time or move in cautiously. I was past that. My feelings were so far past that. I had to make the physical side of things catch up, and the only way I knew to do that was to forget my fear, forget my hesitation, and give in to what I really wanted. Just give in.

"Mallory."

My hands flew to his hair, my fingers winding around each tendril. I could feel his hand on the low slope of my back, and he pulled my body completely flush with his. My back arched and Heath moved over me. It all happened so quickly that I hadn't thought much past the initial my-lips-on-his-lips part of the kiss. I'd seen enough movies to know there was more involved than that. There was movement and rhythm, but I struggled to find the right pace.

Frustration filled me. Heath sensed it.

"Hey," he said near my ear. "It's okay."

I dropped my head to his shoulder. I wanted to hide, to curl up and close my eyes and pretend I hadn't completely butchered my hasty attempt at our first kiss, the one that should've been utterly phenomenal.

"I'm doing this all wrong."

"I can assure you, there is no wrong way to do this."

"This feels wrong," I said.

"Ask any guy, Mallory. There is *no* wrong way to kiss. It's sorta one of our favorite things to do in life."

"But it could be better."

"It could be different."

I'm sure he didn't mean it in the same way I felt it, but Heath only knew it could be different because he'd kissed different girls. I didn't have *differents*. He was my only.

His shoulder nudged me and he took my chin between his finger and thumb, tilting my face to his. "Hey, you."

I smiled, but couldn't look directly at him.

"*Hey.*" He forced my gaze up. "By different I mean you can trust me more, and you can trust yourself and your instincts, too. Just go with it, Mallory. I promise you'll do great."

He was right. I tried again.

I found my confidence, and with that, my rhythm, but not before Nana found us both.

It was less humiliating than if a parent had discovered a boy breaking into their under-aged daughter's room, I supposed. Nana was one-step removed from the responsibility of raising me. She wasn't the type to scold or admonish, but there was an unspoken duty she had to fulfill, the one that didn't allow certain things to happen under her roof, on her watch.

So that first kiss never really happened.

We'd stuttered and stopped and stuttered and stopped once more.

All I could think as my head lowered to the pillow after Heath left that night—through the front door rather than the window—was that I hoped this wasn't some foreshadowing of things to come, of the way our story would unfold.

I doubted life was that tragically poetic.
At least I prayed it couldn't be.

Seven

Heath

Stuff like school, work, and other daily activities were no longer important to me. It wasn't like I hated doing those things, they just seemed to offer little in the way of any rewards. They were the things I begrudgingly did because I knew they got me one step closer to the reward. And that reward was Mallory.

The knowing smiles we'd exchange when passing in the school hallway were the reward. We didn't have any classes together. She said I was on the smart kid's track, and while I enjoyed school and it came naturally to me, it didn't mean Mallory was any less intelligent. She just didn't focus her efforts on her studies the way I always did. Well, at least the way I had up until I met her.

Her kisses were also the reward. Since our first kiss that wasn't quite a kiss, the one Mallory claimed ended up so horrendously, she'd learned and a thing or two about the act of kissing. I swear it was like she had studied those silly teen magazines in her spare time. She would close her eyes a little and tilt her head as though rehearsing before she'd lean in. It was absolutely adorable. I could watch her all day, even though I would rather be making out instead.

Everything about Mallory was my reward.

And I woke up one December morning and realized that I had fallen completely in love.

It was weird how a change that I didn't necessarily want to happen led me to a place in life I wouldn't change for the world. When my parents said we'd be making the move from California to Kentucky, admittedly, I wasn't thrilled. I was generally a happy, simple guy. Go with the flow. So I went with it. But my less than enthusiastic packing of boxes and loading of the trailer must've clued my parents in to my feelings. I wasn't upset with them for plucking Hattie and me from our home and moving us to a new one, but I wasn't stoked, either.

It was merely because I didn't know how happy this move would end up making me.

You couldn't project happiness. Life gave you the good and the bad, often in equal measure, and you never knew which one you'd get at any given time. Moving across the country was the bad, but Mallory was the good.

And I loved how good and happy she made me feel.

It was later that night that I told her. We had finished eating dinner with her grandma and her dad and we were snuggled on the couch watching Survivor together. We'd often do this thing where she'd have me sprawl out and bend my legs a little to create this empty space between myself and the back of the sofa. Then she'd curl her tiny body into that nook there.

"It's like I'm in a boat," she'd said, as though the carpet was water and I had to keep her from spilling over into it. It reminded me of a game Hattie and I used to play as kids that we'd called "lava." Everything but the ground was safe and we'd hop from table to chair to ottoman to avoid falling into the molten and fiery floor below. Mom would get annoyed when she'd come home to find us on the kitchen counters or wedged in the doorway with our feet and hands propped against the frame.

"Why do you call it a boat?" I'd asked Mallory. My mouth was close to her temple and I'd pressed it softly there.

"Because I feel safe here. Like you're my calm place in rough waters."

"You don't feel safe when I'm not around?"

She lifted her chin to look me in the eyes. "No, not unsafe, really. Just uncertain," she'd said. "But I'm certain of you, and that makes me feel safe."

Later that night Mallory led me down the hall. We were headed toward her dad's den, and though I'd always wanted to know what he did in that room, I knew enough to wait until I was invited along.

"Want to see something?"

I nodded.

"Hey, Tommy." She'd dropped a few light knocks on the door as she spoke. "Care for a couple visitors?"

Then she propped open the door to let me through. It was dark and musty. I could make out a wall with a large bookcase at the back of the room, and I studied it. There were hundreds of books, all haphazardly thrown onto their shelves. Some were upright. Others lay sideways. Some looked like they'd been tossed against the case and stayed where they fell. There was a small loveseat off to the side and it was covered in a deep red brocade fabric, the floral, swirling pattern interrupted with tears and snags.

"Go sit over there and I'll see if he's got everything he needs."

I did as instructed and slumped onto the seat with a huff. The springs in the cushions were old and I could feel every individual coil. There was a lamp to my right that looked like it was made from stained glass and I wanted to flick it on, but I decided to wait on Mallory. She'd turn it on if it was necessary. It seemed like she had a routine in here.

"Oh, Tommy," she said, bending to the ground to retrieve a paint tube. "You should've told me to buy more goldenrod. I was just by the store today." The way you do when you squeeze the last bit of toothpaste out of the tube, she rolled the paint between her fingers and a dollop fell out and onto Tommy's pallet. "There, that's all that you've got to work with tonight."

The floor was speckled in every color of paint one could imagine, and there were stacks of canvases lining the walls the way music stores organized their albums and records to flip through. There must've been at least a hundred judging by the ten piles I counted along the wall.

Mallory came over and sat next to me. I wasn't a guy with a particularly long attention span—I'd been known to sleep through movies and lectures and church sermons—but I swore I could've watched Mallory's dad paint all night. The limited movement I was accustomed to seeing from him disappeared altogether. His hand swept across the canvas as though he was a conductor, the paints his orchestra. I almost wanted to close my eyes to take in the concert in front of me.

"Before the stroke, he was right handed," Mallory whispered after an hour or more of silence. "Now he does everything with the left. The doctor says he should be able to speak, too, but he doesn't try. I suppose he doesn't need to speak audibly, though. His work says everything he needs to say."

This piece wasn't what I would necessarily call abstract—it wasn't like Picasso where you'd have to stand on your head and squint with one eye to make out any kind of meaning, but it wasn't realistic, either. There were swirls of yellow that crossed over the entire canvas like wheat or yarn or ribbon. It could have been anything, but the one unmistakable element was the eye that peeked out from under it. It was identical in tone to Mallory's, bright and sparkling.

"What does this piece say?"

I dropped my palm onto her bare knee and left it there. Mallory's eyes fell shut, briefly.

"That he misses her."

Then she got up and padded across the room and came up behind her father, wrapping her arms around his neck. "I miss her, too." She pressed a kiss to the crown of his head and he leaned back at the gesture. She pulled him closer to her and his brush fumbled from his grip and spread thick yellow paint across her arm. She didn't care, she just hugged him tighter. "I miss her every single day. She sure loved the hell out of us, didn't she?"

They stayed like this for a while, and though it was an exchange between the two of them, I felt like I was a part of it. There was a love so present it saturated the space around us. He'd painted more than an image, more than a memory. He'd painted a pure emotion, and in that moment, I couldn't understand how this work of art wasn't on display in the most prestigious of museums with the largest price tag possible. It was one of a kind in feeling and love.

We left him after that and I pulled Mallory into the bathroom off the hallway as we walked away from the den. I took her arm—the one covered in freshly drying paint—in my grip and looked her in her eyes, hard. She held my gaze as I reached around for the faucet and wet a washcloth with warm water and wiped it across her forearm, taking the paint with it.

I set the towel on the counter and stared at her reflection in the mirror for long enough that the connection of our eyes did weird things to my stomach. I didn't know her story, but I knew there was loss—loss of so many kinds. "I'm sorry about your mom, Mallory."

She spun around. I saw the tears well, the quiver of her bottom lip. Then she cried. It wasn't a sob that wracked her body or one of those ugly cries. It was controlled, as though she'd cried this same cry every day.

Like brushing her teeth or doing homework, this was just part of her routine.

I held her. My chin pressed into her hair and her cheek rested on my collarbone. She didn't shake or shudder. The tears slowly and silently slipped down her face and landed on my shirt, soaking into the fibers there. She squeezed me back with her arms coiled around my waist.

I didn't know Mallory's history. I knew I could never take the pain she'd experienced away, but I knew I would be part of her future, and any pain she'd ever face, I would be there for. Be there to comfort her and love her through it. And I needed her to know that.

My voice didn't feel like my own, and when I said it, I could hardly hear it, but I knew she could. I hoped she could. "I love you, Mallory."

She didn't act surprised. She didn't pull back in shock or in excitement at my words. She just nodded against my shoulder and said, "I know. I love you, too, Heath."

Eight

Mallory

Winter didn't hold on as long this year as it had in the past. It was often well into March before the trees turned from brittle looking skeletons with their menacing and bare branches clawing toward the sky into living, budding plants that reminded me of the yearly promise of new life and fresh starts. It was only February and already the town had begun to thaw.

"Good morning, Sunshine," Nana said one Saturday morning when I came down for breakfast. She'd outdone herself with the smorgasbord of baked goods that lined the old pine table positioned in the center of the kitchen. Cinnamon rolls, country-style potatoes, sausage, thick strips of bacon with ribbon-like curls of fat still clinging to their edges. My stomach growled as though letting its appreciation be known. I plucked a piece of bacon from the top of the pile and snapped it between my teeth.

My hair was split into two braids which hung down my back and I wore pink flannel pajamas that had cotton-tailed bunny rabbits patterned all over them. Nana caught sight of me and cocked her head. Her expression was mixed. There was a little nostalgia there, like she was seeing me as the young girl she'd always known me to be, but there was something more in those twinkling, yet unsure, eyes. There was a hint of goodbye.

I chose to ignore it and stuffed my face with a poppy seed muffin.

"Oh, Mal," Nana said. "Why have you grown up so quickly?"

Not quickly enough, is what I wanted to reply. Sixteen was a weird age. You weren't given the benefit of being young enough to make mistakes and merely learn from them anymore, but you weren't old enough to fully own your decisions, either. You were the legal responsibility of a parent or guardian, but the emotional responsibility of no one but yourself. You weren't coddled. You weren't given the benefit of the doubt. You just were.

It was weird that they called those who were ten or eleven in age tweens. *We* were the tweens. We were the ones caught in between childhood and adulthood. Those prepubescent kids were just stuck between being a little kid and an even bigger little kid.

I wasn't a kid anymore. I knew what I wanted out of life, and who I wanted to share it with. We'd been together just over four months. That wasn't a lot in the timeline of life, but my timeline wasn't all that long yet. The space Heath took up felt huge.

For years, I'd wondered what it would be like to fall in love. What steps I would take to get there, how it would happen and who it would be with.

And then one day I was there. Thrust into the thick of it. I thought I was falling in love with him, like it was some process that happened gradually and methodically. But if I thought on those feelings I had when we first met, they were the same ones I had now. My feelings didn't change. They just magnified. Exploded.

I'd burst into love with Heath.

I finished chewing my muffin and took a swig of orange juice as I looked at my grandma, feeling like I had the answer to her question, even though it was probably meant to be a rhetorical one anyway.

"You think I've grown too quickly? Time is relative, Nana. Sometimes it seems to drag on and then others it feels like it's not moving at all. Like everything is frozen."

"Wouldn't that be nice." She laughed. She filled up my glass with a pour of fresh squeezed juice. "To freeze time. A fountain of youth, if you will."

"I don't know about that." I smiled and thought of growing old with the boy who'd stolen my heart, of our years together and memories made over a lifetime of love. "I think I just might like to live my life day by day."

She gave me a pat on my back.

"I think that's the only way to do it."

Nine

Mallory

"Daylight savings is next week. I don't know about you, but I'm done with this dark at five thirty nonsense."

Nana had been flipping through the TV guide, circling the shows she wanted to watch for the upcoming week with a red Bic pen that was close to running out of ink so it skipped and stuttered on the paper. I never understood why she did this since she had her favorites set to record already, but people were nothing if not creatures of habit. And Nana's habits were pretty harmless.

"Hoping for some extra hours in the day to paint the town, Nana?" I'd teased and she just offered me a mischievous smile in return.

I'd finished all my homework for the night, thanks to Heath, who offered to go to the library during lunch to help me find what I needed for my English paper on Flannery O'Connor. I'd checked out one of her novels, *A Good Man Is Hard to Find*, and held it up in front of my face just so my eyes peeked out over the top. "It is not!" I'd exclaimed, waggling my eyebrows and pointing to the title. "I found you pretty easily."

"In all fairness, I found you."

"Maybe we found each other."

"Nope." Heath was adamant. He'd been wearing dark jeans and a Rockley High hoodie with a bulldog in white ink drawn across the front, and as usual, he had his hair tucked under a gray wool beanie. "I'm taking the credit on this one. Remember, I walked two miles in the snow both ways to ask you out."

"Fine. The credit is all yours." I'd winked at him and he launched at me with a *hoomf!* The book dropped and clattered to the ground right as his lips smothered mine. We got the expected shushes and eye rolls from several nearby students and the librarian shot a deadly look of warning from behind her pretentiously tall desk, but that only encouraged us. Heath pulled me behind a bookcase and yanked me closer to his body. He was warm and solid. We kissed like that all lunch recess, sneaking away among shelves, pressed up in dark corners and hallways, his mouth on mine, our hands on each other.

Heath was never shy in showing his affection, and I was never hesitant in receiving it.

If someone had asked me that day how much Heath loved me, I would have said with his whole heart. I'd earned every portion, and he'd taken every bit of mine. It was an even and beautiful exchange, to care about someone intensely and equally.

I gave him all of my heart, knowing that I'd never want it back, hoping he'd never have the need to return it to me.

It was his.

I was his.

Ten

Heath

You didn't remember all moments in life the same. Some held extra weight, others extra clarity, and the very few, significant ones became a part of you, embedded in you like the sharp sting of a splinter. Not just a recollection or a fond memory.

These were the memories that defined you. They intersected and disrupted the trajectory of your life, an unforgiving fork in the road that propelled you another direction, one so very far from the path you were comfortably traveling down.

My direction-changing memory occurred on March 23, 2004.

People called moments like these life altering, and I guessed that was true. But it was never just your life to be altered. There were always others involved. The deepest memories always included multiple casualties.

I often wondered what her memory would be. If we sat down, how would she tell it? What parts would she punctuate with expression? What moments would she gloss over? If I asked her to tell her story, would it parallel mine?

I was beginning to think I'd never know.

This was how I remembered things.

The clocks had changed that day. I always hated having to update every damn watch in our house. It seemed impractical to shift life either one hour behind or ahead every six months. Arizona had something going with their refusal to adhere to daylight savings. Whatever. It wasn't as though my complaining was going to change the fact that I'd lose an hour that day.

I'd lose so much more than that.

Mom and Dad were at the hospital, Hattie at volleyball practice. Back in California, I'd been on the baseball team, but I didn't go out for any sports this spring. In years past, my hands would ache for that familiar grip of the bat. The fresh and crisp smell of the field was a homecoming to me. Hours a day would be filled with the repetitive catch and release of the ball from my glove into my dad's in our pasture by the big red barn.

Somehow I'd missed tryouts. It wasn't really a *somehow*. I knew exactly why I'd missed them. I was with Mallory, helping her struggle through her latest pre-calculus assignment. Numbers weren't kind to her brain. They'd jumbled together and when a few letters were thrown into the mix, it was migraine worthy. Her mouth would scrunch in frustration, the thick line of discouragement creased between her eyes. Shoulders hanging in surrender. She was failing. Sure, we were only juniors, but one failed class led to another and another and she didn't have the luxury of many more semesters to catch up.

I knew what happened to small town girls without their diplomas. At least I'd heard stories, ones I could never match with my Mallory. She had so much potential, and potential was not measured exclusively by academic success.

For whatever reason, the day it happened I was out at the ball field. Mallory and her grandmother had plans that afternoon, and when the final bell chimed at the close of the school day, I began walking through the parking lot, right by my dad's car. They carried me all the way to the diamond at the south end of the campus. There were metal bleachers erected behind the dugout, the yellow paint on them chipped and peeling like the polish on Mallory's fingernails. I'd always loved how haphazardly put together she was. She was a jumble of intention, but never quite successful in matching the mold of her more popular and better-dressed peers. I loved her for that, for her originality in every aspect of her life.

I'd watched the boys play for an hour and a half. I'd be lying if I said I didn't feel a stab of jealousy. Of course I did. That pop of the ball into the glove could be felt in my own hands as I sat on the cold bleachers, a spectator rather than a participant. I knew what plays the catcher would signal before he called them. That had been my territory—in the squat behind home plate—and I was damn good at it. I'd winced at every passed ball that slammed into the backstop, knowing I could've blocked it with my knees, my chest, my body. I wore my pitcher's mistakes and made him look good, helped him get the win. That was my job.

I fixed things. I knew how to shadow and pull my glove into the strike position when something came my way a little off center, out of the zone. I'd fool the umpire, the batter, the crowd into believing it was the perfect pitch. I'd changed the outcome by altering the way I received it.

I didn't know how to fix what ended up happening that evening. I couldn't fake out anyone, least of all myself. I'd received the news as anyone would've expected me to, and in truth, it didn't matter how I'd received it.

It wouldn't change the outcome.

The first thing to tip me off was Mom's voice on the other end of my cell. She was working and never called home, not even to check in. My parents were excellent at what they did and wore a professionalism that came with years of practicing bedside manners with their patients. Mom would come home from work and talk without any effect to her tone of a three-month-old flat lining or a teenager recently diagnosed with terminal cancer. It wasn't cruel at all, just matter of fact. Because things happened in life, and that was the truth in it. The world needed people like my parents who could mask their emotions to hunker down to get the job done when the rest of humanity wanted to curl into a helpless fetal position and cry.

Mom's tears that day did not match her hard-earned consistency.

"Heath," her voice quaked out of her. "Heathcliff, honey, there's been an accident." Then she cried softly into the phone, and I knew this wasn't any other patient. She couldn't detach herself from this one. I knew how she'd grown to love Mallory as I had over these past months, and I instantly heard that reflected in her cry. Something in my blood and bones told me it had to be her.

The rest I remember as a blur, both her words and my actions. Something about a drunk driver. Hit and run. Broken windshield. Crumpled steel. Unresponsive Nana. Broken and crumpled Mallory.

I'd leaned over the side of the bleachers and vomited. Twice. Wretched a few more times. Wiped my mouth with the inside of my sleeve. The crack of the bat in the distance felt like it split my skull in two. The players shouting on the field sounded like a stadium filled with thousands of jeering fans, the volume megaphoned in my ears, ringing. Pounding.

Somehow I stumbled my way to the car and the key found the ignition. I remembered sitting there, the engine idling, thinking I had to go somewhere, not knowing how to get there. Not even sure if I had my license or had ever been taught to drive. Brake on the left, gas on the right. That much I knew. It was a haze of starts and stops until I switched off the car in the driveway and sat there, trying to collect myself. Trying to remember how to breathe. The small space in the car was closing in on me, the edges of my vision blackening.

He's home by himself, I remembered thinking. *They were supposed to be back before dinner. He's got to be hungry. And worried. He's worried. I'm worried.*

The front door had been unlocked and it fell open when I rotated the handle. I'd given them grief the week before about how Nana's "crazies" would just welcome themselves into their home and take whatever their heart's desired, but Mallory had corrected me.

"She's only worried about the crazies on the *road*." She'd laughed over dinner, Nana not offering to deny her granddaughter's statement. "Says no one knows how to drive these days, but have you seen her behind the wheel?" Mallory had looked at me above her glass of milk and mouthed, "S-c-a-r-y," and then shot me a wink.

I shook the memory violently from my head. Acid seeped into my throat as I raced down the hall, my feet only slowing up when my shoulder collided with the doorjamb to his den. "Tommy? Tommy!"

Vacant eyes locked onto mine. Innocent, naïve eyes.

"We have to go, Tommy." My feet slipped on wet paint and I skidded toward him like I was on a hockey rink. Whatever he'd been working on broke my fall, my hand punching through the canvas as I landed on my butt. "Dammit!" Anger blasted out of me and I grabbed the frame and slammed it against the ground, over and over, mangling it beyond any sort of recognition. The sound of my brutality mimicked the bat and I'd wished more than anything I had one in my hands. I'd slam it into any surface I could find. Smash it against everything I saw. "Dammit, Tommy!"

That lopsided mouth drooped even more.

"I'm sorry," I'd cried. Snot ran from my nose onto my upper lip. "Tommy, I'm so sorry. I'll fix this."

Fumbling with the piece, I smoothed out the canvas, trying to rejoin the torn sections. I was like a kid finger painting, smearing the colors into a horrible and disgusting brown. I'd ruined his work, but it was all ruined. Everything ruined.

Tommy was terrified. I was terrified. I had to get to them. To her.

"Tommy." My mouth was dry and my tongue scraped with the words. "Tommy, we have to go." He wasn't suddenly going to get out of his chair and follow me. I knew he couldn't do that, so I wasn't sure why I stood there, waiting. I needed someone else to take control, to look at me and say it was going to be okay. *Please tell me everything will be okay.*

"For once it would be nice if you could actually say something!" I screamed. My chest rattled as I roared at the man sitting in the dark in front of me. Then I threw up again, all over his painting, which didn't really matter since it looked like vomit, anyway. Everything spiraled out of control. My words. My actions. My body. My world.

"We have to go," I said once more and his eyes answered me. *Okay*, they'd said. *Okay. Let's go.*

I pushed the mess I'd created out of the way and stooped down to him. He wasn't a small man, necessarily. Standing upright he probably sneaked up upon six feet, but I'd only known the frailty of him, only seen him bent over his work or folded into a chair at the dinner table. I'd misjudged so much about Tommy, including the size of his love for his family.

His eyes were webbed with red veins, cheeks smeared with wet, salty tears. I swiped my arm across my own face, feeling my tears slick on my sleeve. I gulped in air. "Come on, Buddy. We have to go to the hospital."

I picked him up. That was the only way we were going to get to the car. His weight cradled heavily against my chest, and I didn't know if it was his sorrow that sunk his body, making him dead weight, or if this was all he was capable of, the only support he could offer. I'd left the front door open in my rush, but that didn't matter. They could take everything from the house and it would never come close to what was taken from me that day. They could take it all.

After I'd buckled Tommy into the passenger seat, I raced around to the driver's side. Slammed the door behind me and shut us in, wanting to shut everything out.

I locked my seat belt across my lap and threw my head back against the headrest, closing my eyes, welcoming the black.

"Are you a praying man, Tommy?" My head lolled sideways, my gaze sliding to him as my eyelids fluttered open. "I feel like we should pray."

His eyes told me *yes*, I was certain of it.

I'd never prayed before, but I hadn't stopped praying since.

When we showed up at the hospital, Mom was waiting at the entrance. I was grateful someone was there, readied with a wheelchair to help with Tommy, because truthfully, the moment I pulled up, I'd forgotten about everything except for the fact that I needed to get to her. I needed her.

I'd left the car running. Someone shut it off. I'd left the keys in the ignition. Someone brought them to me later. I'd left the world outside those hospital doors *outside* because my entire world was held *within* them.

It was hours and hours of waiting before I was let into the room.

Family Only had been the policy, but having two parents who worked at the hospital offered something in the way of benefits. If you could call seeing your comatose girlfriend a benefit.

She'd looked so small in that cold and sterile room. When finally given permission to visit her, I'd almost backed out. I hated myself for being too scared to join in her tragedy. If I could offer my support from my maroon plastic chair in the waiting room, then I would never know the magnitude of what had happened. My mind could fabricate something else, something easier, something less frightening. Something more hopeful.

I was a coward, plain and simple.

But even cowards did brave things once in a blue moon, so I put on that counterfeit brave face and walked to her room. Room 4D. She had one of those awful blue curtains draped around her bed, and when the nurse pulled it back, it made this horrendous screeching sound as the metal rings scraped on the rod.

My shoulders shot up to my ears to soften the sound.

What I noticed first was that Mallory had no reaction.

She would've made some snide comment yesterday. "Nails on a chalkboard," she would've said yesterday because that was her go-to with anything that made her uncomfortable. Yesterday.

Yesterday.

But it was today.

And I didn't know that I would be able to face my tomorrow.

The nurses and doctors left us alone that night, except when performing their routine monitoring tasks. Overnight visitors of the boyfriend variety must have been off-limits, but no one questioned my presence in her room. And no one questioned me when I'd pulled back her covers and climbed into her hospital bed with her.

It wasn't the same space as the couch, but I maneuvered enough to make myself her boat. "You're safe now, Mallory," I'd whispered into her hair. Her crusted, blood stained hair. I'd kissed her temple which was purpled and swollen. "You're safe."

Nana was in critical condition, my mother told me. Thrown through the windshield, colliding with a tree stump, her body a heap on the pavement at West Street and Magnolia. That tank of a car hadn't been the protection she'd thought it to be. But you couldn't protect yourself against others' mistakes, it seemed.

Mallory was revived at the scene. Revived. The only need for revival was when someone had died, but I didn't want to fit that piece into the story. I hadn't wanted to acknowledge just how close I'd come to losing her completely. She was here now, breathing along with the machine—or maybe because of the machine—but she was here.

And I was with her. I would stay with her forever, I'd promised. *I'll never leave you, Mallory,* I'd murmured against her cold skin all night long. When I kissed her black and puffy eyes swelled shut, I told her I'd always be there. When I held her hand, crippled and scabbed, I whispered my promise again. *I'll never leave you,* I spoke against her mouth as I kissed her, over and over. *I'll never leave you. I love you. I love you.*

I.
Love.
You.

The thing about promises made was that sometimes you didn't hold the power to keep them.

The thing about falling in love so young was that you weren't always responsible for the path your life took, or the decisions that got you there.

We moved three weeks after Mallory's accident.

Dad was transferred to Dignity Memorial back in California. Given a position as Chief of Surgery. A "once in a lifetime offer," they'd said.

I'd had my own *once in a lifetime*, though.

Her name was Mallory.

I never saw her again.

Part Two

Twelve Years Later

Eleven

Heath

"You gotta catch those, man!" My voice carried across the field as the ball rolled to a stop against a tuft of unmowed grass. Summer heat beat down with a sweltering punishment and I felt the sweat collect against my collar and bead upon my brow. I swiped it from my forehead with the back of my hand and shaded my eyes against the glare. Northern California summers were brutal, and though I'd been back for a dozen years now, I still couldn't say I was acclimated to the heat. Not sure I would ever be.

"It had a funny hop to it!" Nico defended. His back was to me as he raced to the collect the wayward grounder. All legs and overgrown feet like a puppy, he stumbled his way to the ball with exaggerated clomping. "There's no way I coulda snagged that!"

"You gotta make the effort. *Always.* Your coach is going to expect it of you. One hundred percent at all times, Buddy."

"And remind me just *how* many years it's been since you've been on a team, Uncle Heath?" He had his mom's quick wit and smart mouth. Everything else was his dad's—down to his unibrow and dimpled, butt chin—but it was those two inner qualities I adored. I absolutely loved that kid, cheap shots and all. He was free to fire them my way anytime.

"As long as you are old, but some things you never forget." I caught his pop fly with ease and lobbed it skyward. "Like the smell of a well-worn glove or the feel of a championship win."

Nico flashed a brace-filled smile. He was an awesome kid, for sure. Though the little brother in me hated to admit it, my sister had done a great job with him. I knew she'd loathe the comparison, but she was her mother's daughter through and through. I watched her with my niece and nephew and it was like she channeled our mom to a T. Her mannerisms, her rules, her love. It was all passed down the family tree and blossomed out of her beautifully.

"Come on, kid. We should head in. Nana's got a killer smelling pot roast in the oven and I hear Papa made his infamous angel food cake, fresh whipped cream and all. We don't want to miss out on that now, do we?"

As he skipped my direction, I made sure to rough up Nico's ebony hair with my balled up fist, and I hip checked him just hard enough that he didn't fall down, but knew he was still lower on the food chain. I was a twelve-year-old boy once and vividly remembered the cocky, false confidence I tended toward. It was my job as an uncle to make sure Nico stayed humble, and it was a job I took incredibly seriously.

Just as seriously as making sure my niece, Natalie, knew that she was an absolute princess. Because she was. I bought her a tiara with more rhinestones than any child had business owning. Whoever she ended up with best be rolling in the dough, because she'd become used to all things that glittered and shone, compliments of her Uncle Heath. That little girl had me wrapped around her ten-year-old finger and held my heart in her delicate, small and perfect hands. I loved that.

Hattie said it was because I was in the delivery room when she arrived—that the bond we had was born out of that lifelong relationship—but I thought it was more than that. I saw so much of Hattie in her spirit, her passion, and her challenging smirk. There wasn't anything that girl set her mind to that she didn't accomplish, and it was an inspiration to me each and every day. I loved that I got to learn from these incredible kids. It was a gift I didn't take lightly, and though I didn't always show my appreciation, I hoped my sister knew how grateful I was to be a part of their lives. She'd given me so much by giving me them.

By the time we reached the porch, my brother-in-law was already there, standing in the frame of the farmhouse doorway, waiting with an outstretched hand and an ice-cold Sierra Nevada for the taking. I swiped it from his grasp and felt the cool glass on my lips, the even cooler liquid sliding down my throat as I took a hearty swallow. "Thanks, man." I tipped the bottle toward him in a gesture of appreciation.

He cracked the cap off his own bottle with the help of his wedding ring and clinked it against mine. "Of course, Heath. Looks well deserved. Hotter than hell out here, isn't it?" He threw his head back and practically drained his beer in one gulp.

Anthony was a great guy—the perfect brother-in-law. He and Hattie met in college and married two months later, which was one month after finding out they had a bun in the oven. I knew it wasn't the way Hattie had planned out her life, but plans weren't all they were cracked up to be. I'd learned that firsthand. Multiple times. Hattie planned on falling in love and starting a family. Maybe the order was jumbled, but the outcome was the same. In the end, the timeline didn't really matter. It all resulted in love.

I nodded toward Anthony and took another swig. "Nico's got a great arm on him. A few more seasons under his belt and I think he could easily make starting pitcher by high school."

"Really?" Anthony's eyes sparked. With one hand, he tugged at his necktie and swiveled it loose, shrugging the day's stress from his shoulders. He was a businessman, not an ounce of athlete or outdoorsman in him, which was fine because it allowed me to fill that role. That was what family was for, wasn't it? Took a village or something along those lines. This was my village and I absolutely loved it.

"Definitely, man. He's got natural talent. You should be proud of your boy." I took a long pull from the bottle and felt the welcome and intimate warmth of alcohol spreading through my veins. "I know I sure am. Love him like he's my own."

Anthony looked at me—right at me—and his eyes softened, which was the exact look I'd been trying to avoid. Soft, sympathetic eyes. It had been six months, and you'd think sympathy had a shorter expiration date than that, but evidently not. It still clung to nearly everyone I came in contact with.

"Listen." I settled the empty bottle on the chipped, white railing and leaned up against its frame, my hands gripped over the rickety ledge. Dad asked for my help last week in repainting the decking, and it looked like it was something that needed finishing sooner than later. I made a mental note to come by this weekend to help him out. "I'm fine. Honestly. Moved on."

"Oh yeah?" With a cocked head, Anthony challenged me. "With who?"

"No one, necessarily. But the *idea* of someone, and that's something."

"Heath." Two hands dropped onto my shoulders. I wasn't sure why everyone felt the need for physical contact when attempting to comfort, but it was getting a bit tired and overdone. I'd been hugged, coddled, stroked, and pet. I was beginning to feel like a damn golden retriever. All I needed was a, "Hey man, your ex-wife was a bitch," and that would suffice.

Instead, I got actual caring and affection, which was not what I wanted.

"I'm *fine*." I pinned him with a stare and he backed off. When he bent down to fetch another cold one from the open ice chest on the porch, I knew he'd made the right decision. Beer—a better comfort than any hug or sage advice.

Anthony knew to leave well enough alone and I appreciated that. We shared a half dozen more bottles on the porch, the dry summer heat oppressive and undesirable, but oddly inviting all the same. We could've easily escaped the temperatures by finding shelter in my parent's air-conditioned, expansive ranch home, but I'd escaped so much already that sometimes it felt necessary to suffer. To stop running. To avoid the false comfort and soak in the real *dis*comfort. Life was not all sunshine and roses. At least not mine. It was once, but that changed, and it seemed like every day since I'd been chasing that lie— the one that said happiness was meant and purposed for everyone.

Because there was nothing happy about the fact that right now—as I drained frosty beverage number eight— my ex-wife was at the local hospital delivering her first child, the one that supposedly belonged to me, but, in reality, shared her boss's DNA.

No, there wasn't any happy in that.

But there was happy on this porch, with this family that I loved and these people who called and claimed me as their own. And there was plenty of happy at the bottom of this longneck of beer.

It might not have been the happy I dreamed of, but I'd take it all the same.

It was hours later and I was in the barn with Mom stacking hay bales from an earlier delivery when my phone dinged in my back pocket, the familiar alert of a received text. I figured it was Paul, wanting to know if I'd be home tonight or if it was safe to bring a woman back to the bachelor pad. My parents lived just far enough away and I was just enough drunk that I had a feeling I'd be crashing in their spare bedroom for the night, which would be fine if I was in college or recently graduated. But I wasn't. I was one month shy of my thirties, which made for a whole new level of pathetic. Possibly a plateau as I wasn't sure it got any greater than this.

I fished my phone out and when the image flashed across the screen upon unlocking it, my hands reacted before my brain and I tossed the device into a muck bucket placed near the door like it was on fire, its burn too much to handle. My eyes reacted quickly, too, because they welled up right away. Maybe it was the alcohol. I'd always been told I was a sad drunk.

Mom tugged her black gloves from her hands with a bite from her teeth and shoved them into the pocket of her denim jacket. She had the phone in her grip, never mind the fact that I'd thrown it in a tub of horseshit. Mom wasn't bothered by things like that. Maybe it was the years of work in the hospital, or maybe it was the cowgirl in her that had recently been reawakened with retirement. Or maybe—plain and simple—it was the maternal instinct to protect her young, and she knew I needed protection from whatever it was that occupied that phone screen. No amount of crap was going to keep her from that.

"Oh, Cliffy." She swiped the phone across her chest to dust it off. When she looked at it again, she squinted deeply. "That's the honest-to-God ugliest baby I've ever seen. Spawn of Yoda if I didn't know any better."

I dropped down onto a hay bale and laughed. "He's not that bad."

"Did you get a good look at this?" She fished her reading glasses out of her jacket pocket and her neck pulled so far back with the second look that she could've gotten whiplash with the movement. "That baby is hideous! No way on God's green earth would anyone think it's yours. If there was ever any doubt that Kayla was a lying, cheating—"

"There's no doubt, Mom. We've been over this."

"All I'm saying is that the proof is in the pudding. And that little puddin' is the spitting image of her ugly ass father."

"Mom!"

"Oh, come on, Heathcliff! We all know Kayla wasn't interested in her boss for his physical looks. It was the looks of his bank account that was much more attractive."

Maybe, but that never made any sense to me. Logan Tallmadge was a successful CPA and I'm sure his income was substantial, but I wasn't completely hurting for cash, either. Anything she'd ever wanted, I'd given to her. The weight on her left hand had to be a reminder of that. The smell of her newly purchased Audi had to be the proof. And the half million dollar Tuscan-style villa, where our life was meant to take place, should've been the backdrop for our ever after.

I gave Kayla everything. Everything except the little life growing in her belly for the past nine months. Someone else gave her that, and when he did, he'd taken over her future and ensured his place within it. I could never compete with a child, and it wasn't something I was willing to even fathom doing.

My life with Kayla was over, and hers was just beginning. I was the end of a chapter for her, and that reality churned my stomach in a violent and tumultuous way. I was beginning to feel like I was constantly the end. A beginning would sure be nice.

Mom sensed my despondent mood. "Know what you need?"

"Another drink?"

"That's a given. Alcohol is always a given," she said with a laugh. "But no. You need a good, old-fashioned, tried and true rebound."

"Not what I thought you'd suggest."

"Oh, come on, Cliffy." Mom slapped me hard on my back, right between the shoulder blades. The barn had been spinning the entire time we'd been in here, but that shove set my eyeballs rolling. My tongue was thick and dry. I was going to pay for this misery tomorrow morning, but for the moment, I welcomed the blur. "Rebound time!"

Then I saw her fingers scrolling. At least that's what I figured they were doing. There was a light echoing palely off her features and I saw the reflection of my contact list arcing across the lenses of her glasses.

"Tanya Bording?" She pursed her lips. "I remember her. Man hands, right? And that hook nose, like Gonzo. Not what you need right now. Let's keep looking."

"Mom."

"Claudia Heldwig. She was that German girl? The foreign exchange student living with Cousin Marty in Santa Clara, ya?" I laughed at the fake accent. "Huge rack if I remember correctly. She's upgraded to the Maybe List just for her tits alone."

I dropped my head into my hands and closed my eyes. What happened to me? What happened to my life that I was twenty-nine years old and hanging out in my parents' barn at eleven o'clock on a Friday night, listening to my mom critique my equivalent of a little black book? Where did life go so wrong for me?

"Mallory Alcott."

There. That was where.

"No."

"She was a sweet girl—"

"*No.*" I stood to my feet and pulled my phone from my mom's hands. I shoved it in my back pocket and grabbed the hay hooks hanging near the door. I shouldn't be trusted with such sharp objects in my current inebriated state, but I had parental supervision so I was willing to risk it.

"Heathcliff, she's the perfect option."

"It's only two letters yet you're having an impossible time interpreting them."

Mom planted her hands on her hips. "I'm well aware what your voice is saying, but your reaction speaks something entirely different."

I pulled another hundred-pound bale down onto the ground from the top of the stack and dust clouded around my feet as it slammed, hay spraying into the air.

"There was never any closure," Mom said as I continued arranging the bales, ignoring her prodding. "And she liked you so much, Cliffy. I'm sure she'd love to hear from you after all of these years."

My neck snapped. "Really?" I didn't condone shouting at women—especially ones who gave birth to you—but my voice rose sharply in my throat and spewed out with enough volume to rattle the barn windows. "Really? You think she'd like to hear from me, hmm? Then why the hell didn't she return any of my twenty-seven phone calls after the accident? Why didn't she reply to the dozen or more letters or the texts or the e-mails?"

The can of worms was flung wide open and they were squirming all over the barn floor. I was drunk enough to think I actually saw them.

"I don't know, Heath, but I'm sure there's an explanation."

I was defeated, plain and simple. I felt like I couldn't breathe.

"Call her."

"It's going to take a lot more alcohol before I'll ever consider calling Mallory Alcott." My thumb was raw from gnawing on it. I wished I could give up my adolescent nervous tendencies like this one, but it was clear I had my hang-ups. Loads of them.

"Seven."

"What?" I looked up at Mom. She was still quite beautiful with her salt and pepper, sleek bob and full lips, feathered with well-earned wrinkles on her face. She wore her concern and her love in her present expression, and I was a fool to assume this whole shenanigan was for anything other than her wanting the very best for me. She loved me deeply, more so with each passing day. So far, she was the only person in my life to ever offer me that. "Seven what?"

"Beers. Seven beers," she answered. "It took seven beers for me to say yes to your father, but it was the best stupid risk I've ever made. Sometimes we need to take the stupid risks in order to get the best reward."

"And you don't think I've taken enough risks? The masters program? Marriage?"

"Those aren't risks, Cliffy. Those are plans. Big difference."

"I don't plan on calling Mallory." My head throbbed to the point where I thought another beer was the only thing that could take the edge off, but I knew it wasn't the wisest of decisions. Hangover remedies often begot greater hangovers.

"Rebounds are rarely planned."

Mom smirked at me like she knew something, like she was privy to some secret I'd yet to uncover. She was keeping something back.

But the thing was, I was the one keeping it back. I was keeping back the fact that it was impossible to rebound *with* the person you've been rebounding *from* all these years.

Calling Mallory wouldn't solve anything.

Calling Mallory would be a stupid, stupid risk, one I wasn't willing to take, no matter how drunk I got.

Some things were always crystal clear.

Twelve

Mallory

"I'll take all four." Cathy Broderick was a woman I loved doing business with, and her order was incredibly necessary music to my ears and my bank account. "You must have them delivered and someone will need to come down and arrange them. I don't have time for that. And I'm not paying for any that show up damaged, even if they're fixable. I don't care that they're being shipped across the country—absolutely no damage. And no charge for the shipping, nor handling."

"Of course." I nodded. It was more work and money on my end, but what I knew of Cathy was that she was a stiff, unrelenting broad and even if I attempt to renegotiate something reasonable into the contract, she wouldn't yield. "Everything just as stated here."

"Have them arrive on the twelfth. The walls will be ready."

"Yes." I stuffed my papers into my leather messenger bag. My hands were clumsy and shaky. The perfume thick on her skin nauseated me and I took several staccato breaths as though by avoiding breathing deeply, I could avoid the pungent aroma that twisted my stomach. I was a smart enough woman to know that wouldn't do any good, but I did it still. "Thank you, again. Always a pleasure doing business with you."

"Always a pleasure doing business with your *father.* He's the real talent here." Her lips were as tight as the black pantsuit she had on, firm and unmoving. Dark beady eyes lowered, casting a judgmental gaze. "*You*, my dear, are a hot mess."

Cathy Broderick was an awful, pretentious woman, but Cathy Broderick was an observant woman. I was a mess. Carrying a fancy briefcase and dressing in the prettiest dress I owned—the one stuffed all the way in the back of my closet, years' worth of must clinging to its fibers—did not a convincing businesswoman make. Even still, I'd felt beautiful as I slipped it over my small shoulders this morning. I'd hoped the charming apricot hue of roses patterned over the fabric would bring out the glow of my cheeks, accentuating them rather than the reddened rims of my eyes, the semi-permanent veins that crisscrossed the whites of them.

Of course, I'd been wrong.

I didn't linger on Cathy's comment. I was out the door after gathering my things and was smacked by the angry heat of triple digits. I reeled back, then adjusted the hem of my skirt, fluffed my hair, and pushed forward.

The car was parked two blocks over in an empty lot and my heels wobbled down concrete which was speckled with black circles of used gum spat onto its sidewalk. Urine stained the brick walls on buildings a century or more old. It could've been a lovely little town if someone took care of it, but I wasn't sure whose responsibility that was. The mistakes of many have led to its current state. Words like revitalization and revamping got thrown around a lot, but they didn't stick like the grime.

Cathy's small gallery offered a bit of hope. Of all the tenants, she certainly brought in the most revenue, many thanks to my father. I knew her ostentatious lifestyle was also a direct result of the commission she made on his paintings. Everyone knew that. I didn't have the heart to tell her these would be the last she'd ever purchase from our family.

Maybe it wasn't the heart I didn't have. Maybe it was the balls.

By the time I made it to my car, my skin was sticky with perspiration. I could feel the dampness of my underarms and frowned at the fact that I'd have to dry clean this dress. Back into the closet it was going to go. Now I had yet another bill to add to the pile.

I slammed the door to my car and sunk into the driver's seat. It was the kind of heat that made you fight for breath, and I cranked the air on as soon as the key hit the ignition. Minutes went by before the blast was cool enough to do anything to my current body temperature. Dried sweat now chilled made me shiver, as did the tears that burned the backs of my eyes. I slammed the car into *Drive* and backed out of the parking lot.

The road home was under thirty minutes, but I didn't remember much of it. There was a broken down vehicle on I-5 going north, I thought, because I remembered slowing for the first responders with their red lights as warning beacons, pulled off to the side to aid in the rescue. I remembered speeding back up again to keep up with the flow of traffic.

Keep up with the flow.

That's what I'd been doing for the past year and a half. Keeping up.

My bottom lip quivered and I scolded it with my teeth. There was a permanent groove settling into the flesh there.

The tears won their way, spilling over and down my cheeks

I couldn't keep up with the flow anymore.

I couldn't keep up.

I didn't know why I even tried.

Tori was on the couch when I got home, her neck bent at such an angle that her head was square with her chest. The way her fingers flew over the phone made me pause to take in the scene. I'd bet money that the good majority of Tori's conversations with friends took place in written text rather than face-to-face. It made me wonder if she really did laugh out loud, or if it had merely become a three letter, typed reaction for her.

I pushed the garage entry door into the jamb with more force than necessary to startle her into awareness as I walked into the house.

"Mallory!" Tori jumped from the couch. Her curly blonde hair twirled around her face as she spun toward me. "You're back early."

I slipped my bag off my shoulder and my high heels from my feet. My arches ached as they flattened onto the cool tile and I paced across the kitchen toward her. "Well, you know Cathy Broderick. She's nothing if not extremely efficient."

"And extremely awful."

"A little of that, too." I laughed and placed three folded tens into Tori's hand. She curled her fingers around the bills and then stuffed them into her jean shorts pockets, a toothy grin exposed under glossy pink lips. Her cheeks were so plump with youth they reminded me of when I was that age. When life was an exciting, intriguing, and naïve adventure. "How'd everything go?"

"Same as always. He made a mess with the paint again, but I think I got it all cleaned up this time."

"I'm sure it's fine." I gave Tori a tight hug, thankful to have her here. She'd been a godsend these past several years and I loved her like family. There were few people I could call on at a moment's notice, but I knew Tori was certainly one of them. She'd been on the receiving end of several late night, incoherent phone calls and texts, and thinking back on those moments made me feel bad for criticizing her social skills. Sometimes the heart emoticons she'd send my way were exactly what I'd needed. "Same time tomorrow still work for you?"

"Sure thing."

As I walked her to the door and watched her get into her brother's metallic blue car, my heart squeezed, a vise grip of emotion taking hold. Her tires squealed faintly against the curb and the sedan rocked onto the street as she switched the vehicle into gear, the movement jerky and unpracticed. Tori tossed me a wave out of the rolled down window and I lifted my hand to return one of my own.

Then I got as far away from that window as I could. I'd spent countless days waiting by it and I wouldn't do that again. With hasty movements, I dragged the curtains shut even though it was only six thirty-six. The rest of the neighborhood surely suspected things, the way the house was always buttoned up, the garage closed and blinds drawn. They must've thought something was going on inside this quiet place. The truth was, I didn't know how to cope with what was going on outside of it. Sometimes shutting oneself in seemed an awful lot like shutting others out.

I backed away from the window and bumped squarely into a wall like it hadn't been there for the past five years. Like I'd missed out on the remodel taking place and it was some new addition. My head rocked back and I leaned against the drywall, eyes closed.

I could hear him faintly on the other side.

It was enough to pull me from my stupor, from the trap of memories in my mind. More than enough. I jogged around the corner to the second bedroom on the right, and I pulled on the doorknob, rotating it softly so as not to make a sound. The room was dark, but he sensed me right away like always. The tightness tugging at my heart unraveled and my body filled with the warmth of unconditional love.

"Hello, my sweet boy. Did we have a good afternoon with Auntie Tori?" Two small coos answered my question. I heard his chubby legs kick, kick, kicking against the crib mattress, springs coiling squeakily in response.

I promised myself I wouldn't fall asleep in the rocker again tonight, but as I lifted him from where he lay and we settled into our favorite space, Corbin's sweet breath fanning against my neck, his tiny heart beating on top of mine, I knew there wasn't any good reason to place him back into the empty crib to sleep alone. We had each other, and while most children sought their mothers for comfort and assurance, I relied on Corbin equally as much for those two things.

I was sure of the life I once owned when I looked into his eyes. He wore so much of his father on his cherub face, in his crooked smile and long, long lashes. They were the kind that would be the recipient of comments for the rest of his days. He'd grow tired of hearing how unreal they were, become annoyed at how jealous the girls got that a boy would have such beautiful and full eyelashes. He'd grow to hate them, but I'd make him learn to love them.

That was my job now. To make him learn to love *him*.

I wasn't sure if it was innate. It could be one of those things where the stories told by firesides and dinner tables built an imaginary relationship where the real memories were missing. Layer upon layer added in like a tale from a book of fables. A book full of them. A book full of life.

"He wanted you so badly, Corbin," and "He named you the minute I showed him the pregnancy test," and "He planned to take you fishing at three, hunting at twelve. Already owned the rod and the rifle."

Each milestone in my son's life would be tagged with the disclaimer that his father would've "loved to be there for this."

There would always be a missing piece, a gap in his future. Like playing chess without a king or making cookies when you'd run out of sugar, but on a scale not even measurable. Just this gaping, yawning, and noticeable hole where something wasn't quite right.

My world had more missing pieces than usable ones, so of course I got it.

Mom.

Dylan …

I broke my promise and woke up the next morning with a slumbering baby on my chest, sleep lines from the rocker's cushion pressed deep onto my cheek.

But I'd broken a lot of promises in my life.

I wasn't sure it was actually possible for anyone to really keep one.

Thirteen

Heath

Congratulations, Mr. McBride!

Big, swirly letters were scrawled across the entire length of my white board.

I'd already eaten up a good ten seconds staring at the dry erase words, my back turned to the thirty-two pairs of eyes that greeted me for first period Honors English. I settled my leather messenger bag onto my desk without looking down, my fingers fumbling, my words not doing any better. I was buying time, but high school seniors weren't necessarily known for their grace and patience in giving it.

There were two options here, really.

Option One: I could ignore this hulking elephant in the room and continue our section on Flannery O'Connor and the weaving of her faith into her works as planned.

Option Two: I would address this monstrous oversight on my part. The one where I forgot to mention that my ex-wife's new addition was added without the seemingly necessary help of me.

Tabitha Contreras, one of my seniors who I could count on in any situation to answer questions, no matter how challenging or difficult, came to my rescue. She was going to bail me out, just like she bailed out her classmates when the silence became too thick, when the others avoided the answers and waited for the more astute and dedicated peers to come to their aid.

I locked eyes with her and practiced my best telepathy. *Come on, Tabitha. Bail me out. Please.*

"We have a little something for you, Mr. McBride!"

She stood, slipping out from behind her desk. Metal feet scraped against the puke green linoleum. Her arms tucked behind her, hiding something from view. While walking toward me, she swung her ebony hair over her shoulder and offered a smile. It was like she was the spokeswoman for the class, and I knew that curlicue message must've been penned by her hand.

I gulped back the bite of acid that bubbled in my throat. That triple shot Americano wasn't the best breakfast choice, but I needed something strong to combat the hangover I'd incurred from my weekend antics. The ones that involved me getting wasted at my parents' ranch and shutting out the sun under drapery-drawn windows and patchwork quilts, my head hidden from the outside world and the land of the living. Total zombie style.

I was going to need another highly caffeinated drink by noon at this rate.

"My mom works at the hospital and told us your news! We're so happy for you, Mr. McBride. You're going to be an absolutely awesome dad!"

Like a runway, Tabitha shimmied to the front of the class and just as I was about to correct her (at least it felt like I was going to correct her—I was aware I hadn't done anything to contradict the class's assumptions), she shoved a haphazardly wrapped gift into my hands. Baby rattles, blocks, and a stuffed teddy bear repeated in a nauseating pastel pattern across the paper. It crinkled in my palms.

"Oh, how thoughtful, class," or *"You really shouldn't have,"* were two options that failed to make their way out of my parched and numb mouth. The shape my lips took must've been terrifying. I wasn't grimacing, but I certainly wasn't smiling. Just this frozen, wide open gape, like a clown. Clowns were scary as hell.

I was a freaking clown, in more ways than I cared to admit.

"Mr. McBride?" Tabitha's doe eyes went wide. "Mr. McBride, are you okay?"

There was a scattering of *He doesn't look so good,* and *What the hell is wrong with him?* among my students.

When I heard Toby Kincaid, the six-foot-four, long-haired quarterback, stutter, "Big congrats to your swimmers, McBride!" I knew this shenanigan had to come to a screeching and abrupt halt.

I'm not one of those throat-clearing teachers, but some situations called for it.

Swallowing past the lump in my throat, I began, "Listen, class." My gaze swung over the beige painted room, at the bright eyes of my students assembled before me, their expressions eager and equally concerned. "I seriously appreciate all of this. You guys are incredible. Truly."

"There's a but," Mark Dwayne jeered from his seat in the front row. "I'm sensing a but." I moved him up there last week because he couldn't be trusted to pay any amount of attention in the back of the class unless it was to the girls that sat on either side of him. But I saw he had no problem focusing now. Touché.

"Class—Kayla and I split up six months ago."

"Last I checked," Mark started, his expressive, dark brows cocked up to his hairline, "It takes nine months to grow a kid."

Tabitha still occupied the walkway, and when it clicked, her small hands flew to her mouth. "Oh, God, Mr. McBride! I'm so sorry! I just figured—"

"That I'd be the one to have a baby with my wife?" I laughed, genuinely, because it actually was sort of hysterical, in a pathetic way. There was an uneven echo of insecure chuckles across the room. "Yeah, me too."

Apology was written all over Tabitha's face as she had clearly been the orchestrator for today's baby shower. "We are total idiots."

"Since I have access to the grade book, I beg to differ." I sat on the edge of my desk. The button-down white shirt bunched at the sleeves and I pushed them back more before folding my arms across my chest. "Only about half of you are idiots."

That got the chorus of laughter I needed. I felt the energy shift, everything guided back on track. I loved these kids and knew they wanted the absolute best for me, which might've been a strange thing for a teacher to say. Of course I had those same feelings for them, but there was a mutual respect and admiration here. In a way, I felt like I'd let them down in letting my marriage down. A hopeful celebration was something we all could have used.

"I'm going to be completely candid with you all for a moment if you'll let me." Tabitha found her seat again and I took the reins now that the class was somewhat in order. "Kayla and I went our separate ways just before Christmas," I began to explain as I swept the eraser over the white board, each letter blotted away with a stroke of my hand. I settled the felt brush back onto the tray and swiveled on the heels of my leather loafers and they squealed. "In reality, she went her own way long before that. I didn't mention anything at the time because, as your teacher, my personal life is not meant to be on display nor become a burden and distraction to you in any way."

Sabrina Temple's red head snapped up from her place in the second row. Her thick-rimmed glasses slipped down her nose and she adjusted them as she said, "You're not a burden, Mr. McBride. We care about you, just like you care about us." As though surprised by her sudden and quick response, her gaze diverted back to her four-book-high stack adorning her desk, a tower of fictional escapes. She fanned and flipped through the top one, though I knew for a fact that she'd read it three times already. Meek and quiet, she wasn't the one I'd expected to speak up in my defense and I smiled at the surprising gesture.

"I agree, sir."

Lucas Hawthorne.

He was the guy. The one I knew had my back because I definitely had his. I knew parents weren't allowed to have favorites, but that was the beauty of being a teacher. We could (and did) totally have favorites, and over my six years of teaching, Lucas took the number one spot, hands down.

"We're here for you. I know I don't just speak for myself when I say you've always been there when we needed you the most." He turned in his seat, surveying the class like he was rallying them together. "Like last week when Principal Higgins threatened to cancel Senior Ball because we all skipped class on Senior Ditch Day, even though it's a tradition that's been around for the past thirty years. You came to our defense and changed her mind. We owe you big time for that."

Mark narrowed his eyes, nodding. "Or like the time when Vanessa broke up with me and you totally played along with the new girlfriend story I created to make her jealous. You didn't question my elaborate, unnecessary details and specifics about said made up girlfriend."

"Not sure lying was the best decision on my part in that instance, Mark—"

"You had my back, McBride, when it seemed like no one else did."

Lucas planted his hands on his desk, resolute. He shook his cropped brown hair from his forehead and looked directly at me with thoughtful, hazel eyes. "What we're saying, sir, is that you aren't just any teacher to us. You're not some old, tired dude that's only here for the paycheck. You genuinely care about us, and we care about you."

"Which is why we wanted to throw you a shower," Tabitha chimed in. Her voice fell in disappointment as she swiveled in her seat at the back of the room to make eye contact. "And to tell the truth, why we're a little hurt that you kept this from us."

I saw their point and saw the confusion in their eyes. I knew I wasn't a peer—that as their teacher I had to be set apart even just a little bit—but I also understood that much of teaching, of mentoring, involved transparency and the ability to relate on the same level as people. Forget the divide that came through the gap of years, education, and experiences. I'd taken that from them.

"We just wanted to be happy for you, sir." Lucas pulled at the collar of his plaid flannel, clearing his throat. He reminded me so much of me at that age—inevitably and awkwardly stuck between a boy and a man. His Adam's apple lifted as he said, "We just want you to be happy."

"I am happy." Overwhelmed, a little hung over, and exhausted, too. But these kids—they made me happy. "Happiness is not circumstantial. It can't be because there will always be something to bring you down."

"Like your ex-wife shacking up with another dude," Mark blatantly told it, yet refreshingly so.

"Exactly like that. Just when you think life is going smoothly, something juts in your path and throws you off course."

She wasn't one of the usual talkers, so it surprised me that Sabrina spoke up in again. "Always?"

"No, not always. Of course not. But what I'm trying to say is that you can't base your happiness on things out of your control."

"I'm not sure any of it really *is* in our control, sir," Lucas said. His large shoes planted underneath him as he sat up straight in his chair. I noticed the way Sabrina watched him from her seat next to him, how she tracked his movements, and it was something I'd never recognized between them, this interest on her part. I wondered if he was at all aware. Probably not—he was a high school-aged boy and being clueless often came with that territory.

"I don't think much is in our control, except for our choice in choosing happiness," I answered.

Mark laughed. "You sound like a greeting card."

"Do I?" I chuckled. "I sure as hell hope not, because I don't want to give you the wrong impression. Life sucks sometimes, plain and simple. I'm in the suck of it right now."

"Preach it, Teach!" I didn't know who hollered it out, but I took it and rolled with it.

"You think love and life is hard as a teenager? I hate to break it to you, but it's not any easier at my age. You don't suddenly figure it all out. You might think you have, but then someone makes a choice that affects your whole world. They pull out that one wrong Jenga piece and it all crashes."

It was May. I'd had this particular group of students for nine months now and their attention had never been as rapt as it was in that moment. Eyes wide and perceptive, ears alert, minds focused. Maybe I'd been teaching them the wrong things this entire time because my audience had never been so captive.

"Kayla was your latest Jenga piece," Tabitha said.

"One of many. But you have to keep playing the game. Keep restacking the pieces."

Lucas shifted toward Sabrina, unintentionally, I figured, but she sensed it. I saw the nerves straining her brow and quickening her breath. "Who pulled out the first piece?"

"My parents. They yanked me from my school when I was a junior—moved me back across the country away from everything I loved. *Everyone* I loved."

"What was her name?"

They were quicker than I gave them credit. "Love of my life."

"Aww!" Tabitha cooed.

Lucas looked right at me, ignoring his classmate's fawning. "Where is she now?"

"I have no idea."

"You have no idea?" There was a bit of anger in his voice, at the very least, annoyance. "How could you be in love with someone and not know where they ended up?"

I officially scrapped today's lesson.

"I *was* in love with her. A long time ago. Back when I was your age."

Mark hissed disapprovingly through his teeth. "I will always know where Vanessa is. Until my dying day."

"And that, my friends, is what we call a stalker," Lucas teased with a nudge to Mark's elbow so that his arm slipped out from him and slammed onto his desktop. His friend shot a glare, but it was playful in nature. They had the sort of relationship where they could get away with being an ass to one another, and I was admittedly jealous of their easy camaraderie. It wasn't so simple the older you got. There was baggage and walls and insecurities that only deepened over the years. Age and time complicated so many things.

"We lost touch."

Not fully a lie, not entirely the truth.

"You do realize that we live in the era of the Internet, don't you, Mr. McBride?" I didn't know why I kept Tabitha in the back of the class when she so eagerly engaged and interacted. She had to raise her volume so I could hear her from the front of the room, but she had no problem doing so with her cheerleader lungs. "There's this really incredible thing called Google."

"I've Googled her."

"And?" Mark, Sabrina, Lucas and Tabitha all formed one loud, inquisitive voice that caught me off guard.

"And she's married. I stopped searching after that." Just in case they didn't catch my drift, I added, "Off-limits."

"In fairness, McBride, you were married until recently, too," Mark said. "And now look at you."

"Thank you for that reminder, Mark. But I can guarantee she is still happily married." Emotion sneaked up on me, a force unexpected but not unwelcome. There was a hollow feeling in my stomach, this dip-on-a-roller-coaster type of sensation. My seventeen-year-old self crashed in. I was sweaty. Nervous. I was flustered, all from thinking of her.

"How are you so sure, sir?"

"Because she isn't the type of girl you willingly leave."

Again with the surprises, Sabrina looked up suddenly from her book, the one she'd been fake-reading for the last five minutes. "I don't consider you to be the type of person someone would leave, either, Mr. McBride." She closed her book sloppily and it tumbled to the floor. Clearly embarrassed by the commotion, Sabrina's freckled cheeks reddened, and the pigment only deepened when Lucas bent down to retrieve her novel. "Thank you," she muttered as he placed it into her hands.

"Sure." He smiled back. He wore the grin even after she'd looked away.

I cleared my throat for the second time this period. "Why are we talking about my teenage love life?"

"Because you are sad and lonely and maybe looking up this chick might make you not so sad and lonely." Mark flashed a toothy grin. He was all muscle and dark features, cocky and confident. The girls adored him. The guys wanted to be him. And apparently he was also a cheerleader. He broke into the chant, "Google her, Google her," and the entire class joined in, their voices of encouragement pulsing around me.

"If it will get you all to move forward and focus back on your schoolwork, then yes, I'll Google her." I surrendered, but it wasn't that hard. It was one thing when my mom suggested calling. That was a step I wasn't about to take, to hear her voice—matured and full—on the end of the line. But a simple Internet search—this I could do. I pushed up from my desk and grabbed my reading glasses from my top drawer, then closed it shut as I pulled my book from my messenger bag, readying for some Flannery O'Connor.

"I expect a full report tomorrow," Mark said, one last request before we started today's studies.

"Be sure to cite your resources," Sabrina added.

"Be sure give us all the juicy details," Tabitha interjected.

Lucas looked me square in the eye. "Be sure to take a deep breath and just remember that whatever you find, the girl you once loved is still in there and chances are, she's probably thought about you a few times over the years, too."

I cocked my head, perplexed by his insight, but appreciative all the same. "Deal."

"Deal," they all agreed back.

Deal.

Fourteen

Mallory

I snapped awake.

Breathe, breathe.

Sweat slithered down my back. My heart sprinted.

The space where I lay was damp with perspiration, all clammy and uncomfortable like I'd used the sheets as a towel after a swim, my body's outline wet and chilled.

I looked to the monitor on my nightstand and the angelic scene of my baby deep in slumber met my eyes. It slowed my breath. *Steady, steady.*

I let the relief slide out as I leaned against the headboard.

A year and a half and yet it was like yesterday to me.

It was actually every night, stuck in a dream.

It was a dangerous job, we knew that. He'd been an officer for a year already when I'd first met him, so it wasn't as though I'd had a say in his profession. Even if I had, though, I would've encouraged it all the same. Some people were meant for that line of work. Dylan certainly was.

He was brave beyond belief.

Now it was my turn to be brave.

I grabbed my terrycloth robe from the closet and slipped into it, tightening the belt around my waist before making my way to the kitchen. The fluorescent lights flickered on, stuttering to illuminate.

2:08 a.m.

Coffee. That was in order for this sort of hour. I took the grounds from the freezer and put a pot on, waiting for it to brew. My stomach growled, encouraged by the smell, and I tried to remember if I had eaten any dinner. The plate in the sink reminded me of the chicken enchiladas Mrs. Scuttle from church brought over this afternoon. So I had eaten, tonight at least. That was good.

Once the coffee was ready, I poured myself a steaming mugful and took it with me to the den, my fingers curling around the handle, my palm cozied against the warm ceramic. There was one of my favorite vanilla candles on the desk and I lit it with a match. The flame flickered against the dark as the aroma dispersed sweetly into the air.

That tension from being thrust awake seeped slowly from my body, more importantly, my mind. I could do this. I *could*.

Dad did it for years and we were good. When Mom was first diagnosed, I think he knew the inevitable outcome. The way he enjoyed her—enjoyed all our short time as a family—it was as though each moment would be a last.

I wished I'd paid more attention to how he was able to do that. Treasure the lasts.

I slid into the desk chair and tucked my feet up underneath me, the robe blanketing my cold legs with fabric. With the mouse in my hand, I stirred the computer to life. It hummed angrily, reminding me of another inevitable expense. The windows on the screen were still open and I clicked through the tabs. I'd done all the math and every way I calculated it, I came up short. I'd give anything to be with Nana and Tommy again, but the way the market was, there was no way I would ever get back what I owed on this house. I'd be stuck here until things eventually leveled off.

Stuck.

Even still, I busied my mind by searching cottages and townhouses back in Kentucky. Ones that shared the same zip code as my family. Ones where Corbin could walk to his great-grandmother's house after school for fresh baked cookies or for help with his reading homework. Ones where I could send him over for a cup of sugar. Ones where we felt as one again, living life together, even if not within the same walls.

But I had two families now.

Tori was here, at least for another month before she left for college. And Sharon and Boone were just fifteen minutes away. I'd never had a sister, and it had been years since I had a mother and father in the mother and father sense that most people had, but I had *them*. I wasn't willing to let that go, even though I've had to let Dylan go.

So I'd stay up late at night and dreamed of an old life back in Kentucky. I'd decorate the rooms in my head. Practiced writing my name and address on an envelope, just to see how it looked. All my current return address labels still had Dylan's name printed on them. I tried using a Sharpie to black it out once, but something looked off. A little morbid. But I'd ordered a roll of 500. It seemed like such a waste of a perfectly good label.

My eyes blurred. The screen waved in my vision and I sniffed the tears back, using my sleeve as a tissue.

"Pull yourself together, Mallory Quinn," I instructed. It didn't work.

I let myself weep into my coffee mug until the tears were gone and there was nothing left besides a few sighs and the shudders that follow a hearty cry.

"Okay. *Now* pull yourself together." I let myself have second chances when it came to things like this.

Two hours passed quickly, one click leading to another until I was looking at plantations in Georgia where I could own a "small piece of history and huge portion of southern charm." I had no idea how my search led me to the opposite coast, but it was a distraction and I welcomed it. In this particular house I'd found, Corbin and I would breed and raise French bulldogs and compete in chili cookoffs with the award-winning recipe we'd discover behind a broken board in the pantry. We would call ourselves the *Chili-Bulls* because it was convenient to lump our two titles as one and because that was as creative as I got at four in the morning. Our prize pup, Sir McDoodle, would win the 2025 National Dog Show, allowing Corbin to go to Duke and major in neuroscience with the earnings.

I giggled to myself.

Was that the life I really wanted to lead? I'd never even made homemade chili.

This was crazy. Maybe I was crazy. No *maybe* about it.

But what was really crazy to me was that one move—one decision—could change so much.

I'd told Nana to turn right that day.

Dylan offered to cover his partner's shift.

So here I was, a twenty-eight-year-old widow and mother.

And I was lonely. I was so *lonely.*

I reached for my cell phone and unplugged it from the computer where it had been syncing.

Three rings and she picked up. "Nana?"

"Mal, sweetheart." Her voice was thinner than it used to be, shakier. Despite the frailty to it, she spoke with a chipper tone and I could tell she'd been up for a while. I was thankful for the three-hour time difference between us on nights like this. "Can't sleep?"

"Not even a little bit."

She huffed into the mouthpiece. "Not even a *little* bit. Well, that certainly will not do."

"Do you own a large pot for cooking chili?"

"No, I can't say I do," she answered, then paused. "Do you need a large chili pot for something?"

"Not in the immediate future, but someday."

"Okay," she said. I could hear her smile, even through the phone. "I'll be sure to grab one on Black Friday this year. You know, just to have on hand."

I sighed.

"Another bad dream?"

I was a grown woman with a child of my own, but the only place I wished to be right now was snuggled under Nana's patchwork quilt, her reassuring hand stroking through my hair, her soft words telling me everything would be okay.

"Yeah, bad dream."

The computer dimmed, the screen saver turning on. It was a terrible idea to have the *Pictures* folder go into slideshow mode when the mouse sat quiet for too long. Dylan had set it up. He thought I would be grateful for the digital album that highlighted our good memories. But it was hard to look at his wide smile. Our smiles. Even the computer couldn't sleep without his face flashing across it.

I swallowed and shook the hell out of the mouse.

"I'm thinking of moving back to Kentucky."

Through the earpiece, I could hear Nana's hesitant breath release. "Oh, Mallory. You know that's not the best idea."

"Why isn't it?"

I was looking for a list of pros and cons here. For the good to outweigh the bad.

"Sweetheart, it's nice for Corbin to be near his grandparents."

"What about you? And Tommy?"

"Let's face it, I'm no spring chicken." She laughed. "And with Tommy's declining health. He's stopped painting and …" She trailed off. I didn't have to ask her to elaborate. "Boone and Sharon would be devastated if you took their only grandbaby from them. Rightfully so. There's no real reason for you to come back to Kentucky, sweetie. California is where your life is now."

She was right and I knew it. I just had to hear her speak those truths to me once again. To help convince my heart what my head already knew.

Switching gears, she asked, "How's the job hunt going?"

"Nothing permanent yet, but I've got a position I'm starting on Monday at a flower shop about twenty minutes away. It's their busy season with proms and weddings, apparently."

"That's great, Mal!" she said, her voice hopeful and kind. Nana was so good at being those two things. "Maybe it will turn into something."

"Maybe," I agreed, hoping—*needing*—something to keep my feet planted in California when my roots felt half a world away. "Maybe it will."

I swiveled the mouse on the desk and clicked out of the websites until they were all closed down, cleared from the search history.

Then I shut the computer completely off, letting my irrational dreams fade black with it.

Fifteen

Heath

She was either military or an ex-convict or in the Witness Protection Program.

Those were the options I was going with. Other than a marriage license, there was very little in the way of Internet presence when it came to Mallory Alcott.

Mallory *Quinn*.

It was a beautiful name, even though someone else gave it to her. She deserved a beautiful name, though. McBride just made me think of a wedding catered by McDonald's or something. Maybe if I'd suggested that to Kayla things would've gone in a different direction. Instead, we had a five-course meal enjoyed with our 350 best friends on a beach one hundred miles from our house with a reverend neither one of us even knew. Many of these so-called friends Facebook blocked me the day Kayla walked out. How odd was that? That *she* left *me*, yet took our entire social circle with her.

All I really had left were my family, my students, and my roommate, though I supposed that was all I needed.

Maybe I didn't even need the roommate.

Actually, at this late hour, as I listened to whatever bedroom Olympics were taking place behind the wall shared with mine, I decide I *really* didn't need a roommate. Not this one, at least.

Paul was a good enough guy. He didn't touch my food in the fridge and he bought toilet paper when we ran out. Those were definite marks in his favor. And he was a Pre-Cal teacher at Whitney High, so carpooling cut down on gas money. He had a great collection of vintage Grateful Dead LPs that were on constant rotation and he hadn't mentioned Kayla's name even once since moving in, so those were the obvious reasons I liked him.

But the slumber parties, those had to stop.

This guy was a sex athlete because just as I thought his date and my ears were about to get a little reprieve, he was back at it again, going for the gold.

I needed to escape this. I slammed my laptop closed and grabbed my wallet and keys. Our apartment was on the second floor and though it neared ten o'clock, the air was still heavy and hot and I was sweating by the time I made it down the flights of stairs. I clicked my truck unlocked, the beep echoing off the carport roof. The cab was musty with the stench of decomposing fast food still left in crumpled brown bags. I'd take better care of the junker if I thought it would mean I could someday sell it for Blue Book pricing, but this thing didn't even register on there. It was the equivalent of Fred Flintstone car, for sure. But it continued to run fine enough, so I kept it.

I hit the gas as soon as I eased out of the complex's parking lot. I didn't bother with the radio anymore, it had been on the fritz since I purchased the vehicle, so I pulled out my phone from my back pocket and scrolled through the playlist, one eye on the road, the other on the phone.

And then both of them on the rearview mirror and the flashing blue lights that sparkled like a house all lit up with a Christmas display.

Groaning, I slid deeper into my seat as I angled the jalopy off to the shoulder of the road and readied my license and registration.

"Good evening," a clean-cut officer about my age greeted as he peered in my rolled down passenger window. I jutted my hand out with my documents and he took them from my grasp. "I gather you already know why I'm pulling you over."

"Yes, sir. For doing the very thing I caution my students not to do on a daily basis."

He nodded and smiled as his pen scrolled across his notepad. He had a high and tight hairstyle going on and a tan that looked more inherited than sun-given.

"A teacher, huh? Locally?"

"Whitney High School just down the street."

"Excellent football team." He still didn't look at me and I was eye level with his broad chest and shiny badge adorning it. *Officer Douglas.*

"Back in the day, definitely."

The Matadors hadn't had a winning season in nearly a decade, but for five solid years there we were nationally ranked champions. It was funny that those few good seasons earned us a positive reputation that we couldn't shake. In a way it was good we were able to hold on to that claim to fame, but it was reliving the glory days at its finest, and at some point that became tired.

The officer was still studying my information when he crouched down and rested his elbows on the window ledge of my car. "Heathcliff McBride?" he asked, a strain in his gaze. I thought through all the things I'd ever done wrong and wondered if maybe, just maybe, there was some outstanding warrant for my arrest that I was totally unaware of. Panic stabbed me in my stomach.

"Yes, sir."

It seemed like maybe I was supposed to know him, the way he scanned me for recognition. "Heathcliff McBride, please don't let me find you on your phone again while driving, okay? California is hands-free."

I tried not to let him see the huge breath I had to release. I hissed it slowly between my teeth. "Understood." I reached down and grabbed my cell phone and chucked it over my shoulder into the back seat. That elicited a laugh from Officer Douglas and he slapped the inside of my door as he pushed up to stand. He tossed what I assumed to be a ticket onto the passenger seat, along with my registration and ID.

"You seem like a good guy and a fine teacher. Thank you for all you do for our community."

"The same to you," I said though it didn't feel like enough.

He flicked me a quick salute and headed back to his cruiser.

I took a few minutes to clear my head and get the car in gear to continue to my original destination. Staying at home would've been the smartest decision—and likely the cheapest given I'd already got a ticket and I was only ten minutes in.

But there was comfort in the neon yellow light that flickered above Pint and Pail, like a beacon for the downtrodden and discouraged. That was a touch melodramatic, but I honestly loved this place. They had the best beer on tap, no question, and the bucket of peanuts was pretty awesome. Who didn't love throwing the shells on the ground, knowing you wouldn't be the one to clean them up? After my years bussing, I took full advantage of being able to make a mess and have someone else deal with the aftermath.

Reggie was behind the bar when the door swung in and he immediately nodded toward an empty stool near the end of the establishment. "Over here, Champ! Saved you the best seat in the house."

It was the only open stool. Reggie was a jokester like that. I admired the fresh ink twisting around his arm and nodded my appreciation as I made my way down the bar. "New?"

"Yeah." He rubbed at the colorful tattoo. "I had to come up with something to disguise Tatyana's name. Why the hell did I have to be engaged to a chick with such a long name? It was quite the feat to get it to even look this decent."

"I bet." I settled onto the barstool and emptied my wallet and phone onto the counter. Reggie had a square napkin ready and slid it toward me. "It does look good, though, man. You can only see *"ana"* left on it, and that could be really convenient if you happen to meet a hot girl named Ana. Immediately score some points with that."

Reggie flicked his head to the person seated to my left. I hadn't noticed her when I first came in, which seemed absolutely crazy now that I looked at her. She had blonde hair in perfect long waves and the fullest lips I'd ever seen. Not the kind that appeared pumped full of toxins, but just naturally pouty and kissable. I found myself biting my own as I studied her more.

"Your name happen to be Ana?" Reggie asked with a deep, flirtatious grin plastered on. He was burly and mildly intimidating, but she didn't appear the least bit phased by any of it.

"Nope." She smiled politely. "Sorry."

"Damn shame." He hit his fist against the counter and shot her a wink. "*Damn* shame."

Nervously, she glanced my direction. I was surprised when she offered a shy smile, but grateful that Reggie's failed flirting only made me look that much better.

"Hi," I mouthed.

She took her straw between her teeth and murmured a soft, "Hi," back.

"What'll it be, Cliffy?" Reggie shouted over his shoulder as he pulled down on a carved wooden handle to fill a pitcher with amber colored beer. "The usual?"

"Nutty Brunette tonight," I called back and then turned my attention back to the blonde next to me. "You?"

"I'm fine." She waved me off with a manicured hand. "For now."

It looked like she was drinking soda and I took the necessary moment to look her over and make sure she was of legal drinking age. She didn't have wrinkles by any means, but she'd lost just a bit of that childlike softness to her face. She was still youthful, but definitely out of her teen years, which allowed me to breathe a sigh of relief. To anyone else, I was sure she'd appear quite young, but being around teenagers all day gave me a good gauge on judging someone's age. Based on what I could see of her, I guessed her to be twenty-two, newly turned.

We caught eyes again and she looked down at her lap, then back up at me, her gaze coy yet intentional. Then she locked in on my hand.

"You're married?" It was nearly a yell though she tried to keep her volume controlled.

"What?" My head snapped up as Reggie settled my drink in front of me. "No, why?"

The blonde nodded her head to my left hand. "Your ring tan. Dead giveaway." She pushed up to stand. "Sorry, I'm not into being with a cheater. Better luck with someone else."

"Neither am I, which is the exact reason for my recent divorce."

Like I'd thrown a bucket of ice water on her, she pulled stick straight, only relaxing once the words really sunk in. "Oh God." She covered her mouth. "Oh God, I'm so sorry. I'm awful."

"You're not." I tugged out her stool from under the counter and tried not to stare as she slipped back onto it, her bare legs exposed under her short black skirt. "I'm not really good at this."

"Me neither."

She twirled her straw in her drink and the ice cubes spun around. "In fact, I don't do this. I don't come to bars and hit on guys twice my age. Like, ever."

The sip of beer I'd had held in my mouth nearly spat out across Reggie's sticky counter. "Twice your age? Just how old do you think I am?"

"I don't know. Forty?" Her light eyebrows raised to her widow's peaked hairline. "Forty-five?"

The ale in my mouth was bitter as I swallowed it down. "You can't be serious? I've had a rough year, but I didn't think it aged me that much!"

"You're not that old?"

"God, no." Relief washed over her as panic invaded me. Maybe she was much younger than I originally suspected. "I'm not even thirty."

She slumped down in her chair and threw her head back with a cackle. Blonde strands swung around her body as she brought her head to my shoulder. She shoved at my side. Clearly there was a little something else mixed in with that Coke. "That's really, really good news."

"Yeah?"

"Yeah." She lifted her head and took another sip from her drink. Her lips pressed to the straw and stayed there like they tempted me on purpose. They were so incredibly plump and damp from her drink and I couldn't look at anything but them as she said, "Seven years isn't nearly as bad as seventeen."

So she was twenty-two, just as I'd thought. I didn't know if I should be happy about this, but the fact that she seemed pleased that I wasn't the grandpa she'd originally assumed did make me feel better.

So did the three other beers that I consumed as the night lingered on.

Reggie was the type of bartender that kept them flowing, and though I'd never needed his heavy hand when it came to pouring before, since my breakup with Kayla,

I'd relied on Reggie to get me wasted more times than I liked to admit.

But I wasn't wasted tonight. Buzzing, but not hammered.

Just drunk enough to no longer be offended by the fact that the blonde thought I was nearly elderly, and just drunk enough pretend that part of our night never even happened.

The only part I chose to focus on was this moment— the one where this stranger straddled me in the front seat of my truck, her honeysuckle-scented hair fanning across my face, her chest pressed to my chin as I laid kisses across her porcelain neck. The windows fogged, an opaque layer of steam keeping the outside out and whatever happened inside the truck, in.

"Mmmmm," she moaned into my ear as I ran my jaw over her ample cleavage, playfully biting at her collarbone. My hands grabbed her ass and lifted her closer to my body. "I really like that."

I did, too. At least, my body did because I was a guy. Guys liked hot girls pressing their bodies firmly to theirs. That was just the nature of things. My brain, though, that was a different story. He'd been scolding me all night, an internal lecture that didn't relent.

She's not for you.

This will go nowhere.

It's not fair to do this with her when you don't even know her name.

But then my body whined back, spouting off how unfair it was that he'd been celibate for over a year now, and during half of that time, he even had a wife. How was that for unfair?

My mind finally agreed with my body. Totally unfair.

The blonde from the bar went home with me.

I still didn't know her name.

Sixteen

Mallory

Leaving Corbin this morning was harder than I expected. Sure, Tori had watched him many times when I'd had a meeting about Tommy's paintings or when I'd had to run a handful of errands that would be more easily executed without an eight-month-old in tow.

A flower shop was no place for a baby, anyway. That was how I justified it. That and the fact that it was typically frowned upon to bring your infant child to work, especially on the first day and especially without permission. There really were no scenarios where Corbin would be able to be with me right now, and that was what I hated the most. That I couldn't just take him with me everywhere I went, like he was an extension of me.

Of us.

When Corbin was with me, I felt like Dylan was with me. Maybe that was unfair to my son, to saddle him with that, but I couldn't help it. He was my living, breathing reminder of Dylan.

Dylan's shirts had lost his smell. Three months. That was the amount of time it took for him to dissipate from the fibers. I'd stand in our walk-in closet and breathe him in. I'd slip on his sweatshirt from the academy and could feel his arms wrapped around me. I could inhale him, until one day I couldn't. Until one day his shirts just smelled like detergent and no longer like him. It felt like a piece of Dylan died all over again.

The things I thought I'd always have to remind me of my husband slowly began to fade. The phone calls from his fellow officers gradually stopped coming in. The pieces of mail addressed specifically to him were no longer left in the mailbox. His favorite television series would continue on with a new season, a surprising plot twist that everyone would be posting on social media, but he'd never know it.

They might've been small and silly things to others, but they were huge to me.

Dylan slipped out of this world, but Corbin kept him here, so very alive within it. Within my corner of the world, at least.

Which was why it made it that much more difficult to leave my sweet baby this morning. I was leaving much more than just my son.

I tried not to let that thought rattle me as I drove to the shop. It had been a long time since I'd had a first day on a job. I knew I was a fast learner and that my tendency toward the obsessive and compulsive side of things could only help me in this line of work. I'd spent the good majority of last night watching YouTube videos on the art of floral arrangement and thought that in a pinch I could create something pretty impressive, even on day one. With training and a little guidance, I was certain I had the potential to become a valuable member of their team. It was a goal I planned to work toward, and having goals felt incredibly good.

The drive went more quickly than I expected for this time of day, and as I pulled my sedan into the parking spot just behind the brick building, my nerves finally caught up with me.

"Breathe, Mallory Quinn." In through my nose, out through my mouth. "Breathe."

My eyes closed as I drew in air deeply and rolled the tension from my shoulders.

I could feel myself relax, that was until the *tap, tap, tap,* on my window shot me through the roof.

"I'm so sorry! I didn't mean to scare you, ma'am."

His voice was muffled through the glass and since I'd already shut the car off, I popped open the door in order to communicate with him. "I didn't even see you there!" I stepped onto the concrete and the boy who startled me backed up in a rush. He stumbled against the silver Jeep parked in the space adjacent mine.

"I didn't mean to sneak up on you. Just wanted to greet you before heading into the store." He looked to be young, in his late teens, I would guess. There was an endearing air to his reddened cheeks and faint pockmarks that wouldn't be all that noticeable, except for the fact that he stood just a foot from me. His hair was neatly cropped high above his brow and he wore a collared green shirt with *Grow* embroidered on the chest pocket. "There's a security code for the back door to get in—7986—and I wanted to let you know before you tried the front. We don't unlock that for another hour."

He jutted a hand into the space between us and impressed me with the firm shake he gave. It wasn't what I expected from our flustered original dialogue. "Nice to meet you …" I started, as though requesting his name.

"Lucas." He bore his teeth with a wide grin. "And nice to meet you, Miss Quinn. My mom told me you'd be starting today."

"You can call me Mallory—"

"No." He stopped me suddenly with a palm thrust into the air. "Miss Quinn will be fine. As long as that's all right with you."

I cocked my head. The morning sun beat down on us in the parking lot, the glare like a starburst of light. I squinted into Lucas's eyes and tried to decipher why he insisted on being so formal. I did have to admit, it was a nice change. So many kids didn't know how to show respect for anyone, and it was apparent that someone had taught Lucas well. That was an admirable trait.

"Of course it's fine with me," I said. "But I have no problem with you calling me by my first name, either."

"I have a problem with it. Doesn't feel right to me, to address an elder so informally."

"Well, Lucas, that just makes me feel really, really old." I smiled and followed him toward the rusted metal door on the backside of the building. I watched as he punched the four-digit code into the pad and heard the click of the lock turning over. Lucas yanked on the handle and tugged the door open, holding it for me to pass through first.

"Shouldn't make you feel old. Should make you feel respected. That's my only intention."

I liked this kid. He had a decent head on his shoulders and manners to boot.

"Thank you, then. I appreciate the gesture. It's incredibly refreshing."

And so was the floral shop. All at once I was met with the scent of hundreds of species of flowers, each giving off their own unique aroma. The room was decorated in a beautiful chic style, not the sort that involved large amounts of distressed woods and chalk-painted furniture, but there was a tone that felt feminine and fresh here. The walls were a pristine white with gold shimmering vinyl lettering adhered to them. I didn't read all the quotes in their entirety at first glance, but caught words like "adoration" and "serendipity" and knew I was in exactly the right place. There was a bit of magic here and I was grateful to be part of the spell. It was charming.

"Mom will be in at nine forty-five, which is when I leave to head to school. She told me to have you start with the notes first. Most customers order online and we have to write their messages onto notecards which we'll stick in the arrangements. You have good handwriting?"

"Decent enough."

"Good to hear. Mine is atrocious. Almost feel bad for the recipients of the flowers when they get a card written by me. Pure chicken scratch."

I laughed at that, but wouldn't doubt it. I'd yet to meet a guy that had nice penmanship.

"I'll show you how to log in and which cards to use, but it's all pretty self-explanatory. Should only take an hour or so and once Mom has the arrangements done, Trevor will come in to take everything out for delivery."

It sounded simple enough, which I was thankful for.

Lucas flipped on a computer that sat on top of a zinc table with chunky wooden legs. He pulled out one galvanized stool from under the table and slid another out for me. Everything in this place was so my style from the Mason jar pencil holder to the barnwood picture frame showcasing the stores hours on the front glass window.

As Lucas opened up a program on the screen, I decided on a little small talk. Always a good idea to get to know your coworkers, I figured. "How come you go to school so late?"

"I have ROP for first period, so I get school credit to help out." Lucas stared at the screen as he spoke. There was a hesitation before he added, "Plus, after my dad left, my mom needed more hands here at the shop."

"She's lucky to have you here."

My stomach knotted and suddenly I missed Corbin even more than before. In a way, this boy before me embodied the fast-forwarded version of my son. Fatherless and feeling indebted to his mother. There was relief in the fact that Lucas didn't appear to hold resentment for his mom, at least not any that was outwardly visible. I hoped Corbin and I would grow into that same sort of relationship as the years continued on.

"Here we have it," he said as he maximized the window to pull up the notes section. "Looks like eight orders since yesterday. All of the memos are in this column." His fingernail grazed the staticky screen. "Just go through them one by one, print out their order form, and paperclip the message to the top of each. Make sense?"

"Makes sense, and if I happen to have any questions, I'll be sure to ask."

"Please do, Miss Quinn." Lucas grinned as he stood. "I'm more than happy to help."

People sent flowers for bizarre reasons.

One was in sympathy for a friend whose ferret had died. Another to a teacher as an apology for a child who puked in class. And another written to someone who the sender, *H,* affectionately referred to only as *Not Ana.*

There were the traditional congratulatory well wishes for newborn babies and new employees, but it was these odd ones that stuck out to me. They also made me realize that maybe working wasn't going to be as daunting as I'd originally thought. This could be my most entertaining occupation yet.

Lucas headed to school just as I finished up with the cards and his mother, Vickie, was eager to train me in the art of arranging. Over the course of our morning together, I'd discovered she was the sort of woman who enjoyed sharing her talents with others—a true teacher. She was encouraging and engaging, a person you felt instantly comfortable with. In a way, she fit right into the shop so seamlessly, so refreshingly. The fact that she looked like she could grace the pages of an Anthropologie catalog was just the icing on the cake. She was so well put together, with even her outfit arranged like one of her stunning bouquets.

I knew it would be a while before anything I created would make it into the hands of a customer, but Vickie let me choose flowers for several the pieces and showed me how to she would arrange them. It was a beautiful talent and I was so thankful for the mentorship.

As we worked on the bouquet for *Not Ana,* I couldn't keep quiet my laughter. I wondered if this woman would take offense that the sender hadn't addressed her by name, just by a name that happened to be someone else's. It wasn't as impersonal as a *To Whom it May Concern*, but right up there.

"So strange."

"Oh, Mallory." Vickie wiped her palms on her green apron and blew her dark bangs from her eyes with a light huff. "I've seen it all. Sometimes I even like to make up stories based on the limited information I have from these often cryptic messages."

"That's a fantastic idea!" I handed her a sprig of baby's breath and she slipped it into the vase. "How fun is that?"

"Incredibly." She winked at me. "But not as fun as *H's* night last night, I'm guessing."

"Or maybe his night was just the opposite, hence the reason for the flowers."

Vickie shrugged her shoulders. "I like to think people send flowers more often out of love than from regret. It might be a naïve wish of mine, but I'm old-fashioned that way."

"I really like the way you think."

"You'll find that working here changes your outlook on things. Sure, there's sadness, but I find the main intent in sending flowers is to brighten someone's day. It's become impossible for my days not to become just a little brighter as a result. It's like magic."

For the first time in a long, long while, I noticed that glimmer of hope bloom in my chest, and I almost laughed out loud at the thought that a literal flower shop made it so.

It had been more years than I could count since I'd been able to witness magic created on a daily basis. I thought I'd have to move back to Kentucky for that, but maybe there was a bit of magic everywhere.

Seventeen

Heath

Not Ana seemed like a nice girl.

A nice girl who I owed a very large apology.

Dating sucked. I knew our night at the bar and what I had planned for when we left it didn't constitute as actual dating, but still, it sucked big time.

Being married wasn't much better. The first few years with Kayla were good, filled with marital bliss. It wasn't like I could lie and say our relationship was doomed from the start, the dire outcome written on the wall. It wasn't like that, not entirely, at least.

We were in college, both majoring in English. The lecture hall was packed deep with other first years hoping to one day teach or publish or write. That was my guess. I didn't really care about any of the rest of them and their future plans, though. I had my eyes on someone else.

It was two minutes before our professor would take to the podium when I caught her attention. Her catlike, amber-hued eyes collided with mine, tucked under a fringe of dark lashes. She smiled at me with them, so innocently. They were not the eyes of someone who would later throw away our marriage for a romp in another man's bed. They were the eyes of a young girl, new to campus and new to the game of flirtation and all that it entailed. On the cusp of womanhood, and it was incredibly sexy.

I'd winked at her. Mallory was the only other girl I'd ever winked at and that was all shy and sloppy. With Kayla, it was intentional. College was my stage for a new chapter, one where I had newfound confidence and charisma. I'd been with enough girls between Mallory and Kayla to know that for some reason, they found me attractive. An educated guess could be the dimples, another the hair. Whatever it was, there was an exchange between us in that auditorium that day.

One day we were sitting side-by-side, drawing in each other's notebooks while Professor Metcalf droned on about sixteenth-century literature, the next we were rolling around in one another's beds, kissing away sunlight into dark. Days turned into years and we were signing our marriage license, then everything turned upside down and she served me with divorce papers.

Life changed quickly.

Feelings moved fast.

Like last night. When I'd pulled into my apartment complex, things were still looking in my favor. The girl from the bar and I managed to make our way up the stairs, lips connected, hands roving and insistent. I felt like those alpha males in movies as I pushed her roughly up against the door and opened it with my free hand, swinging us into the entryway with a chorus of growls and giggles. We stumbled through the family room, collapsing onto the leather couch, bodies pressed together, legs entwined. Her fingers gripped my cotton shirt and forced it up and over my head. I was contemplating doing the same to hers when it all came to a disappointing and screeching halt.

"Good for you, Cliffy!" Paul's meaty hand slapped against my bare back and I bonked foreheads with the woman I'd brought home. "*So* much hotter than Kayla."

Nothing like a drunk peanut gallery to squelch the mood. The blonde from the bar shimmied backward on the couch cushions, tucking herself into the corner, her dress hiked up her toned legs. "Excuse me?" she demanded. Her drinks had worn off, that cloudy fog of alcohol lifted. She was no nonsense and gruff.

"I said you're *way* hotter than his ex-wife," Paul called out over his shoulder as he headed to the kitchen and pulled on the refrigerator door handle. Light from the fridge blasted into the dark space. "And she wasn't bad to look at. Her boobs were a little on the small side, but Cliffy's more of a butt girl anyway and yours seems to be right up his alley."

My date dipped her head and whispered, "Can we do this somewhere else?" Her gaze scanned the apartment, landing on my open bedroom door at the end of the hall. "Please?"

I didn't acknowledge Paul, at least not then. I had serious plans to throttle him the next day, but that would have to wait.

Standing, I took her hand in mine and led her to my room. The sound the door made as it softly clicked closed made my palms sweat. It felt taboo, to bring a woman home when I didn't even know her name. I had no intention of asking for it, and as far as I could tell, she had no plans to offer it. There was no question we were both using one another for some other, unspoken purpose. Hers could be anything, but it didn't matter to me. She needed me to fill some void, and the expanse I needed her to fill within me was so deep that I knew she wouldn't even come close to making a mark. A drop of water in an ocean of pain. That was fine. I just needed *someone*, and someone who didn't ask any questions seemed like the perfect someone.

It didn't take long before we were on the bed. It had been unmade, my sheets peeled back from the mattress and pillows everywhere, but we were everywhere and the fabric just tangled around us in a way that was invigorating and wild. Our breaths were hard and short. She was an incredible kisser. The way her plump lips would slip from my mouth to my ear to suck on my earlobe made my stomach weightless. She was great with her hands, fantastic with her body, the rhythm of a dancer. On paper, our night together should have equated to something unforgettable. Something so enjoyable and passionate that it all other nights would forever compare.

But when I woke up this morning, the pillow next to me was cold and empty, and I felt exactly that. Cold. Empty.

Alone.

I figured she didn't want a relationship. I didn't really, either. I thought I could find solace in knowing that she was using me just as much as I was using her, but it was so hollow. Impersonal. As much as I liked to think I was capable of a casual one-night stand, for me, there was nothing casual in being that intimate, when you shed your clothes, your reservations, your fears.

I was not that guy.

I didn't want to be, and deep down, I doubted she wanted me to be him, either.

She had mentioned during our car ride that she worked at a day spa downtown as a receptionist. She'd said she spent all last week preparing for the grand opening, so after a little Internet searching, I was able to narrow it down to *Refresh Salon and Spa,* which had opened on the fifth of this month. I reassured myself that it wouldn't be creepy to send flowers. I really didn't have to do too much investigating, just the right amount to show her I was interested, and not a genuine stalker.

That thought made me laugh. What I'd gone through to show up on Mallory's door back when I was seventeen was *so* in the realm of stalker status. But we were kids and flattery was the first response, not fear. It was so much easier back then because second guesses rarely happened.

Now it seemed like I second-guessed everything I did. I supposed having your spouse walk out would do that to you.

But I didn't want to be *that* guy, either, the one who wallowed. Wallowers were total downers.

God, I didn't even know what guy I *wanted* to be, just a bunch that I didn't want to be. Maybe that was how life worked, though. You made enough mistakes and had enough things happen to you and it chipped off all that you didn't like until you were left with a person you did like underneath. I hoped I was getting closer to finding that guy.

Sending flowers was a predictable attempt at repairing whatever damage I might've caused last night, but I did it anyway. I found a shop online, just down the street from her spa and the prices were decent and the arrangements pretty. Plus, they handwrote the notecards, which wasn't as common as you would think. Most florists printed them out, and to me, that was canned and impersonal. Even though it wasn't my handwriting, it was someone's, and that carried with it the bit of emotion I hoped for.

Just as I got into the truck to drive to school, my phone rang. I knew better than to test my luck after being pulled over once this week, so I let it go to voicemail. When I arrived at Whitney, I punched in my code on the security screen and lifted the cell up to my ear to hear the missed message. High school kids bumped into me and jostled against my messenger bag that swung at my side as I threaded my way through the congested hallway, nodding toward students that shouted various takes on "good morning." I had my phone pressed between my shoulder and my ear and my free hand giving high fives and fist pounds. Nothing beat this feeling—having these kids in my life, greeting me every day.

The message was long and I made it all the way to my classroom at the other side of the campus by the time it finished. It was Hattie. Apparently Mom filled her in on Operation Rebound and she was calling for the details. How the two most important women in my life were now involved in my love life was beyond me. I couldn't say I was incredibly thrilled about it, but I admit it was nice to have some support in my corner.

I glanced at the clock on the back wall of my classroom. I had five minutes until the first bell would ring. I punched Hattie's number into my phone as I got my desk ready for the day.

"So you send me straight to voicemail now, huh?" She picked up on the first ring. "That's the F-you of phone etiquette, you know. I feel like I should be offended."

"I was driving."

"Just giving you a hard time. So?" She said it as a question.

"Tell Mom there haven't been any changes since the last time we spoke."

"Okay," Hattie said, her voice prying like she was trying to get more from me. "I'll tell Mom that. But what are you going to tell me?"

Women. For as much as Paul irritated me, we could communicate in grunts alone and knew exactly what the other was attempting to say. Ladies, not so much. "Hattie, I don't have a lot to tell."

"Then just tell me a little."

She wasn't going to give up. "I met a girl at a bar last night."

The groan pierced through the phone and I fumbled it from my ear and caught it right before it hit my desk. "Puh-lease, Cliffy. You are *so* not that guy."

"Exactly what I tried to tell myself."

"Did you at least get her name?"

134

I paused.

"Please tell me you got her name."

Students started filtering in, slipping into their desks. I was going to have to wrap this up, but I knew Hattie wouldn't let me off the hook that easily. "I know it's not Ana."

"Oh dear Lord." She switched into older sister mode instantly. "Okay, we can work with this. Flowers are a first."

"Already on it."

"Then maybe chocolates. Or a puppy."

"Hattie." I lowered my voice so my students couldn't hear. Luckily, there was a lot of white noise that went with the start of a school day, and my classroom hummed with activity. "For the record, she was just as willing and into it as I was."

"Still, puppies are always a good idea."

"I'm not getting her a puppy."

She expelled an irritated harrumph. "Okay. No puppy. You have to find out her name, though. You'll feel much better about the entire situation if you do. I'll feel much better about you if you do."

"I'm already on it."

"Good. And an actual date wouldn't be a bad idea, either."

"I can see about that."

"It's not a bad thing that you're putting yourself out there, Heath," Hattie said. Her voice shifted and it was full of sincerity. "I just don't think you need to put *all* of it out there."

I laughed. "Thank you for that advice, Oh Wise One."

"I'm serious. I don't want to see you get hurt again. Kayla messed you up, big time, and understandably so." There was a quiet on the other end of the line that she filled with a slow, measured exhale. "I love you. There are lots of people who love you, including one little girl who is counting on you to show up at her recital next week. Still on for that?"

I smiled, thinking of little Natalie, her shiny tap shoes clicking across the travertine floor the many times she'd practiced and performed at my house. That was one thing Kayla was really good at, supporting the kids in their interests and talents. I knew the divorce has been hard on them, too. Even though I'd made my ex-wife out to be the villain, she still adored those kids and they felt that loss. Everyone felt it.

"I wouldn't miss it for the world."

"Good," Hattie said, satisfied. "And we reserved you two tickets, so feel free to bring this Not Ana chick if you like."

That was easy.

Not Ana's name was Monica, as printed on her name badge pinned to her lapel.

"Hey." Her voice was soft and sexy. She looked up from her desk, almost startled to see me walk through the doors of the trendy salon, but it was a startle filled with anticipation more than surprise.

"Hey."

A bouquet of peonies and hydrangeas was just to her left and she lifted her slender fingers to toy with the card placed in the arrangement. "Got the flowers. They're just beautiful, but you didn't have to send me anything."

"I know I didn't have to, but I wanted to."

Her smile deepened, those plump lips spreading wide. "*H*." She eyed the inscription on the card. "Harrison?"

"I wish. That's way more sophisticated than I deserve."

"Hank?"

"Nope." We could be at this all day. "It's Heath."

"Heath." She rolled my name around on her tongue like it was the actual candy bar. "I like that."

I knew we were in a salon, so by nature everyone spoke in a hushed tone, but her voice was so smooth and sultry that I started thinking with my body again and not my brain, which proved to be a bad move for me in the past.

"Listen," I said as I took a step closer and placed my hands on the desk. "I feel really bad about last night."

"I don't." Monica shook her head. Her blonde hair was wound into a sleek bun and it bobbled back and forth. "I feel really good, actually."

Those weren't the kinds of comments that made slowing things down any easier. "Me too, but that's not me. I'm not the kind of guy that brings home a girl without even knowing her name and then doesn't call the next morning. And I hate that I'm standing here saying I'm not that guy because so far everything I've done just proves that I *am* him."

Like she was taking in what I'd said, Monica twisted the stem of a flower between her manicured fingers and then shrugged nonchalantly. "Fair enough. That was *Not Ana* and *H*. We'll let them have last night because I don't want to forget it altogether. But I'm fine with Monica and Heath having a different start if that's what you want."

Was it? Was that what I wanted? Before I had time to think on it, I answered, "That's what I want."

"Listen, I get off work tonight at six, but I've got some boxes I need help unpacking. Any chance you're free and feel like a little physical labor? I could take advantage of that body of yours."

Statements like that were no good for my recent vow to behave. I swallowed thickly. "That's perfect."

Monica scribbled something on a notepad, ripped off the top sheet, and slid it toward me. "Meet me at this address at seven. I'm looking forward to it."

I took the paper from her and studied the writing.

As I turned to go, I sneaked a look over my shoulder and caught the small grin accompanied by a flirtatious wink and my stomach went sour, knowing this was all backward, every bit of it.

But honestly, I didn't even care.

Eighteen

Mallory

"You're just in time, my dear. The lady of the house has a mouthwatering lasagna in the oven and your finest dollar store wine uncorked and ready to pour." Boone pulled me from the front stoop into his burly chest, enveloping me in one of his famous bear hugs that reminded me of the ones his son used to give, solid and strong. Old Spice wafted into my nose. It was a woodsy scent that I affiliated with all men his age and it was welcome and comforting in its familiarity. "Once we're all around the table, I want to hear about every second of your day. No details left out."

"Mallory, is that you?" I heard Sharon's voice before I saw her peek around the corner. Corbin jutted out on her full hip. He was dressed in a new outfit I didn't recognize and I realized it must be one of his grandparents' new purchases. They spoiled that boy of mine rotten, and I was so very grateful for it.

"Hi, Mom." I walked toward my mother-in-law and Corbin stretched out two chubby arms. His upper half leaned forward and I scooped him into me. "Smells wonderful in here."

"I do my best." Sharon shrugged, humbly.

"That's a lie, my sweet." Boone deposited a chaste kiss on the crown of his wife's gray head of hair. "Stouffer's does its best. You do the bare minimum."

With a devilish grin, Sharon elbowed her husband in his stomach and then whipped him with the checkered dishtowel she had draped over her shoulder. He shrugged away from her attempted assault, but not before he got in a playful swat on her backside.

"Corbin just got up from his nap about twenty minutes ago. He's been begging for a snack, but I figured he could wait until dinner."

"That's perfect." I followed my in-laws into the heart of the house, where it opened up into a large family room with overstuffed, distressed leather couches and chairs. The ceiling vaulted steeply and exposed wood beams slanted across the pitch of it. There was a stone fireplace that stretched two stories high and even though it was hot out and no fire currently blazed in the hearth, the room felt just as warm and inviting as it did on a cozy winter's day.

"Tara said they went to the park and his music class down at the church this morning. Apparently his girlfriend, Lizzy, was quite the flirt today, slobbering all over our little guy."

I turned Corbin around in my arms to look into his sweet blue eyes. "Is that so?" I teased. "We can't have any of that, now can we? Much too young to have girls chasing after you."

Corbin gurgled and babbled on cue.

From the dining room, I heard Boone click the tray off the highchair and then he came walking toward me, hands flapping in a "give it here" sort of way. Corbin all but dove into his grandpa's arms, but not before I smothered him with a kiss on his cheek.

"Let's leave the women to the kitchen where they belong."

"Thomas Boone Quinn! You are fixing to sleep on the couch tonight!" Sharon yelled.

"Don't let the angry one scare you, my boy. She's more bark than bite."

Sharon looked at me and rolled her eyes. "God bless him," she muttered as she retrieved a bottle of merlot from the counter. Her dark eyes raised as if asking if I'd like a glass and I nodded my answer. "He'd be lost without me." She smiled as she withdrew two glasses from the cupboard and poured them full of the dark purple liquid. She slid one my way as I retrieved a barstool under the counter to sit down.

"Good first day?"

I took a sip and immediately felt a warm tingle seep into my body. There was nothing like a glass of wine at the end of a long day. "It really was." I thought back on the things I'd learned, the new people I'd met, and the hopeful opportunity before me at the florist. "Truly."

"That seems to be the case for you lately, Mallory. More good days than bad."

If anyone had the right to speak about something like this, it was Sharon. I may have lost my husband, but she'd lost her eldest child, her only son. I recognized the good days for her, too, the ones where her eyes were a little less swollen, her tone a little less soft and far off, like she longed for someplace else. But there was heartbreak in the good days, underneath the layers of happiness. Moving on held its own sorrow, maybe not in equal part, but it was there, shrouded in guilt. I often felt guilty for feeling good.

I took another slow drink from my glass.

"I wanted to ask if it would be okay if we had Corbin overnight one of these nights. Boone finished with the crib last week and I finally sewed the bumper for it." She looked into my eyes and tilted her head. "I understand if you're not ready to be away from him for that long." She lingered on her words a moment before saying, "I know it will be hard to be home alone in the house."

I shook my head, too quickly. "No, of course. It's fine. In fact, I think he'd love that. Staying over at Grandma and Grampy's, waking up and watching cartoons." Of course I knew an eight-month-old was too young for Saturday morning television, but I was trying to convince myself that it was for his best to spend more time with his grandparents. It was, I knew that. He needed more than just me.

"It doesn't have to be anytime soon. Just know that we're here, and maybe a little break might be good for you."

I reached across the counter for Sharon's hand. "I appreciate that, I do. I love you guys." Without warning, a tear skated down my cheek. They had a way of doing that, of escaping one by one. It was like they were always right there at the edge of the dam, just waiting to make their way out and ambush me.

"And we love you."

Just then, Boone and Corbin bounded into the kitchen, only to stop short when they glimpsed our exchange occurring before them. "Oh, Corb. We leave them alone for five minutes and they become a heap of hormonal tears. Women."

"You, sir, are two comments away from a good beating." Again, Sharon came at him with the towel, flicking it repeatedly at his backside as he dodged and hopped away from her. They had so much fun together that I couldn't help but smile.

"Is that a threat or a promise?" Boone joked.

I laughed into my glass of merlot, loving all the banter and loving this family. It was so, so good to be loved.

Dinner and the conversation during it was just what I needed. We laughed when Corbin slung his lasagna from his tray, sending it across the room to splatter on the wall like an abstract painting. Babies got away with so much. I figured their innocence allowed them to misbehave every once in a while and go without proper punishment. Boone and Sharon adored that child, and their new wall decoration sent them into a fit of laughter, which only encouraged him to add one to the adjacent wall. In their eyes, he could do no wrong.

Sharon and I were washing up dishes, Boone on the floor stacking colorful learning blocks with Corbin, when my mother-in-law spoke up in a way that indicated she'd been storing this conversation for this precise moment.

"Mallory." She said my name too formally for my liking. "I'm not sure how to broach the subject, but there's something I've been wanting to talk with you about."

My heart stuttered nervously. "Yes?"

"Have you thought about dating anyone?"

Of all the things the mother of my dead husband could ask, that was not one that came to mind. I chuckled a little in relief, a little in embarrassment.

"I'm sorry. It's not my place to ask. It's just," she stammered on as she vigorously scrubbed the dried on lasagna from the pan. "It's just, I think ultimately it would be nice for Corbin to have a male role model in his life. I understand that Dylan's only been gone a year and a half, but I worry if you never let him go, you'll never be able to fully move forward."

"Move forward with someone else."

"As odd as that sounds coming from me, yes, with someone else."

"I don't know, Mom. I don't think my heart is there yet." I didn't want to cry again tonight. My shoulders sagged and I shook my head. "I'm sorry."

"Oh goodness, you shouldn't be apologizing for loving my son." Her hands were wet and soapy but she wrapped them around me still. "Don't ever apologize for that."

After things were cleaned up, we joined Boone and Corbin in the family room. Sharon carried the bottle of merlot and tilted it toward me. "Another glass?"

"I'm good." I waved my hand. "Actually, if you don't mind watching Corbin for a little bit longer, there's something I need to drop off real quick."

"You hear that, Buddy?" Boone scooted closer to my boy and he rolled a small soccer ball toward him over the rug. Corbin batted at it, squealing. "We get to play *even* longer."

"Of course," Sharon said as she took her seat on the floor next to the two. "Take all the time you need."

"I shouldn't be long." I stood to gather my purse and keys and as I walked to the entryway, I heard the three chatting to one another and for the first time in a long while, it didn't feel like something—or someone—was missing.

When I got to my car, the reality of that washed over me.

Then I burst into the tears that had been saving themselves for this exact moment.

Nineteen

Heath

"This place is great."

I looked at the high ceilings and exposed ducts, their glints of metal an appealing addition against the deep, matte black ceiling. The walls were high, about twelve or more feet and it was industrial, yet modern.

"Thanks," Monica said, but she didn't shift her attention to me. She was counting boxes on her fingers and was lost in thought as though it required all her brainpower to sort this out. "My mom put both a lot of time and money into it."

"You can tell."

It was a small studio, so I made my way around as she busily organized the delivery. There were tiny lights hung on the walls, spaced evenly apart in order to showcase paintings, I guessed. Four corrugated metal wrapped podiums stood near the entrance, their stands empty, and reclaimed wooden shelves jutted from the south wall. The gallery was bare, but obviously awaiting something.

"I could use some help with these."

I jogged over to Monica. She was dressed in a baby pink sweat outfit, her hair slicked into a ponytail that still hung well past her shoulders, even when pulled back. In silver glittered lettering, the word *ADORBS* was plastered on the backside of her pants. I cringed, wondering what on earth I was doing here, with her, with a girl that had writing on her ass.

"Okay, put me to work."

Monica pointed to a box leaning against the wall. It was as tall as myself and about four feet across, though thin in depth. "Open that up. Mom wants them to go on that wall over there, but I think they're going to be too big." Her eyes moved to the wall I had just been looking at with the canned lighting and display hooks.

I began peeling off packing tape. "What are these all for? Some kind of show?"

"Yeah," she said as she crouched down to open smaller boxes that were more square than the ones I was tackling. "The theme is *Truth*. Mom commissioned a bunch of her favorite artists to create their take on the word. We already have a life-size, chicken-wire Jesus in the back that we're going to have to wheel out here once all the paintings are hung. These ones I'm opening are from her favorite Italian artist, Leonardo Vitalli. Not sure what he created, but it's bound to be something outrageous. He tends to be that way."

"What about these?" I still hadn't gotten my box open. Whoever packed it secured it like it was Fort Knox. "Who are they from?"

"An artist in Kentucky my mom discovered a few years back on a trip she took to the Derby. She happened to stop into a coffee shop where his work was on display and fell in love with his technique. He's pretty much a nobody when it comes to the art world, but Mom likes his work and it actually sells for a lot out here."

Kentucky. I didn't let myself linger on that and focused my efforts on opening the box instead. The paintings were wrapped in copious amounts of bubble wrap, so much that I couldn't distinguish anything about the pieces unless I peeled each layer back. There was a long strip of masking tape stuck across the front and in Sharpie pen, the words, *True: Emotion.* I scanned the piece and saw two more similar labels. *True: Love* and *True: Heartache.*

"Do the paintings come titled?" I asked. I wasn't sure how I'd be able to figure out which belonged to which unless the images clearly indicated one way or another.

"Not sure. Open them up and we'll have a look."

Monica came to my side and grabbed the corner of bubble wrap from one end and I took the other. Underneath the protective layers, there was a covering of paper that she used her long nails to claw at, pulling it free. Only half of the image was exposed, but it was more than I needed to see.

"Oh my God."

"He's good, huh?" She peeled the rest of the parchment off the first painting and discarded it to the concrete floor. "That's phenomenal. A little morbid and sad, but totally beautiful."

I couldn't breathe.

"I love how he can make something so abstract feel so real. I mean, just look at that."

I needed Monica to stop talking.

"Let's open the others."

I threw my hand up and it met her shoulder. "Wait."

Her eyes went wide and then she stepped back, giving me space. "Okay." Her response was hesitant, but she allowed me the moment I needed. "I'll finish up with these. Let me know when you want to look at the others." There was a wary look in her gaze. "But that's a good response. Mom's gonna be happy with that one. Super emotional."

My mouth was tacky, numb. I couldn't feel my fingers. The percussive heartbeat in my chest pounded intensely, clanging against my ribcage. My face heat, palms sweat.

I couldn't look away; I was drawn into the image. Catapulted back. Back in time. Back in heartache. Back in emotion.

Back in love.

This painting in front of me was all three titles in one. I didn't even need to see the rest.

From behind me again, Monica took cautious, slow steps. Her head peeked over my shoulder. "I don't really get it," she said, her minty breath hot on my neck. "I mean, I get that they're in a boat of some kind. But the machines and the tubes, it's like a hospital bed, too."

I forced a swallow.

"And she kinda looks dead."

The boat. Our boat. Her safe place.

"I love how their bodies are all tangled, though, like you can't tell where he begins and she ends. Like they're one person."

Because they were.

"They look so young. It's sad."

I stepped toward the painting. It was just an object, I told myself. But it wasn't, there was no truth in that thought. I ran my hand over the paint that bubbled up and hardened on the canvas. I had to feel it under my fingers. It was the closest I'd been to Mallory in the last twelve years and my body needed to feel that. I needed to feel that.

"Umm." Monica's tone was scolding. "We don't really want your dirty prints all over these. You shouldn't be touching that."

I ignored Monica's demand and stooped down to study the scene, the way the colors wove and blended to create a story in sweeping, heartbreaking strokes.

"If you like it that much you can bid on it at the auction." Monica left me where I was and I could tell she was pissed that I wasn't paying her any attention. I didn't care. I couldn't deal with that right now. "Or take a picture or something …" Her voice trailed off with her footsteps.

I remembered the two remaining paintings and tore their covers from them. There was relief in the fact that they weren't of Mallory and me, but it didn't make them any easier to look at.

The second was drawn from the same bird's eye view as the first, but rather than a hospital bed underneath her, thick green grass grew around Mallory's prone body. There wasn't anyone at her side here, only a headstone at her crown. She curled in on herself, her body full, her stomach round.

My breath caught.

Mallory, pregnant. And grieving.

True emotion, love and heartache all over again.

I could hardly bring myself to view the third.

The front door to the studio chimed just as I slid out the last painting and I heard Monica's voice when she greeted the visitor. I was glad for her distraction and that I could take my time here without Monica peering in on me. The shock still clung to me, so fresh and raw.

And I felt it even deeper when I looked at the third image. It was Mallory as a little girl, sitting on her father's lap. Two wings enveloped them, layers of white and gray feathers that looked so real I imagined they would be soft to touch, like velvet. Hair that appeared almost spun as gold wrapped around them. It took me immediately back to the image Tommy painted in the room on that day long ago when I watched him work—the painting of his wife. It was essentially the same one, only with Mallory and Tommy added into the frame, their family of three.

I was lost in the paintings when the murmur of voices crept up behind me, and it wasn't until I sensed the two bodies right there that I turned around to break from my trance.

"I'll just put them on the back table and your mother can decide what she wants to do with them. The hydrangeas will only keep for a few days, but I know they're her favorite."

The blood ran from my face, the feeling from my limbs.

She was absolutely, impossibly stunning.

The woman I'd imagined her becoming during the time apart was nothing compared to the one who faced me right now. I couldn't fathom any man on earth laying eyes on her and not giving up everything to make her his. She radiated and captivated. My God, she was even more perfect than I remembered her being, and she'd always been perfection in my eyes and in my memories.

Out of every piece in this studio, she was the truest form of art. Scrap the rest, all of it.

Mallory was my truth.

Her gaze met mine, softly and unexpectedly.

The vase faltered in her grip and I saw the recognition on her face, in her features that pulled tight.

"Heath." She breathed my name.

My body vibrated. I'd wanted this day to happen for longer than I should have. Even when I was with Kayla. And it was here. She was here. I reacted the only way I knew how. With two long strides, I was inches from her.

She searched me with a look that no one had given me, ever.

"I'll just be taking those." Monica jutted her hand angrily in between us and tugged the vase from Mallory. I saw her shaking her head in a way that should've frustrated me, but I didn't think about it. I couldn't think about anyone or anything but the woman right in front of me. Everything else faded away.

"Mallory." I wanted to shout her name, to shout everything I'd felt for the last twelve years, but it slipped from me, protected in a whisper. "I can't believe it's you."

She laughed quietly and there was some relief in it. "It's me."

I brought my hand to her cheek, no second-guessing.

She could have shrugged away. She could have jolted at my touch. She could have slapped it down, asked me what I was doing or why, but she didn't.

She didn't.

She closed her eyes and leaned into my palm.

I still love you. The promise from all those years ago was fresh in my mind and heart. It took more power than I had to keep it in those places instead of letting it fly out into the open, into the space between us.

Like she knew, she smiled sweetly. She was beautiful. As a girl, she was adorable. As a woman, she was incredible. Her strawberry blonde hair curled around her shoulders and her green eyes were alight with the kindness that always defined Mallory in my memories. She'd grown into herself in a way I didn't think possible.

She glanced at the floor and swiveled her head back and forth, and broke our connection along with it. "I have to go," she stammered, her breathing labored and unsteady. I tried not to notice the way her chest rose and fell under her silk blouse. "It's late and Corbin and the floral shop tomorrow and …" She wasn't making sense, but it was okay. I let her have the moment to take it all in. "I have to go."

"All right." I smiled and she flashed me a grin that made my knees completely unbuckle. "But I need to see you again."

Mallory expelled a huge breath through her mouth. "Heath."

"Please." I took her slender hands into mine. "Please, Mallory."

Whatever wall she was trying to build crumbled and she let me in, a little at least. That was all was asking for. "Okay."

"Give me your phone."

Without hesitation, Mallory reached into her purse and pulled out her cell phone, handing it to me. She looked up at me with trusting and expectant eyes.

I dialed my number and when I felt it vibrate in my pocket, I pulled mine out so I could save her number there.

But it was already there. *Mallory Alcott.* After all these years, she'd had the same phone number. A different name, but the same number.

If only I'd had the courage to call it. If only we had connected years before. If only.

Fate didn't care about my if only's. And I only cared about my what now's. I was tired of waiting on fate, on destiny, so I took things into my own hands when I asked, "What do we do now?"

"You call me."

"When?"

Another smile from her full lips. "When you want to talk to me."

I clicked the button on my phone and the room filled with the trill of her ringtone.

She laughed, deep and heartily, so much that she bent at the waist.

"You're not going to pick up?" I nudged my chin toward the phone in her hand.

Humoring me, she answered. "Hello?"

"Hi Mallory, it's me, Heath." I saw her nerves surface as she bit her bottom lip between her teeth. I couldn't look at anything but her mouth, remembering what it felt like against mine back when we were kids. "I know it's been a while, but I hear you're in California now and funny thing, but so am I."

There was a touch of sadness in her look and I wanted to take it from her immediately, so I kept talking. "Anyway, I was wondering if you'd like to hang out sometime. No pressure. Just two old friends catching up."

"I'd love that." She grinned. "Truly."

"Me, too," I said as I lowered the phone from my ear but kept my eyes pinned on hers.

Monica came back from wherever she had disappeared to and Mallory left like she said she needed to, but I remained standing still, unable to move for so long I had to shake myself out of my daze. I gave Monica the huge apology she was due, but she waved me off, saying she got it.

"First loves will do that to you," she'd said with a laugh and added, "I can't say I wouldn't have done the same if I was reunited with mine. But we were able to have a little fun while it lasted, huh? That's all I think either of us were looking for."

I hugged her and thanked her for her candor and we set back to work getting the studio ready.

I wanted to tell Monica that her mother's *Truth* showcase would never come close to the exchange that just took place right in the middle of this studio between Mallory and me, but I didn't because not everyone had the same truth.

I knew mine though, and it was Mallory. It was us.

I just hoped with all my being that I could become her truth again, too.

Twenty

Mallory

"I'm so, so sorry."

"Stop." Boone dropped his hand heavily onto my knee. "Family doesn't apologize."

"I should've been paying more attention. The light had been on since this morning."

"It's no problem, Mallory. Honestly. It'll be fine to leave it overnight where you parked it. I'll come back with Sharon in the morning to get it and I'll bring a gallon of gas, too." He stroked his beard and switched his focus forward through the windshield. It was dark out now, the sun finally sliding from the sky. Lights flickered on at establishments that dotted the road as we passed, their illuminated colors an amber blur spread across my window. I let it lull me as the car rocked down the highway.

"So, are we going to talk about the tears?" Boone asked. "I'm not good with the emotional stuff, but I can sure try."

I sunk into the passenger seat of the truck. There were cracks from the wear of time that spliced the leather and I curled my finger into one that had tufts of stuffing popping from it. It didn't distract me the way I hoped, though. "I feel like I've just seen a ghost."

"I feel that way a lot about Dylan."

"Oh. No." What an insensitive thing for me to say. I felt like an idiot. Of course it should be Dylan I was talking about. Dylan I was thinking of. "Just an old friend."

"Of the boy variety?"

I smiled without meaning to. "Yes, an old boyfriend."

"And you weren't expecting to see him." The truck swung wide around the corner and the Quinn house came into view at the edge of a court. I'd be staying there tonight, which was one part comforting and one part confusing. I didn't want to be in a place that reminded me so much of my husband when I had thoughts of someone who wasn't him. It wasn't rational, of that I was well aware, but emotions rarely were.

"I honestly never thought I'd see him again."

"Are you glad to have seen him?"

I bit my lip to tuck back the tremble. I only answered with a small nod.

Boone's eyes met mine. "Then I'm very glad you saw him, sweetheart. So very glad."

I needed that more than anything. I needed permission to feel again because on my own I didn't know that I'd ever allow it. To feel anything other than the loss.

"Thank you, Boone," I said as we pulled into the driveway and parked. I climbed down from the truck and shut its door. "For everything."

"This is not the sort of thing you need to thank me for. I'm your dad. I'm happy that I get to come to your rescue."

He held the front door open to allow me to step inside once we got to the house. The lights were off downstairs, all but the glow of the baby monitor in the kitchen that flickered in a rainbow arch from Sharon's singing voice as she lullabied my boy to sleep.

"Sounds like our little munchkin is just getting to bed," Boone acknowledged, his eyebrows waggling my direction. "I know you'd probably like to go tuck him in, but do you think it would be all right if Sharon settles him down first? I have to admit, she was quite excited to hear that he'd be spending the night. That little man has her wrapped around his tiny, sticky finger."

"Of course. In fact, she can do the honors tonight." I rubbed the back of my neck. "I actually might have spent the other night with him all snuggled in my arms in our rocker, so I think it's definitely Grandma's turn."

Boone gave me a hug before he headed to bed and even though I wanted to slouch into his arms, I tensed. If I let myself really feel it, I'd lose it. I didn't want to lose it again tonight.

The hallway was long and I shuffled my way down it. Pictures varying in size and frame dotted the walls but I didn't look at them. I'd seen them all a million times. So many were of my husband, youthful and vibrant. He was the star quarterback at Whitney High and there was no shortage of recognition for his performance here. It was practically a Hall of Fame.

I tugged on the door handle to his room and entered. It was quiet. Of course it was quiet. It didn't smell like him, either, and I knew that, but I still took a deep, lung-filling breath. If anything, it was musty and dank. There were cleats and trophies and leather footballs on shelves and his varsity jacket pinned to the wall, all flat and stretched out, missing any form. I didn't know him then and in a way, it made it easier to be here—surrounded by so many of his things and memories that didn't involve me—than it was to be at home where his absence in *our* life was so noticeably strong.

I peeled back the covers on the twin-size bed as I toed off my shoes and slipped my jeans from my hips, tossing my purse to the nightstand before doing so. My shirt would have to do for pajamas. I knew I could rummage through his dresser and find an old, worn t-shirt, but I didn't do it. Moving on from my husband was not made any easier when I wore his clothes.

The Quinn's used this as a spare bedroom, so there was a weird comfort in the fact that it wasn't just Dylan's space anymore, like some shrine to him. I slumped onto the mattress and the pillow wrapped softly around my head. My body was tired and welcomed the promise of rest.

Many times when I lay here, I thought of what Dylan was like as a teenage boy, if he would've been someone I would have been interested in or even dated.

But my heart wasn't available then.

It belonged to Heath McBride.

Our encounter tonight at Caroline's studio must've been the reason for the phrase, "What are the chances?" I'd thought about him often over the years, less in the current ones, but still, there was always a piece of me that held on to him, on to what we had. It wasn't an easy love to let go.

And he looked so good tonight. Amazing, actually. The dimples that won me over the first time I laid eyes on him were even more appealing now on the face of man. They pricked deeply into his cheeks when he smiled at me, his grin wide and warm. There were times when I'd thought about what he might look like all grown up, but I never let myself dwell on it.

I was dwelling now. Completely dwelling.

Dwelling so much that I felt the stupid smile sneaking onto my mouth. I pulled the pillow out from under my head and smothered my face with it, trying not to giggle.

The thought of Heath's dimpled face made me giggle. I was certifiably crazy.

I was about to scold myself, tell myself what a senseless woman I was that I was in my dead husband's teenage room, thinking of my old teenage boyfriend when I registered a low buzz coming from deep inside my purse.

It pulsed once more after few moments of going unchecked. I'd gotten texts before, thousands of them, but my heart raced at this sound like it was unfamiliar and unknown.

"It could be anybody," I actually said aloud.

I didn't want it to be just anybody.

Five minutes lapsed and my willpower was no match for my curiosity.

I pinched my eyes shut while I dug my phone out and held it in my palm. When it pulsed another time, I threw it across the room, the grenade launched from me with force.

"Good grief, Mallory!" I trudged to where my phone landed on the carpet. It should've been cracked across the screen, but the rug cushioned its fall. "You are absolutely ridiculous, you know that, woman?"

Crouching, I folded my legs up underneath me and slid right down into the middle of Dylan's room, staring at the words on my phone's screen.

Heath: Hi.

And then a second text, longer than the first.

Heath: This is probably none of my business, but are you married, Mallory?

My shoulders bounced with the unanticipated laugh that elicited.

Me: No, not married.

I fired off the text and then seconds later added, *Are you?*

Waiting for the returned message was more challenging than waiting on a pot of water to boil. The longer I stared at the device, the more certain I was that the answer would be one I didn't wish to see. It only required a yes or no, but there was an explanation here and I was impatient and expectant for it.

> *Heath: Me neither, but it's complicated.*

> *Me: I'm fluent in complicated.*

> *Heath: LOL*

I cringed. That was teenager speak, something I most definitely was *not* fluent in.

You couldn't really end a text on an LOL. It just wasn't possible. The other person would always wait for another, more adequate response, some way to finalize and button up the conversation with full words rather than abbreviations. I was doing just that as the phone buzzed again.

> *Heath: If you don't have plans this Tuesday, I have two incredibly hard to get, super sought after tickets for one of the most highly anticipated events of the year. I'd love to offer one to you.*

My cheeks flushed and there was a welcome enthusiasm from that invitation that did strange things to my belly.

> *Me: You've got me curious. Where to?*

> *Heath: My ten-year-old niece's dance recital.*

A laugh leaped from my throat.

> *Me: Sounds fantastic.*

> *Heath: Really? I might have played it up slightly.*

Twelve years. Twelve years without any communication and we slipped right into this easy banter so effortlessly. How was that even possible?

Me: What time should I be ready?

Heath: I would love to say right now, but I suppose 6:00 on Tuesday will do.

Me: I can't wait.

I stared at the phone for a heavy pause when he finally answered.

Heath: I guess we'll only have to wait a little longer.

Those words were dense with meaning. Not definitions, but emotion and story. One sentence that, to anyone else, would be easily skimmed over and forgotten. But there was something weighty in his words, and I felt it. Nerves rattled around in my heart, the one he'd owned so fully when we were kids.

The one a piece of him probably still owned.

But the one that had also been burst into a million other pieces, some pieces that I didn't even have anymore. Some pieces that someone else would always have and some pieces that were gone forever.

But maybe, *maybe* there were pieces that I could try to get back.

I smiled to myself and shut my phone off for the night.

Twenty-One

Heath

Friday passed quickly. I gave out tests in each one of my classes and filled the silent time with Pinterest searches on appropriate first date attire. Not information I ever thought I'd look up on a women's crafting site, but I was all about making a good impression. And let me just say, there were a lot of sharp and dapper dudes out there. Mustaches that curled upward like they were made from pipe cleaners and beards that had glitter strewn in them like a unicorn vomited directly on their face. That wasn't the exact vibe and the look I aspired to, but you had to give it to them for the ingenuity. It was definitely there.

All of this led me to my Saturday activities which consisted of a much-needed haircut and first ever professional shave at a barbershop. I wasn't a wuss. Of course I liked manly things such as guns and four wheelers and fine whiskey. But knives? I could appreciate a knife so long as it stayed away from my jugular. A close shave did not allow for the distance I required between a razor sharp blade and myself. One accidental sneeze and I'd be bleeding out on the floor.

The unnecessarily amount of perspiring I did during my barber shop experience led me to the department store on Sunday to purchase a package of brand new undershirts, which then forced me to visit a neighboring town on Monday after school in order to pick up the gray button up shirt they had on hold for me since the original store didn't have my size.

All in all, I was extremely successful in distracting myself for the five days necessary.

But now it was Tuesday. Not even halfway through the workday, either, and my distractions had officially run out.

"You got some place you need to be, McBride?"

Leave it to Mark to call me out. I peeled my gaze from the clock to meet his. "Nope. Just focus on finishing your assignment, Mr. Dwayne."

"Oh, I'm all done." He pushed his packet so it lined up with the edge of his desk and swung his sneakers onto the desktop. Then, like he was Mr. Cool, he bit the eraser on his pencil between his teeth.

"Off," I instructed, raising my eyebrows toward him. I was all about being the good guy, but respect and manners were non-negotiable. "Bring it to me if you're done."

I'd released the hounds. All students bombarded me at once with their assignments in hand, ready to turn in. I collected them at a rapid rate, but I was unsure how they all finished so quickly.

"You underestimate us, Mr. McBride," Tabitha said as she dropped her assignment onto my desk. "That was hardly what I'd call a test."

"Give him a break, he's been a little distracted lately," Lucas murmured, but he was still finishing up his work, head hunkered down.

"Distracted?"

"Yeah, you know," Mark interjected. "With your date and all."

My eyes flitted his way and I didn't wear the surprise well at all. "Date?"

"Sir." Lucas flipped the last page of his packet over and held the papers by their stapled edge. Sabrina snagged it on her way to turn hers in and handed both papers to me. "You've hardly been secretive about it."

"I haven't?"

"The haircut?" Tabitha nodded toward my freshly cropped scalp. "And the smooth-as-a-baby's-butt chin? You're clearly cleaning up for someone. Bachelors don't do that much manscaping unless they're trying to impress."

"Manscaping?" I was about two conversations behind.

"And the constant glancing to your ring finger. I promise, none of us can see your ring tan anymore. It's not noticeable."

What the hell? How on earth were these kids recognizing things I wasn't even aware of? "Anything else?"

"You've been biting your thumb," Sabrina offered, her voice characteristically quiet. Her eyes were downcast under a fringe of thick bangs. "A lot."

"And you've been muttering under your breath. Like reciting a conversation or something. Freaky as hell if you ask me," Mark said.

"All right. That's enough. Let's move forward with today's agenda." I ran my index finger over my notepad, but I wasn't reading anything. I'd expected the quiz to take up the majority of class time, and now we had twenty minutes of empty lesson planning. Major teacher fail on my part.

"So." Tabitha leaned toward me and kept her voice a hushed whisper. "Who is it?"

"Back in your seat," I instructed. She scrunched her face in disappointment.

"Seriously, Teach. Who's the chick?"

"She's not a chick. She's a woman. Women aren't chicks. For that matter, neither are girls. You could benefit from expanding your vocabulary a little, Mark."

"Ouch!" He slammed his hand down onto his desk but was all smiles. "Looks like someone's nervous!"

"Of course I'm nervous! I've been waiting twelve years for this night!"

"Oh my God!" Tabitha screamed. "It's her! Your high school sweetheart? Oh! This is soooo good."

Lucas looked up. "Is it really, sir? Is it her?"

I felt like I was about to puke. Talking about the date catapulted everything to a new level, one where I was suddenly aware of the potential for tonight to go very, very badly.

"Yeah, it's her."

"So she's in California?"

"Yes." In California. In the same zip code. Unbelievable. Absolutely unbelievable. I hadn't let the enormity of that coincidence settle in yet, but as I reiterated it to my class, it made my chest tighten with anxiety.

Tabitha clapped her hands together wildly. "This is like the sweetest old people fairy tale ever!"

"I'm not that old," I murmured as I grabbed a dry erase marker and begin writing Faust's words on the whiteboard. "Seriously, I'm not even thirty."

I wasn't a teenager, either, though. And neither was Mallory. For as much as I wanted to believe we could pick things up where we left off, I knew that might not be possible.

But that sure as hell was not going to keep me from trying.

Twenty-Two

Mallory

The car ride was longer than I had expected. I'd assumed Heath's family lived in town, but Natalie's performance was at a theater twenty-five minutes from my place—all highway miles—and parking took another fifteen to find. I wouldn't say we caught up on much during the drive, but we filled the pauses with pleasant and enjoyable conversation. Heath told me he was a high school English teacher and I'd smiled at that. He always was such a great student of literature. It only made sense that he'd make a career out of that passion. I'd told him I was a mom and a budding florist and he'd laughed at the pun and didn't dwell on the mother part so I couldn't read how that news made him feel. Either way, it felt good to let him know about Corbin right off the bat. I wouldn't let him become some secret.

By the time the blinker on Heath's old truck flicked on to turn into the performing arts center, my jitters subsided, replaced with a warm, familiar ease. From what I could tell so far, Heath was the same Heath of my memories: charmingly witty, smart, and subtly flirtatious when the moment was appropriate for it. He'd held my door wide open to allow me into the truck when he'd picked me up and I could feel his gaze land on my bare legs, skimming them up and down in appreciation. Then he'd given me the most adorable grin through the window as he closed my door into place. I had to collect my breath and myself as he jogged around to the driver's side.

This was a date, clearly, and it surprised me at how okay I was with that.

I could do this.

Heath parked the vehicle at the edge of the lot and his truck was so big and the car next to us so far over the line that I had to shimmy across his bench seat to get out on his side. He extended a hand out to help me down, and I grabbed right on to it, probably a little too eagerly, but not enough to make me insecure. Then we walked quietly side by side toward the entrance. Heath wasn't wrong in saying this was a highly anticipated event because the proud parents and grandparents and siblings in their Sunday best sure made it feel like a red carpet event.

I loved seeing the excitement on the dancer's faces that congregated in the lobby before showtime. It was a kaleidoscope of sequins, taffeta, and stage makeup. Tonight was their time to shine and even though I didn't know a single soul in the building other than Heath, my heart swelled with pride for the performers. For them, this was a really big deal and I was thankful to be a part of it.

"There she is." Heath's eyes lit up when he locked in on a dark-haired girl, her pin curls bobbing like springs. She giggled with a group of friends who were similar in age and costume. "Nat! Hey, Natty!"

Other pre-teen girls would be mortified to have an adult calling out and frantically waving their direction, but Natalie's reaction was anything but embarrassed. Immediately, she abandoned her crew and shimmied through the throng of bodies, trying to reach her uncle like a salmon swimming upstream.

"You came!" Her rouged cheek smacked into his chest.

"Wouldn't have missed it for the world." Heath dropped a kiss onto the top of her head. "Not really sure what that phrase even means, but all I can say is that there's no place in the world I'd rather be right now."

"Well, since I *am* your whole world, it's good that you're here." Natalie turned to face me. She had deep-set dimples and they were fantastic, like her uncle's. "You must be Mallory."

I reached out to offer my hand in greeting but Natalie confidently went in for a hug instead. "Uncle Heath hasn't stopped talking about you. I just hope he shuts up long enough to actually watch the performance."

Heath shook his head violently and stammered, "Don't you have some last minute warming up to do?" Taking her by the shoulders, he swiveled Natalie away and pushed her toward her friends like she was a ticking time bomb of words and potential humiliation.

I bit my lip to pinch back the smile, but clearly still wore it when Heath returned.

"Hmmph. Kids sure say the darndest things." He shrugged as he rubbed the back of his neck, and then he pulled two tickets from his back pocket with the other free hand. He flapped them against his palm and asked, "So, what do you say we find our seats?"

I hadn't thought of holding anyone's hand in a long, long while. Dylan wasn't the touchy-feely type, which never bothered me because, under the circumstances in which we met, we didn't begin our relationship in a way that allowed for much physical contact.

But this—this sitting here next to Heath—the memory of it all was too much. I thought back to when he'd taken me to the movies when we first dated in high school. It was a popular romantic comedy at the time, and it took until right before the credits rolled onto the dark screen for him to grasp onto my hand, which had been conveniently waiting on the armrest between us. We sat there until they flicked the houselights on, stealing away every second we could to finally have our hands joined.

It was presumptuous for me to think Heath had any interest in holding my hand now, though. "As friends." That was the qualifier he'd given for this night. Maybe it was forward to assume he'd invited me here for anything more than friendly company. I might have jumped to an embarrassingly wrong conclusion with this.

Even still, I couldn't deny that I was sitting there as girls in glittering tutus pirouetted across the stage, hoping he wanted my hand. Because I certainly wanted his.

When the number stopped and the applause broke, I let the point of my elbow land on the rest between us. From the corner of my eye, Heath's Adam's apple lifted and dropped, worked with an agonizingly slow swallow. His fingers came to his tie and he swiveled it loose, slightly. It made me blush. I was staring at him, at the way the lights from the stage flashed over his strong features. They sparkled his gray eyes, and when he blinked, his blond lashes fluttered and made my stomach do the same.

Realizing one of Natalie's dance troops was about to perform, I switched my attention forward, but the pull to glance over at Heath was almost more than I could withstand. My hand lay there between us, palm up, and it was desperate and needy and brave all combined.

"This is what you want, Mallory," I told myself, silently. "You're a grown woman and if you want to hold hands with a guy on the first date, there is absolutely nothing wrong with that." I laughed at the innocence in my pep talk but gave it still.

The problem was that there was an opportunity for rejection here, and I felt it deep down, in the part of me that worried I'd mess this up, read into it all wrong.

He'd rejected me before.

He could do it again.

But rejection was not the worst thing to happen.

I wriggled my fingers and left my empty and willing hand there, open for Heath to take.

Twenty-Three

Heath

Her hands were ice. They always had been. She wasn't the sort of person whose body regulated with the outside temperatures. No, even when it was a hellish 110 degrees, her fingers were as icicles growing out from chilled and brittle knuckles. Her palms never sweat. Mine, on the other hand, pooled with it. Maybe nerves gathered them there, or maybe I just ran a few degrees hotter than her. Whatever the reason, we were opposites in this, and in so much more.

She'd cocoon herself in our bed every night. I'd throw off the blankets even in the dead of winter. Like a squirrel, she'd scramble for my discarded quilt and bury underneath the body heat it still held, taking advantage even there.

Kayla was frigid.

Always.

And she'd become so cold to me in every possible way. Her hands were the starting point and I swear she could use them to cast a spell like some ice queen. She'd frozen me out, frozen me solid.

Tonight, when Mallory stepped out from the dark porch covering and into the hazy yellow light from the lamppost, I thawed.

Instantly.

She was warmth. I wondered if her hands were, too.

I'd mustered all my courage and found out eight numbers into tonight's performance.

I could see her eyeing me throughout the night, trying to be discreet and it was cute as hell. Every time I'd angle my head a couple degrees her direction, she'd flinch and whip her gaze toward the front of the auditorium. If she'd been driving, she'd be in oncoming traffic with the way she overcorrected. It was cruel, but for the length of an entire dance routine, I kept playing like this: me looking over and her looking away.

She had to have noticed it, this game of ours.

But then I did it. I used the commotion that came after intermission to my advantage and effortlessly slipped my hand in hers, right as the noise and lights died down. I could feel her surprise in her fingertips, so I wrapped my thumb around and rubbed small circles on the back of her hand to let her know how intentional this was. It wasn't like I'd accidentally dropped my hand onto hers. I'd taken it within mine.

Oddly enough, for a guy who had a one-night stand just a week before, this felt incredibly forward, but even more so, it felt right. Sometimes taking things slow was more of a turn-on than going all the way.

I couldn't say I watched much of the dance recital. I paid just enough attention that I could later recount to Natalie how spectacular she'd been in the piece with the lavender harem pants and how her flying leap across the stage in the Tchaikovsky number was on point. Everything else focused on a four-inch space on my body, resting on a four-inch space on Mallory's body.

When that final tap clicked across the black stage, we all waited for an expectant pause, the customary moment it took to recognize the performance was over. Then, someone near the back started to slow clap and we followed suit. Applause was such a strange thing, how we latched on to one another, some leader who set it into motion, indicating when to begin and end like a clapping conductor.

For me, this leader was a complete buzzkill.

It wasn't like I wouldn't have clapped. Of course Natalie's performance deserved that. Probably a standing ovation. It was the fact that, had the round not been initiated by someone else, I'd have never realized the evening was over. My hand had no other purpose than to hold Mallory's.

I prayed that she wouldn't move, that she'd let our fingers stay together like they had been for the past fifteen minutes, but she yanked her hand free and pressed her palms together emphatically, just like everyone else in the room.

From the stage, makeup emphasized my niece's features and her braced teeth appeared even more brilliant behind her ruby lips, pulled taut with a beaming smile. I looked at Mallory. Her face wore the same, proud expression. Proud of a young girl she'd only recently been introduced to. This woman had so much joy it was contagious.

My hands finally found one another and I clapped along, knowing that I'd just have to gain more courage later.

That courage finally came after the event when I asked if Mallory was ready to head home or if she'd like to stop and grab a cup of coffee.

"Coffee," she replied, instantly. "That sounds amazing right now."

"Great. There's a little shop off Hickory Avenue that I love."

"The Roasted Bean."

My eyes went wide. "You know it?"

"When I was pregnant with Corbin, I craved their decaf peppermint white mochas. They're the only shop I know that carries the peppermint syrup year round."

When she was pregnant.

She was a mother. I knew that, she'd told me earlier this evening, and I'd also had an inclination when I saw Tommy's painting, the one with her body so round with life.

She'd been a wife.

She had a family.

That was huge. Someone else existed that—each time she looked at him—she was reminded of the deep love which created him. I didn't have that. All I had as a reminder of the love I thought I shared with Kayla was the narrow line on my fourth finger where the pigment was just a shade or two lighter.

But even that faded with the memories I would replay time and again, like a rerun of a sitcom that once brought me laughter.

Now my life seemed so rehearsed.

But this, with Mallory, was new.

And she was new. There was so much newness to her that I didn't know where to start with the questions once we ordered our drinks and settled into two plush, overstuffed chairs at the cafe, right near the window where passerby's walked just a few feet away on the other side of the glass. I gazed at Mallory over my coffee mug, the steam rising in curly and smoky tendrils. She looked up from the chocolate cakepop I'd ordered her and she beamed at me. I should've told her about the clump of frosting that stuck to her bottom lip, but I didn't. I let her savor her dessert because this was the old Mallory—the one who loved and appreciated everything so fully, even down to a bite of cake.

"So, Heath. Tell me about the person you've become." Her lips met the mug and she held the warm liquid in her mouth before swishing it down. "The Californian. The teacher. The ex-husband."

"That's a loaded question."

She offered an innocent smile. "Is it? I guess you're right. You don't have to answer if you don't want to."

"No, no. It's all right, I'm just trying to see if I can give you the condensed version."

"It doesn't have to be condensed."

"I'll spare you the boring details," I said. "Promise."

Mallory shifted in her chair. Her dress was beautiful, even if a little outdated. There was an effort she'd made here, and it was so endearing I found myself giddy over it. The paisley pattern on the fabric looked like something cut from Nana's couch, but I loved knowing that she picked out her best for our night together. It wasn't what I would call a terribly sexy dress, but it suited her. I sincerely hoped I'd get to see her in it again.

"I want all your boring details." She laughed, then her gaze diverted to the floor when she said, "It's kinda what my life has become lately."

That truth was too melancholy so I didn't let us pause and instead started right in. "Well, as you know, I moved to California when my dad got that promotion as chief." I waited for the recognition on her face and when I didn't get it, I kept rolling. "Went to Sacramento State for undergrad. Met a girl. Got married out of college. Got my credential. Got a job as an English teacher. Got my masters. Got a divorce. Got an apartment with my buddy. Got the courage to text an old friend." I tipped my coffee cup toward her. "Got a delicious cup of Joe."

"That's definitely the condensed version. I have a feeling you left out a whole lot there."

"Maybe." My shoulders shrugged to my ears. "Maybe not." I took another slow and appreciative sip. "Damn, that's one good Americano."

"The best."

There was something between us. Not really tension, but some barrier that kept all we want to say back. A protective layer we were shielded behind. That was natural, of course. It wasn't realistic to expect vulnerability after so long, but I wanted it. God, did I want it. From her, and out of me. I wanted to be vulnerable again, more than I'd ever realized.

"So, tell me about your life, Mallory." I knew I'd need to encourage this out, coax her story from her. "How on earth did you end up in California of all places, after all these years?"

"Dylan had an opportunity to transfer two years back. He's got family out here." She caught herself. "I mean, he had family out here. Well, his family is still here. It's just … he isn't. He died last year."

That was not the condensed version. That was a freaking novel right there, exposed in her words, her demeanor, her nerves that fidgeted out of her.

"I'm so sorry."

Her eyes misted. She sniffed lightly and wiped her nose with a brown paper napkin that had a wet ring in the center left from her drink. "It's okay."

"It's not, but you can say that if you like."

"Ha!" She sniffed again, kind of snorting with a laugh. "You're right, it's not. But so goes life, huh?"

"I suppose." I studied her until she caught my gaze. It didn't throw her off. Her eyes crinkled behind another smile that got even bigger when I asked, "So you have a son, huh?"

All pretense sloughed off, melting the opaque and secretive layers she tried unsuccessfully to wear, leaving her transparent with the obvious emotion and affection she held for her child. Mallory slid deeper into her seat and the cushions surrounded her small body. "I do have a son. Corbin. He's the absolute love of my life."

"Tell me about him."

"Really?" Her cup stopped short as she brought it to her lips.

"Yes. Of course. What's it like being a parent?"

"In a nutshell, it's letting someone else carry around your heart, outside of your body."

At that moment, a young, hipster-looking couple shuffled past and bumped Mallory's elbow as they walked to an empty table behind her. Her cup jostled with the movement and brown liquid splashed out onto her floral skirt, but she offered the same, honest grin when they apologized, to the point of profusion. I swore I could watch her interactions all day long. She was so genuine it was nearly alarming.

I handed her my extra napkin. "If that's the case, parenthood sounds amazing."

"I'm pretty sure I plagiarized that from a greeting card, but it sums it up for me, at least."

"And Dylan?" His name was different coming from my mouth than I'd expected. I figured it would be tinged with jealousy, but it just wasn't there. "Did he love being a dad?"

"He never got the opportunity."

"God, Mallory. I'm so sorry."

"Don't apologize." She stopped me before I could properly wallow. "Dylan died when I was three months pregnant. The day before he passed, we had our appointment to hear the heartbeat. I'm forever grateful he got to experience that. It's sort of silly, but in a way it feels like he got to meet Corbin."

"There's nothing silly about that. It's actually really beautiful."

Her tears were spilling and she didn't try to blot them away anymore. "It kinda is, isn't it?"

"Absolutely."

Our gaze stayed locked for so long I wondered who would break first. Only when the door chimed as another patron entered the coffee shop did we allow our gazes to fall elsewhere.

"I might be saying too much, but this is really, really nice, Heath. I've missed you."

"Mallory—"

"I mean, I know we were just kids, but what we had was real, wasn't it?"

"It was real," I said quickly. "For me, it's always been real."

Mallory seemed satisfied with my answer and the content expression on her face proved it. We were wordless for a while more and it felt right and appropriate so I let the silence stay.

"How long have you been alone?"

"Oh." I jolted. My eyebrows raised to my hairline as I asked, "You want to go *that* complicated tonight?"

"Complicated is all there is anymore. We're adults."

"Unfortunately, I think you're right about that," I agreed. "Well, Kayla left me about six months ago. Legally, at least. She'd left long before that."

"I can't imagine how awful that must've been." From across the gap of space, she extended a hand and it fell softly on my knee. A fiery heat licked across my cheeks and my heart forgot a few beats, but I loved how all that felt deep inside. I wanted her to keep her hand there forever.

"I think you must know exactly how it feels, having lost your own husband."

She pulled her hand back, but not in recoil. "I didn't lose Dylan's love, just Dylan. There's a difference. He never stopped loving me, he just *couldn't* love me anymore."

I wanted to tell her that I never stopped loving her, either, because I got the sense she thought I had, that she could relate to losing love in that way.

I didn't say it, though. I let the elephant hang out in our room a little bit longer.

"I'm sorry your wife left, Heath." Her coffee was drained but she swished the empty cup in her hands, the dark residue pooling in the bottom of the mug. "Are you at least still friends?"

Bitter liquid burned my throat. I had to clear it with a cough, then I settled my drink onto the side table next to me. I looked directly at Mallory. "Is it ever possible to remain friends when someone breaks your heart?"

Her lips pursed. She nodded slowly like she understood what I was implying, but I wasn't sure what I was saying, or why I'd said it. It was just something that had to come out. "I hope it is."

"I do too, Mallory." I hid behind my cup as I said again, "I really do."

Twenty-Four

Mallory

"Why does the water have to be this cold?"

My fingers were prunes, all puckered and lined. This was the normal state of them lately, and it had never bothered me before, but now, with the potential for someone to actually hold my hand, I suddenly wanted to avoid old lady wrinkled skin at all costs.

"You ever see flowers in a pot of boiling water?" Vickie slipped another piece of greenery into the rose bouquet but, unhappy with its placement, she plucked it from the vase just as quickly and threw it to the counter. She curled fingers over the edge of the table. "You get used to the chill. I don't even notice it anymore. Must have ice water running in these veins."

Over the last week, I'd come to genuinely look forward to my days at the shop. Vickie turned into an instant friend and confidante. Along with that—as if it weren't enough—she'd transformed the break room into an unofficial day care center. The moment she'd found out I was a single mother with a little one to care for at home, she'd insisted that Corbin accompany me to work. I'd refused her offer for a solid two hours until her offer was no longer an offer, but had become a genuine demand. She could not, in good conscience, allow me to leave my baby behind when there was a perfectly good crib, playpen, and changing table on the premise.

The thing was, there weren't any of those things. At least, not until after I'd returned from my lunch break that afternoon, only to discover the small room in the back of the building remodeled to comfortably welcome the stay of a young child.

The word *no* did not belong in Vickie's vocabulary; she just wouldn't allow her ears to register its meaning. I'd recently learned to allow others the opportunity for generosity. That was a game changer. There was no sense in being stubborn for the sake of politeness when the polite thing was to let others extend a generous hand if they so desired. Sometimes we needed to give. Sometimes we needed to receive. This was the sort of give and take that made the world go round.

"So, tell me about Heath." I couldn't see Vickie over the foliage she now stuffed into a hollowed out birch log, but something in her tone gave away a playful expression. "Other than the fact that he's drop-dead gorgeous."

"Vickie!" I squawked. "He's just a friend."

"Oh, sure he is. I saw the friendly way he looked at you yesterday when he came by. That is one absolutely lovesick man."

There was no color in my face. All blood drained from my cheeks and I could feel it leave, the plug pulled. "Honestly, he's an old friend. We've only recently reconnected."

Vickie's penciled eyebrows sprang up. "Just *how* much have you reconnected?"

"Would you stop?" I swatted her arm as I headed toward the glass case and to place our three most recent arrangements on display. As I was sauntering back to the counter, I bumped into Lucas, my shoulder smacking against his chest.

"I'm so sorry, Miss Quinn!" He was apologetic and flustered, a typical state for him. "I didn't see you there."

"It's no biggie, Lucas. I wasn't watching where I was going, either."

"No, she was too busy daydreaming about her long, lost lover!"

"Vickie!" She was relentless with the teasing, though I wasn't actually bothered by it. I'd become a giddy schoolgirl and the butterflies that tagged along weren't unwelcome.

Heath and I had been texting all week since the recital, with the occasional phone call in between. Hours ticked down along with daylight and conversation filled the dark moments of night, ones which usually held sleep and dreams. There was never any shortage of topic or story. In fact, he'd just texted me a half hour earlier and my fingers were eager to reply, but I'd planned to wait until my break to respond. There was an anticipation present that birthed a few more butterflies, and I liked having them around.

"That is really bizarre," Lucas said as he placed a cardboard box on the counter. "My English teacher just reconnected with an old high school girlfriend. Must be something in the water."

"Mallory? What is Heath's last name?" Vickie asked, her wheels spinning.

"McBride."

In choreographed unison, Vickie and Lucas's mouths popped open.

"Someone's hot for teacher!"

"Mom!"

"I can't believe you're in love with Lucas's teacher! This is too perfect!"

"I'm not in love with him." This conversation was slipping from me. "I mean, I used to be, but that was a long time ago."

Lucas brought another large package from the back room and deposited it next to the other. "I'm not sure it was so long ago for Mr. McBride, the way he talks about it."

"He talks about it? I mean, about me?"

"Yeah. Just yesterday he was asking the class what the latest baby trends were. Not completely sure why he thought we'd have any idea. Maybe because we're closer in age or something? I don't know."

"Has he met Corbin yet?" Vickie's voice lifted more octaves than should've been possible. "Oh my gosh, when is he meeting Corbin?"

"Tonight. They're meeting tonight."

With her hands clasped to her chest, Vickie swooned, her eyes closed shut. "This love story keeps getting better and better!"

I smiled, albeit hesitantly, hoping she was right.

He wouldn't remember this. Of course, he wouldn't. Memories began much too late in life. My first was from when I was five years old and I'd fractured my arm when I took a hard spill off the swing at the neighborhood park. First formed memories always seemed to be of the tragic kind.

I supposed there was some protection in that, though, to be able to introduce Corbin without him knowing the enormity of it. Because this felt enormous. I'd kept Corbin away from other men, unintentionally, but still, I hadn't let anyone significant into his life. I couldn't say if Heath would stay a significant part of mine, but there was significance in what we once had, and from that alone it felt appropriate for the two to meet.

"Corbin," I whispered against his chin. His skin smelled like sweet potatoes and had a sugary, orange film on it. "Corbin, I have someone very special I'd like you to meet."

With his palm, he placed his hand to my cheek, the way he always did. He was dressed in a yellow onesie with an embroidered blue monkey across the chest. I loved him in this, where his legs peeked out and his rolls were accessibly squeezable. There was nothing better in this world than a squishy baby.

"We don't need to be nervous," I convinced, but it didn't work much to alleviate the anxiety forming in my chest, churning in my belly. "He's going to love us."

I'd spent more time than I needed getting Corbin ready. Three times I'd rehearsed in front of the mirror that hung over his changing table. *Mirror, mirror, on the wall. Please let this go well.* That hadn't rhymed, so for another ten minutes, I tried to come up with words that flowed nicely until I realized the absurdity in my procrastination. It was a time waste, and chances were Heath wasn't even waiting in the family room where I'd left him anymore. Maybe he'd lost interest in the introduction altogether. I couldn't tell if I was dreading that, or hoping for it.

Finally, I made up my mind.

"Let's do this."

I strode out of Corbin's room, baby on my hip.

Twenty-Five

Heath

"Heath?" Mallory's voice wavered with her uneven footsteps. "Heath, this is my son, Corbin."

I stared at them, in absolute, unabashed awe.

He had her mouth, the easy smile that curled her upper lip just a little too high and revealed her pink gums. But he was all gums. He had her coloring, too. Fair and redheaded with a hint of blond waving through his fine baby curls like highlights of gold.

But the eyes belonged to someone else. It startled me, almost, to know that looking into this boy's eyes was to glimpse into his father's.

They braved a cautious step forward.

"Heath." Mallory extended her hand. "Corbin." She patted her son on his round stomach. "Corbin, Heath."

I gulped back my nerves and said, "Hi."

She grasped Corbin's hand and lifted it up, gesturing a wave. "Hello."

I took them in. I didn't know this child at all, but something burrowed sharply in my chest. I couldn't pinpoint what it was, or if a name existed to define it.

Maybe it was gratitude. Gratitude that Dylan gave Mallory such a perfect little person. Whatever it was, it was a sensation I knew I wouldn't quickly forget, and I hoped Mallory would give me the chance to let this feeling grow even deeper.

It was a gift I was well aware I needed to earn: the right to join into their life.

"Would you like to hold him?"

Hold him, raise him, either one.

"Of course." A false confidence accompanied my exuberant response. The last time I'd held a baby was at one of Kayla's friend's coed baby showers. I'd had no idea why baby showers for couples existed. Very rarely were the men even remotely interested in the corny games, boxes and boxes of newborn diapers, and spit up that occurred during them. This couple had waited until after their baby was born to celebrate. I figured it was because they weren't finding out the gender until she delivered, and a shower would be more successful gift-wise once everyone knew if they were buying for a boy or a girl.

Holding that particular baby didn't go well. She'd had a blowout, whatever that meant, and for the remaining two hours of the party, I'd sported a mustard seed-looking stain in the shape of an owl on the thigh of my jeans. I didn't figure I was the baby type.

Until Corbin reached for me.

"Are you sure?"

"Of course," Mallory said, stepping closer to hand him off. "He doesn't have stranger anxiety yet. You'll be fine."

Babies were funny things. I could not think of any other creature on earth that you could hold which would give such an overwhelming feeling of peace, just by taking it into your arms. Maybe a puppy. Puppies loved unconditionally and were equally as cute, and slobbery, too. But for the first time in my life, I thought seriously about what it would be like to be a father. Mallory had said

Corbin wore her heart, and as his beat, pressed up against my chest, I could feel hers there, too. It was remarkable.

"He likes you."

"You think?"

I didn't want to delude myself into believing it meant anything when she stepped closer, her body sandwiching Corbin between us. "I definitely think so." She wrapped her arms around us both. "Absolutely."

A date with a baby made for a casual evening. Rather than a meal that required cloth napkins and waiters in penguin suits, we'd headed down the road to Harvey's BBQ, where the tablecloths were checkered, and wet wipes provided. Watching Mallory annihilate half a rack of ribs was just about the sexiest thing I'd ever seen. And when I thought she was ready to throw in the towel, she'd snag another piece, devour it with ease, and toss it on the pile of discarded bones like she was a carnivorous animal.

"You got a little something." She motioned toward my cheek as we were finishing our dinner.

"Oh, yeah?" I teased. "Well, you got a whole lot of something all over." My hand made an all-encompassing, sweeping movement across her face.

Ripping the packet with her teeth, she unfolded the wet wipe and pulled it over her mouth, dragging the contents of about a bottle's worth of barbecue sauce with it. "There really is no attractive way to eat this, is there?"

"I disagree completely," I said but didn't add anything more.

I was informed that eight months was the age when solid meats were introduced into babies' diets, so Corbin even got to join in on the meal. About halfway through, though, his eyes drooped and his head lolled, fighting back sleep that came in waves.

"It's past his bedtime." Mallory pointed a half-eaten rib toward her son, who was now slumped low in his highchair, eyes shut. "Actually, it was over an hour ago."

"We should get him home then." The restaurant hummed with chatter and I scanned the room for our waiter. I flicked a finger at him to indicate the check and he nodded and scurried off to retrieve it. "You should've told me."

"I wasn't ready to leave."

"Leave me? Or the ribs? You seemed to really enjoy the ribs."

She popped her thumb into her mouth and sucked it clean and I swear the room shot up to about a thousand degrees. I could not have her doing things like that, especially not with her baby right there. My entire body responded not so innocently to that one purely innocent gesture.

"I enjoyed both equally."

I shrugged, coy in my movements. Flirting with Mallory was an easy rhythm. "You are more than welcome to keep enjoying me."

"Heath McBride! Are you inviting yourself back to my place?"

"Not if you invite me first."

When the waiter came by, I signed the check, but I didn't look up to hear Mallory's answer, worried that maybe I'd taken things a step too far.

"Would you like to come home with me, Heath? I can't promise anything more exciting than giving the baby a bath and possibly finishing the half-eaten box of truffles I've had since Easter, but you're welcome to join us if that sounds like fun."

I snatched the diaper bag from the empty seat next and slung it over my shoulder. "That sounds perfect, actually. Let's go."

Corbin's bedtime routine didn't take long but the poor little dude could hardly keep his eyes open during it. If it were up to me, I would've placed him in his crib fully clothed and worried about the bath and the outfit change in the morning since we literally had to wake him in order to put him back to sleep. But there was a pattern here and Mallory insisted that babies did best when they kept a consistent and predictable schedule. You learned something new every day and tonight had been my crash course in toddler rearing. But I also knew there was so much more to learn, and I was eager for that opportunity.

I was currently waiting in the family room while Mallory sang her son goodnight. Her voice was that of an angel as it trilled out of the monitor on the fireplace mantel, and I closed my eyes to listen. I'd traveled a little while in college and as a result had visited two of the wonders of the world, but it felt like this should count as a new one. Mallory's voice was something to marvel at. I'd become so lost in the notes, that when she suddenly appeared behind me, I snapped from my reverie with a jolt.

"Sorry," she said, always an apology readied. "I didn't mean to startle you."

"Where'd you learn to sing like that?" When we'd been together, it wasn't something I knew about, this musical talent of hers.

"I took a few voice lessons down at the church right after Dylan died. Someone had said it was good to keep busy, especially in the beginning. I also registered for a belly dancing class, but I promise you, I'm not nearly as skilled at that."

"Oh, I think I should be the judge of that." Playfully, I reached my fingers out to graze her stomach and Mallory's eyes shot open. "I'm sorry."

She took a prolonged breath and let her air back out with her words, those coming in a rush. "No, it's okay. I just wasn't expecting that. That's all."

Confusion was a challenging emotion. Ironically, there was room for hope where it was involved. If things had been black and white, then I'd know exactly what next move to make, good or bad. But the fact that moments of uncertainty passed between us like some current or charge, that gave me something to cling to. This wasn't a complete rejection, but it wasn't an invitation, either.

"Mallory? What are we doing?"

Relief crossed over her features. "Honestly? I have no clue." She swept her hair back from her face to tuck it behind her ear. I'd done that so many times when we were together, and my fingers begged to do it again. I jammed them into my pockets to keep them from making a fool of me or acting out on their own accord. Those damn things had a mind of their own.

Mallory continued, "All I know is one moment we're together, the next you're gone and I never hear from you again. And it's like you took all of those feelings with you, and now you're back—now *they're* back—and I don't know what to do with it all."

"You never heard from me? What about all of the phone calls? The e-mails?"

Her eyes narrowed. "I never heard from you, Heath. You abandoned me in the hospital and left me to question everything I knew to be true about us. It was horrible. I thought we had the lasting kind of love, and yet you moved away without a real goodbye. You broke my heart."

She was right. I'd never given her the appropriate goodbye she was due, but that opportunity was never there. Mom and Dad didn't leave their jobs on the best or most amicable of terms, so showing up at their former place of employment was off-limits. They'd decided that for me. I'd tried calling, knowing that a goodbye over the phone was just as pathetic as avoiding one altogether, but Mallory never picked up, never had the chance to hear my voice on the other end of the line or offer an opportunity to speak my peace.

Now was my time.

"I called you every day for two weeks, Mallory. Every single day. At what point does sincerity turn into stalking?"

"Stalking?" She laughed the words. "That never stopped you. If I remember correctly, that's how this whole thing started."

I doubted she meant it, but hearing her refer to us as "this"—as something present and still ongoing—made my stomach drop. My mouth went dry, my face burning with heat. "I never would've left you if I'd had a choice in it, Mallory. I never stopped thinking about you. Wondering about you." Loving you.

"That was twelve, long years ago."

"Yet it feels like yesterday. At least to me, it does. Everything reminds me of how it used to be."

Her gaze fell away, dropped to the floor. With my finger, I hooked her chin and angled it up slowly, bringing her eyes to mine. God, she was gorgeous, even in her frustration.

"Me too," she whispered, and then my whole world shifted on its axis when she asked, "Will you remind me what it's like to kiss you?"

Up was down and down was up and the earth spun just a few extra rotations. I couldn't keep myself grounded in the moment. I floated, completely untethered.

Did she want me to describe it like I had back then? When we were pajama-clad teenagers all hot and bothered under the covers. Or did she want me to show her? To remind her lips what the pressure of mine felt like when they met.

"Kiss me?" Her voice was the sweetest sound.

But her mouth had always been the sweetest taste.

My throat caught with a swallow. "Yeah?"

"Yeah."

Had there been an earthquake at that moment, I wouldn't have felt it. My body pulsed. My stomach rolled.

My breath wavered. It was all tremors of emotion, the need for her that built over a decade of time.

Mallory tilted her head a fraction and grinned. "What are you waiting for?"

And that was it. I was done waiting.

Twenty-Six

Mallory

Heath blinked slowly. And then he didn't blink anymore.

One movement forward and his mouth touched mine, his lips light and cautious and feeling like nothing and still everything. Just the tip of his upper lip brushed my mouth and it was the feather that teased me into delirium.

My senses spun at the tinge of whiskey that lingered sweetly on his breath and the faint scent of leather and the spice of his cologne that melded and made up Heath. It was a drug to me, to smell him this close, to breathe him in and out and in and out, a high that I'd chased for so long.

Time had changed his body. Where he'd been lanky, he was now solid. Filled out from boyhood youth into a man that took up all of his space so completely with muscle and strength and a presence that weakened my legs, unbuckled my knees. He pressed in, possessively dropping both large hands to my waist.

"Mallory." There was pain in his voice, in the strain of his brow pulled impossibly tight.

Then his mouth covered mine. From the back of my throat, a moan vibrated and it urged him closer. Brought his lips down harder. I grasped for his shoulders, yanking him to me. He'd grown after high school and I loved the new way his body bent over mine. His hands came up to close over my jaw, thumbs rubbing against my skin.

Then his lips started to move. It was one thing to have them pushed onto mine, connected but still hesitant, as though we'd break away before we even came together. It was something different to have them moving, tugging. We alternated between sucking on top lips and bottom lips and it was perfect and warm and reminiscent of another life. Of a time when we'd been madly in love, the future a promise afforded only to us. It didn't feel much different than now.

When his tongue licked into my mouth, that groan from earlier gritted out and Heath took that as his cue to keep going, to keep making me senseless with his mouth, his hands.

"Is this okay?" he asked. His words accompanied each step toward the sofa, our bodies moving together, his forward, mine backward, a dance with Heath in the lead.

"Mmm, hmm."

He pushed me down on the couch. His hand cradled my head as he lowered me onto the cushion, control something he fought to maintain. Heath's strong legs slid between mine. His chest dropped onto me, his hands twisted in my hair. I turned my head, exposing my neck to his lips and he trailed kisses down the tender slope of it, running his nose along my skin. His breath panted into my ear, hot and erratic, uneven and without rhythm.

"Mallory." My name became a growl from his lips. I shimmied under his weight, laced my legs around his. "I've missed you so damn much."

While his breathing was rhythmless, our bodies were not. We moved together, against one another, with each other. It was all motion and friction and lips and moans and I lost myself in it. In Heath. His mouth was at my neck, the swell of my chest, my chin, my cheek, my eyelids.

Anywhere Heath could find to put his lips, he placed them there.

We were teenagers in our eagerness, but adults in our need.

Kissing warped time, did something to the clock that only it could do. It twisted the hands round and round until it could've convinced me that time didn't even exist at all. It might've been hours, might've been minutes. It was hurried up and slowed down, the blur of our mouths and emotions smudging out the ability to decipher anything other than the here and now.

He gave me answers with his lips, not his words. The way he touched them to me, letting me know that it wasn't over in his mind, was all I needed. We were never over. We'd picked back up where we left off, if even a lifetime existed in between.

"Incredible." He breathed against my jaw as his hand palmed my chest. "Absolutely incredible."

My hands were just as eager, searching for their own satisfaction. I pulled up the hem of his shirt. Crawled my fingers up the hard ridges of his stomach. His abs clenched, then released with the air that hissed through his lips. I crashed my mouth to his and took everything Heath was willing to offer.

It was only out of loss of breath that we pulled away. Heath dropped his forehead to mine, his eyes searching. Then, with the sweetest grin, he left a kiss on my nose before flipping onto his side.

"Scooch on over." He nudged me deeper into the back of the couch and he spread his long body across the edge.

The boat.

With two arms around me, Heath drew me solidly to his chest, his leg thrown over my hip. To be wrapped up in him was the safest place, now as it had always been. It wasn't easy to look at him, being this close, but I arched my neck and kissed him directly on his dimpled cheek.

"You are powerless when it comes to the dimples," he teased. "They have you completely under their spell."

"Something like that."

"By the way," he continued, all the while raking a hand through my hair, tingling my scalp at the roots. "Did you know that manmade dimples are an actual thing?"

"Get out." I swatted him on his shoulder. "They are not."

"No joke. I'm dead serious. People get them all the time now. I think it's like second only to breast implants or something."

Trying to keep from erupting with laughter, I buried my head in his chest.

"Okay, I might be making up that statistic, but it is a real thing. You can Google it. You were very prophetic with that back in the day."

"Hardly. I wouldn't say I'm all too great at telling the future."

"I'm quite good at it."

"Yeah?" I asked.

Heath's heart raced against my ear. There was a speed to it that didn't match the cadence of his voice, like he'd managed control over one part, but not the other. His heart ticked wildly. "Here's my future: another date, with you."

I laughed. "A date? That's it?"

"Hey, I didn't specify how far into the future I can tell. I'm really only good at predicting like a day or so ahead."

"What about even shorter term?"

"Like how short?"

My mouth smothered Heath's before he had another opportunity to speak. I worked my lips against his, my tongue finding its way into his mouth with rough assertion. It was bold and wet and made my pulse press through my veins so thickly that I could feel it beating in my wrist, pounding against my neck. Heath bit my lip and I matched his intensity when I climbed up onto him, my knees pinned on either side of his hips, digging into the cushions underneath. In one motion, I crossed my arms over my waist, gripped the hem of my t-shirt, took a breath of confidence, and lifted the fabric from my body.

Or tried to, at least.

Just as my arms were about to slide from the armholes, Heath frantically reached up and tugged the shirt down. Rolled it over my stomach. Then, with the most solemn expression I'd ever seen him wear, he pulled me from my straddled position and righted himself on the couch.

"Mallory." He crossed his legs up underneath his big body. We sat there, face to face.

Any confidence I'd gained over the course of the evening dissipated instantly, a vapor. I'd done such a good job shutting out that nagging voice all night, the one that reminded me this was not the same teenage body his mouth and hands had been familiar with. This was a body that had been stretched and shaped with the life that grew inside it, molding it, changing it. To me, it was exceptionally beautiful, but to a person who had no ties to the reason for its transformation, I could see how it would be a disappointing turn-off.

Heath's reaction was what I'd expect from any man, but it hurt all the same.

"I'm sorry," I said, not wanting to utter it, but feeling obligated to offer the excuse. "I know this is probably not what you'd hoped for."

I could've slapped Heath across the face and I think it would have been better received. His eyes sprung open, mouth slack and dropped wide. "You've got to be kidding me right now."

I didn't know how to answer.

He pulled at my chin with his thumb and finger. Challenged me to meet his eye. "God, Mallory. Never, for one moment, think there is anything about you that you would ever need to apologize for. That is completely crazy." I could feel the heat of embarrassment full on my face. He leaned closer and cupped my jaw in his hands. "If it were completely up to me, I'd be taking you to your bedroom this very second. Making love to you the way I've always dreamed about. Giving you every part of me that has belonged to you since the first time I saw you."

I gulped back my nerves. "So why did you stop?"

Heath dragged a hand down his face. "Damn, this is hard." He looked away before looking back. "Because you're someone else's wife."

I bristled, caught off guard. "Someone's wife?" My heart was in my throat and I felt the intense sting of tears prick the backs of my eyes. My chin trembled, my lips quivered. "To death do us part. That was my vow to Dylan. That was our end when he left this earth. Has it been hell? Absolutely. Do I think about him every single day? Of course, I do. Will that ever change? Honestly, probably not." I took a breath, then continued. "But I'm not his wife anymore, Heath." The hot tears spilled over. "He's not mine, like your ex-wife isn't yours."

There was a hint of understanding in Heath's eyes, but then he said, "There's no love left between me and Kayla. That's over." His throat pulsed with a swallow. "But you will always love Dylan. And it feels like those vows are even stronger. I don't want to be the one to break them for you."

I bent at the waist, shuddering with a sob. Heath scooted across the couch swiftly and took me into his embrace, holding me steady, letting me cry.

"So what?" I sniffed. "I don't get to move on?"

He shushed against my hair and rocked me back and forth in a way that no one had ever been able to comfort me. And I let him.

"Of course you do, Mallory. And I hope to God I'm the one you choose to move on with. But I want *you* to be the one to choose *me*, and not in the heat of the moment like this. I want your heart to choose me first," he whispered against my temple and left his lips pressed against my skin as he said, "Because mine already has and always will choose you."

Twenty-Seven

Heath

For the past three years, my parents have held a graduation party at their property to celebrate my most recent batch of students heading off on their next grand adventure. I'm usually a big participant in the planning and orchestrating of the event, but this year I've had my mind on other things. I wouldn't say I've developed as advanced a case of senioritis as many of my kids have, but I was getting close.

Every moment I wasn't in the classroom or Mallory wasn't at the florist, we were together. Grocery shopping. Doing yard work at her place. Taking Corbin to his baby music class at their church. It had been almost a month since we'd reunited. Our relationship was progressing in the way I'd always wanted, but there were still the things of our past that we kept to ourselves. I knew that, in order to ever take things to the next level, we'd have to empty our closets of our secrets. You could only go so far on the path of a new relationship without studying the roads in life that led you there.

"You going to ask her about him?" Mom threw down the last bale of straw from the rusted bed of my truck, then stepped back to analyze its positioning. We'd created a semicircle of bales in a seating arrangement with the logs for tonight's bonfire stacked high in the center like a teepee of sticks. "I think it's time you both opened up a bit more."

"We're open." I slammed the tailgate shut and walked around to the front of the cab. My boots were caked with thick mud and it dusted along the hem of my blue jeans. Mom followed on the passenger side and climbed in. "We talk about stuff."

"He needs to stop being a ghost in her past, Cliffy. It's romantic to think there was just a temporary pause in your relationship, but the truth is, you both went separate ways. Had different lives. Sooner or later, that gap is going to catch up with you, or swallow you whole."

I hated that she was right. Mom had an annoying habit of always being that: dead on when it came to relationship advice. I admired my parents' marriage, though, how they fought to protect it, nurture it, and keep it fresh and alive. She could impart her wisdom with authority, and though it was easier to believe Mallory and I could coast along like this, when it came down to it, I knew my mother was speaking the truth. As always.

"Speak of the devil." Mom smirked. Her eyes were cast up ahead, at the long bend in the red road that curved into their tree-lined property. "I have to admit, Cliffy, I'm a little nervous."

"You've met her before, Mom." I pulled my truck off the grass where we'd set up the bales and parked it in the dirt ruts that my tires settled into like a mold made for them. "She's the same Mallory. Just even more incredible. More gorgeous. More motherly."

"That's the part I'm nervous about. It's been so long since we've had a baby around here. What if I forget what to do? How to hold him?" Mom was stammering. "Or maybe I shouldn't ask to hold him. That would be really presumptuous of me. Why would I expect her to trust me with her baby?"

"Mom, you were a pediatric nurse for over thirty years. She's going to let you hold him."

My mom's hands came to her chest, clasped together. "Oh, I sure hope so." Then she shoved me hard against my shoulder as she said, "Go get over there and help her out! I raised a gentleman, not a slouch."

Smiling, I shrugged away from Mom, got out of the truck, and jogged down the drive. Mallory had her head ducked into the backseat, reaching into the infant carrier, and when I came up behind her, my arms wrapping around her slender waist, she let out the faintest gasp.

"Heath!" She spun around in my arms and smacked my chest. The women were sure handsy today. "You scared me!"

"I gotta sneak this in before my parents steal you from me." I leaned over her, my fingers falling lightly on her spine, and I lowered my mouth to hers. Is was slow and sweet and only when Corbin let out a squawk from his car seat did we pull away. "To be continued."

"You are insatiable, Heath."

"You have no idea." Reaching around her, I unhooked the buckle on Corbin's carrier and scooped him into my arms. "By the way, my mom's unreasonably nervous to meet you again. It's sort of endearing, sort of obnoxious."

"I don't find that obnoxious at all. I have to admit, I'm in the same boat." She lifted a hand into the air and popped up her fingers, one by one. "Nervous to meet your mom, your dad, your sister, and brother-in-law. Your students. Don't get me started on your students."

With my free hand, I slung the diaper bag over my shoulder and closed the car door. "My students are fantastic. They've learned all they know from me, so obviously they are amazing."

"Do they share your humility, too?"

I loved to play like this, flirting under the guise of banter. But there was still a lot of work to be done. As soon as the three of us set foot on the porch, Mom and Dad swooped in with greetings and flailing arms that wrapped in hugs and pulled us into the house. It smelled of spicy marinades and sweet treats and all the fixings necessary for an event of this scale. The counters were layered high. You couldn't see one centimeter of butcher block underneath the pilings of food.

Mom sent me straight to work, but Mallory didn't make it past the foyer.

"She looks just the same," Dad said as he shucked an ear of corn over the farmhouse sink. Stringy hairs stuck to the porcelain, our fingers, and clothes. We'd cleaned about twenty ears, but easily had another thirty to go. "More mature, but still has those adorable freckles and beautiful red hair."

"Should I be concerned that it sounds like you have a crush on my girlfriend?"

"Oh, please." Dad passed me another ear when I held an empty palm up. "You sure about what you're doing, Cliffy? I mean, she seems great and all and I remember how head over heels you were for her when you were young, but you're adults now. Both of you have been married. This isn't high school anymore."

"I know that." I'd only been at my parents' since mid-afternoon and we were already two lectures in. "I'm taking things slow. Painfully slow."

"Okay, okay." Dad laughed his deep, bear of a growl. "Maybe with the physical stuff, but I think in this instance it might be the emotional that is even more important. It's only been a little over a year and a half since her husband was murdered, Heath."

My face blanched. I ripped the husk of the corn in my hands harder than I should have.

"I looked it up, he—"

"I don't want you to be the one to tell me." I halted Dad with a corn pressed to his chest. "I'll ask her."

Dad pushed my hand, steadily lowering the vegetable like it had been some kind of weapon. "And just think about how hard that's going to be for her. To retell that story."

"No question, it will be hard. But I'm here for her. Always."

A sigh pushed out of Dad so slowly. "I'm worried about you, too, Son. I don't want you to get hurt again."

"And I appreciate that, but life involves hurt. I'm don't plan on living a safe life just to avoid it. What's the fun in that?"

Shaking his head while smiling, Dad looked down at the growing pile of husks and hairs. "Looks like a tornado blew through here. Mom's not going to be happy with this mess we've made."

"Sir, put us to work." I spun around to find Lucas, Mark, and Tabitha standing at the kitchen entry. They each wore their country finest, Lucas sporting a black cowboy hat to match. He tipped it my direction and yelled, "Let the hoedown begin!"

"I will be picking straw out of my hair for the next week."

Mallory stood barefoot on the deck. The moon washed a silver glow across her pale skin, making her shimmer under its light.

"I didn't expect you to fall off the horse before actually getting on."

"I told you I'd never ridden one before!"

"Well, technically you still haven't ridden one."

Her lips, shiny and plump, spread into a slow smile. "Maybe horses aren't my thing."

I drew a hand to my chest and feigned shock. "You've got to be kidding me! Something Mallory Alcott does not like? This is a first!" Then I realized the mistake in my words. "Mallory Quinn."

She didn't acknowledge my flub. "I can't like everything. Peanut butter and horses don't make the cut, I suppose."

The bonfire roared up ahead. The students' shadowy figures danced around it, the beat of the music that pulsed from the speakers guiding their bodies and movements.

"Looks like they're having a lot of fun. I can't believe your parents put this on every year. That's awfully generous of them."

"They like doing it. Mom always says a house isn't a home unless it's full of those you love. And they love that I love my job, so by default, I love my students and since my parents love me, they love them, too."

"And those kids really love you, Heath." Her green eyes sparked my way. "They care about you. I had a chance to talk to several of them and it's clear you've influenced them greatly. Lucas speaks of you constantly at the shop. You're quite a role model."

Compliments weren't always easy to receive, especially when I was just doing my job. But it did make me feel good to hear it. It made the lesson planning, the paper grading, and the lecturing all worth it.

"It helps that it's a great group of kids this year. Well, every year, really."

I took her hand and pulled her over to the pair of white rocking chairs. Instead of taking the one at my side, though, she slipped down onto my lap and threw her hands around my neck.

"Hey," I said against her forehead. "There's something I want to talk about."

Mallory's frame pulled taut, like a coat hanger straightening her back. "Everything okay?" Tension was thick in her voice and shrouded in her stare.

"Yeah, yeah," I assured. "It's just … I just—I just want to learn more about Dylan. If you're willing to talk about him."

"What would you like to know?" Her readiness eased some of the anxiety from me. I pushed off the deck with my toe to rock the chair.

"How you met," I answered. "How he died."

"Okay." She swallowed, then filled her lungs with a breath. "Well, I was there for the first, but not the second, so I can only tell you what I know, but I'm more than willing to share."

I continued to rock us back and forth. "You're all right with that?

"Of course, Heath. It's not a secret."

"But I'm sure it's painful to relive."

"Well, yeah, it is. But it's healing, too."

I could understand that. It had been healing to talk with the counselor that Kayla had refused to see, and death wasn't even involved in that scenario. Mourning occurred on a much different scale when it was the loss was life and not just a relationship.

"Dylan was the officer who found Nana and me after the accident."

I stopped rocking. The blood in my veins ceased pumping, making me rigid, like every inch of me solidified. I tried to mask my shock when I asked, "You're serious?"

"Yes." It was matter-of-fact information for her. "It was his first year on the job. He was the one to give me CPR. He basically saved my life."

She'd been revived. That was the detail I'd always held closely to, fastened in my grip like a tangible hope. She'd been given another chance at life. In the recent weeks, I'd wondered if I'd been the reason for it—if *our* second chance had been the reason for *her* second chance.

It suddenly felt like the most selfish reason of all.

He'd saved her. And he'd been given the chance to fall in love with her.

"At first he just visited to check in on me. It was purely a friendship. After all, I was only seventeen and he was twenty-one at the time." My stomach roiled. "But once I got out of the hospital, he continued his visits, not often, maybe a couple of times a month. When I graduated, he came to my party and that's when he first asked me out."

"So he was what, twenty-two and you were eighteen?" It felt a little like he was robbing the cradle, but it felt equally as wrong for me to judge a dead guy. I hadn't been there to know the details of how their relationship progressed.

I hadn't been there.

That was the hardest truth to swallow.

"Yes, Dylan was four years older than me." There was no shame in her tone, and it made me guilty over my quick and judgmental feelings. "We dated for three years before he asked me to marry him. We were together on and off in the beginning, but were serious for the last two before he proposed."

He'd been gone over a year now. That meant Dylan had been in her life for an entire decade.

We'd only dated for six months as kids.

How could I ever, in this lifetime, compete with what they had?

It wasn't possible.

"I had no idea you'd been together that long." I didn't want it to come out the way it did, how the sentence fell from my lips like the disappointment that formed it.

"Ten years, give or take."

"Yeah." I'd calculated that. "Wow."

"It wasn't a perfect marriage, Heath." She interpreted my reaction. "We loved each other, but our life wasn't easy. We had struggles to overcome. He wasn't always faithful. He was a decent and hardworking man, but not the best husband."

And now I wanted to punch a dead guy.

"It's hard to think about those things, though, especially with him gone," she continued. Mallory looked out into the pasture, at the fire that climbed into the sky with its flames licking against the black backdrop of night. "By nature, we only want to remember the good in people. And Dylan had a lot of good, so much of it."

"I'm sure he did. For him to be worthy of your love, he must've."

"He was a good man, Heath." It felt like an apology each time she defended his honor. "He loved me in the way he knew how. And he loved Corbin. When he found out we were pregnant, things changed for us. For the better."

My heart broke for her, for the loss she'd experienced with Dylan's death, but also for the pain she'd experienced during his life. "I'm so glad," was all I could say.

"It was just a routine traffic stop, that's all it was." Her voice started to shake with emotion. I pulled her tighter to my chest. "Something went terribly wrong. The man had a warrant out for his arrest. He shot Dylan five times in the chest the moment he walked up to his window. He never saw it coming."

I was nauseous with grief, with the pain I knew Mallory felt on a daily basis. "God, Mallory. I'm so sorry."

"I'd anticipated it our entire marriage, I think. Every time a cruiser would drive by the house, I was certain it was that news. That he was dead. I think anyone who has a spouse in that line of work thinks that way. The worst-case scenario is always tucked in the back of your mind. Maybe not even in the back. Maybe it's always just hanging out in the forefront."

That made so much sense, but I couldn't imagine ever living that—dealing with the day to day worry that the other shoe was about to drop. "His death must've been impossible to live through."

"Oh, I wouldn't call it living." Mallory shook her head. "I'm grateful for his family. They took me into their care and under their wing and made sure I put one foot in front of the other each and every day. Corbin and I might not be here if it weren't for them."

The gratitude I felt for two people I'd yet to meet was enormous. They'd saved Mallory and Corbin. There was not a Thank You big enough or loud enough to ever show my appreciation.

"I hate that I've summarized his entire life in a five-minute conversation, but that's what it is. That's what we were. I hope that answers some of your questions."

"It does," I said. "It does."

"Listen." She scooted back, balanced on the edge of my knee. "I get that this isn't easy. It's not easy to date a widow, I know that. Or a single mother. And if it's too much, it's okay for you to walk away. Honestly, I get it. It's a lot to deal with."

"To *deal* with?" My neck snapped. "You and Corbin are not something to deal with, Mallory. It's an honor to get to be with you. Whether it's me or someone else later down the road, I sure hope you always feel that. Honored. Cherished."

Her mouth crept up at the edges, the hesitant curl of a smile forming on her lips. "Heath. You always were such a good guy." She swung her hair back from her face and tucked it over her shoulder. "I remembered that about you. Your maturity and sincerity. I never thought it would keep growing. I'd just assumed you'd matured emotionally earlier than everyone else."

"I have a feeling the two people who raised me would beg to differ."

"Maybe so," she said. "But I see it. You've become this awe-inspiring person. This beautiful soul."

Our mouths were mere seconds from colliding when a young voice broke our momentum.

"Sir, I just wanted to thank you for all of this tonight." When Lucas noticed he'd all but cock blocked me, he muttered, "Oh, I'm sorry. I didn't realize—"

"It's okay, Lucas," I said, noticing something of my own as well. His hand gripped tightly to Sabrina's, their fingers intertwined. "You two have a good night?"

"The best." Lucas turned his attention to Sabrina, who shed a small smile. She hid her emotion behind the drape of her hair that crossed her cheek. "Couldn't have asked for anything more."

"Then my work here is done," I said. Mallory hopped from my lap and I rose to stand. With an extended hand, I offered it to Lucas, a sort of congratulatory gesture. "It was an honor to be your teacher this year, Lucas. You have a bright future ahead of you. I'm glad I had the chance to be a part of your story."

Lucas took my palm in his grip and gave it a firm and impressive shake. "My story isn't ending and you're still very much a part of it, Mr. McBride. This is just the chapter where I get my diploma."

"I like that way of thinking." I nodded, pulling him in for a one-armed hug the only way guys knew how to hug.

It must've been time for the festivities to wrap up because Mallory and I spent the next half hour saying our farewells and goodbyes. I wanted to tell them all it wasn't over like Lucas had said. That there was hope for more after that graduation cap was tossed high into the air.

Mallory and I were proof of that. Of the potential for more.

That reality spread through me as I looked at her. She was waving at the last car to pull down the long drive, and when her eyes swung my way, she startled.

"I still love you, Mallory."

It flew out, the truth set for escape. Then, like she had so many years before, she slipped into my arms, her head against my chest, as she said, "I know, Heath. I still love you, too."

Twenty-Eight

Mallory

I stared at the open suitcase, studying the garments rolled and crammed into it like some complicated game of Tetris. The nightie lay on the mattress beside the luggage and it mocked me with its pink lace and sheer, billowy fabric. Heath and I weren't in the spending-the-night-together realm yet. Though it was nearing the end of June and we'd been seeing each other a little over two months, things were moving slowly. Crawling. I couldn't say I was upset by that because put together, the two of us had way more baggage than the suitcases we had prepared for our trip.

But a girl could dream, right? Or at least fantasize.

I was surprised when he'd asked if he could accompany Corbin and me to Kentucky for Tommy's birthday. Most people did not willingly sign up for a four-and-a-half-hour flight with a baby in tow. It was a little like electing to have a root canal procedure or an ingrown toenail dug out. Being trapped in a floating prison in the sky with a screaming baby did not make for a relaxing vacation.

And Heath was definitely on vacation. I knew he was a teacher and that he'd have summers off, but I didn't think I registered what that meant. Summer Vacation Heath was a night owl. Though he never technically "stayed over," there were many nights that he left my place when it was, in fact, the next morning, the sun creeping up above the dusky horizon. The hour when the only others on the road were paper delivery boys or those finishing up their night shifts and heading home for sleep.

Since Heath didn't have a job to get to in the morning, he'd push for just one more episode of whatever our current television series binge happened to be, or just one more game of Scrabble or Yahtzee. Which all ended up with us falling asleep on the couch, our arms intertwined, our breaths in sync as we napped away what could've been a deep slumber had we headed to the bedroom, instead.

But that hadn't happened, and from what I could tell, it didn't seem like it was on the table or his radar. I respected Heath enough not to pry. There was a line he'd drawn for whatever reason, and I wasn't about to barrel through it just because I happened to find an incredibly flattering piece of lingerie at the mall this week, on sale no less. Maybe I would sneak up to that line, but I wasn't going to cross it unless he took my hand and led me there.

"Knock, knock!"

Heath's voice rang out as he traipsed down the hall. My stomach jumped into my throat and I jammed the lingerie into the luggage, shutting it closed with clumsy fingers that weren't able to manage pulling the zipper all the way around. When he reached my room, his two large hands hooked the doorframe and his eyes popped open. He looked amazing in his V-neck heather gray shirt and low slung jeans, worn in all the right places. The sunglasses shoved to his hairline were a trendy and sexy touch, too.

"Mallory, why are you sitting on your suitcase?" he asked, pulling down his glasses and bringing one of the arms to his mouth to bite it between his teeth. His brow strained. "Did you really overpack that much? We're only going to be gone for four days." He came over and bumped me off the luggage with a push from his elbow and settled his glasses into the deep scoop of the neckline on his shirt. "Here, let me help."

"No!" My assertion flew from me. I struggled to grab the suitcase from him in a playful tug-o-war. "I've got it under control."

Famous last words, Mallory.

Like a bomb of fabric detonating in the middle of my bedroom, the suitcase burst open, my clothing scattering all directions. My socks landed on the dresser. My jeans, a heap on the rug. And my nightie was now a scarf, flung unceremoniously around Heath's neck.

"What's this?" He pulled at a thin strap. When the lingerie fell from his shoulder and its form became recognizable, his face went white. "Oh. Oh, God. I'm sorry."

I yanked the nightie from his frozen hands and balled it into mine. "It's nothing. Just pajamas. Didn't you pack pajamas?"

Heath was still unmoving. "Yeah, yeah. My Superman ones." There was a shallow quiver in his voice. "Those are not footsie pajamas, Mallory. And here, all, this time, I'd thought you wore a gigantic onesie to bed."

"So is that the reason why you've never joined me *in* my bed?"

Even if I'd tried, I wouldn't have been able to stop that question from vomiting out from my mouth. It had been held there for so long, just hanging out and waiting to fly forth when given any hint of permission. Heath hadn't been ready for it, though, and a look of sheer shock coated his features.

"Wha—what?" He added an extra syllable as he floundered. "Um, no. I mean, I don't know. It's complicated, Mallory."

"Of course. Isn't everything." I was tired of the runaround, of using the guise of life's challenges to keep us from what we really wanted.

"Most things, yes." Sensing my disappointment, Heath strode closer and wrapped his arms around my waist, pulling me to him with a tug. "My feelings, however, are not. I love you, plain and simple. Do I want to see you in that?" He nodded toward the discarded garment that lay on the floor. "Hell yes. More than you could possibly know. Do I hope that happens soon? Absolutely."

I didn't understand the hesitation, in that case. The cautious way he held off.

"So?" I needed to draw more out from him.

"So …" He lifted a hand and rubbed the back of his neck while he looked down at the floor. "Here's the thing. If I'm going to have you, I need to know that I have you … forever."

My ears rang. "Oh."

He shrugged in the most innocent way. "Yeah."

"Yeah," I echoed, still gaping.

"I don't want to lose you, Mallory. If I make love to you and you end up leaving me, it'll just be another piece of you to lose. I can't do that. I wouldn't be able to move on from that."

"Why are you so certain I'm going to leave? Why can't you just trust that I'm going to stay?"

"Because I have trust issues," he said with a laugh. "Clearly."

I bent down to collect the clothing from the floor.

"But trust me," Heath continued. "I *will* see you in that."

I wasn't sure if a full body flush was a real thing, but mine was currently evidence of it. "Maybe I bought it for myself?" I teased.

With all the cockiness in the world, Heath snatched the piece of lingerie from my hands and shoved it into his back pocket as he headed toward the door. Then, without even looking back, he called out, "This is mine and you know it. Just like you are."

"This is your captain speaking. We'll be beginning our gradual descent into Louisville. If you can please return your seats to the full and upright positions, as well as your tray tables into the seatbacks in front of you, we will prepare for landing."

I blinked through bleary eyes, the stale airplane air having dried them shut. Stretching the stiffness from my shoulders, I looked over to the seat next to me and saw the best sight in the world. The one thing I could wake up to every day for the rest of my life.

There, in seat E6, were my two favorite people, cuddled together and fast asleep. Heath's chest rose under Corbin's cheek with each content and peaceful breath, and the drool that pooled under Corbin's parted and pouty lips spread onto the pocket of Heath's V-neck, soaking the fabric. But they were oblivious to it all. Heath had two protective arms draped loosely around my son, and Corbin had one hand pressed to the hollow of Heath's neck. I stared at them, wanting to cry.

This could be my future, I thought. *This could be* our *future.*

I didn't get too long to play it out in my mind as the plane suddenly hit a pocket of air, throwing the jet up with a bounce that awoke the larger of the two passengers.

Heath smacked his mouth, his tongue tacky. "Mornin'," he crooned, his eyes still slivers as he fought the glare of light from inside the cabin.

"Night, technically."

With a hand to Corbin's small back to steady him, Heath dragged the other across his eyes to pull the leftover sleep from their gaze. "How long did we sleep?"

"Pretty much since the pilot told the crew to prepare for takeoff."

Heath slumped in his chair. "I'm so sorry, Mallory. I make a crappy travel partner."

"Are you kidding me?" I said. "You do realize this is the only peaceful plane ride I've had since Corbin's birth, don't you? I read SkyMall cover to cover five times, in complete and wonderful silence."

"Did you buy me any of those wineglass holder necklaces? You know, the lanyard kind?"

I chuckled. "I did not."

"Shoot, no hands-free wine for me." Heath pouted his bottom lip out, then glanced down. "Looks like this little guy will be up all night, huh?"

Corbin remained nestled to Heath, unaware of the bustling around him as the plane touched ground and passengers began unbuckling their seat belts and moving about the cabin.

"That huge nap, along with the time change, is definitely going to throw him off."

Even when Heath handed Corbin to me so he could pull our carry-ons from the overhead bins, my boy didn't stir. I slipped into the aisle and followed Heath as we departed the plane. Crowds of people scurried around us, the commotion of travel alive with noise.

"Hungry? I could use a Cinnabon." Heath's gaze scanned the terminal and he rubbed his stomach in circles. "You?"

"Absolutely."

Heath got us our sugary treats as I called Nana to let her know we'd landed. She and Tommy had just pulled up to the airport entrance and she said they'd make a few extra loops while we waited for our luggage at baggage claim.

We strapped Corbin into a baby carrier on Heath's chest and I couldn't stop looking at the two of them, how Corbin's little legs dangled and kicked playfully, and how

Heath would unconsciously grab and squeeze them as we walked through the terminal.

I'd been in love with Heath before, and certainly loved him now, but this time I fell. Hard. It was the soul grabbing, twisting, crushing intensity that made me feel like I could burst or shatter or explode. Like I needed to stop everyone in this crowded airport and shout at the top of my lungs how much I loved this man standing next to me. Adored him.

I didn't do that, of course. Instead, I gently slipped my hand into his, and when he looked over to me, I smiled and it felt like the same gesture. I could see in his eyes that he knew, and that was all I needed.

I just needed him to know.

Twenty-Nine

Heath

"Let me take care of those," I said, gently guiding Nana to the side with my hands on her shoulders.

"Absolutely not. You are a guest. Sit," she said as she flipped the water faucet on. "That's an order."

I backed away from the sink, my hands in the air in surrender. "All right, all right."

Mallory was in her room putting Corbin down for the night and Tommy was in the den. We'd enjoyed dinner together and it was reminiscent of my first time at the house, back when I showed up with nothing more than youthful confidence and a budding crush. The house was still pretty much the same. Nana was the same, too. Maybe a few more wrinkles, but even those she wore well.

Time hadn't been as kind to Tommy. I didn't ask, but I'd assumed he'd suffered at least another stroke between now and then. The spark in his eye was harder to find. There had been more loss of his physical control over his body, but definitely not over his mind. That evidence was hung all over the house. Every room had at least one of his paintings, some three or four. It was a museum. It was incredible.

While Nana stubbornly washed the dishes from supper, I walked around the house to admire the artwork. The one thing that struck me were the dates written at the bottom, right next to his unmistakable signature. All were created at least six months ago, nothing more recent.

Tommy had put away his paintbrushes.

"I had to load him with Benadryl, but it looks like he's out for the night." Mallory stood in the archway to the family room, her hand to the wall. Her hair was pulled into a messy topknot and she had sweatpants on. She looked incredibly hot and my heart stirred at the sight of her.

"Seriously? That's how you do it?" I turned my attention from the painting on the wall.

"No! I'm totally kidding."

I felt like an idiot for asking. All it served to show was how much I didn't know about parenting. How far I had to go. "Oh. Got it," I said.

"Believe me, I've been tempted before." She came to sit on the couch and curled her legs up under her small body. "Corbin's a pretty easy baby, knock on wood." With her hand in a fist, she tapped on the side table next to the sofa. "And despite all of that sleep earlier in the day, I think traveling still wiped him out." The moment she finished her sentence, her mouthed turned into an O shape, the yawn escaping her lips. "Me too, I guess."

I was still wide-awake, the three-hour time difference messing with my senses. "Traveling will do that."

"Where's Nana?"

"Doing dishes like a beast. Won't let me help, of course."

With another yawn, Mallory nodded. "Yep, that sounds like her." She looked around the room, taking in the pictures I'd studied earlier. "He hasn't been painting lately."

"Do you happen to know why?"

"No muse, I suppose."

"Muse?" I shook my head. "I didn't realize he had muses."

Mallory shifted in her seat. "Well, not in the sense that a person can be a muse. But an event. So much of Tommy's art is centered around something that happened and the emotion that came with it. It's like an article on the canvas, the way he retells the story."

That's exactly what it was, and suddenly it all made sense. The paintings from Monica's mom's studio were exactly that—events retold with his talent.

It felt like maybe it was time for Tommy to have another muse.

"Hey, do you know if he's is in the den?"

Mallory nodded. "Tommy? Yeah, I think so. Want to visit with him?" She started to stand, her body lifting from the couch cushion.

"If it's all right with you, do you mind if I go alone?"

The room was essentially how we'd left it that day. The day when I'd barreled in and pulled him from his work, from his life. When the wreckage was more than twisted metal and steel. When it was my twisted heart, my broken spirit. My broken Mallory.

The books in the back of the room had a decade of dust on them, filling the embossed grooves of titles and author names. I resisted the urge to blow across their spines, to see the dust sprayed into the air like confetti. The brocade couch remained in the same place, with maybe a few more springs popped and broken. The floor was thick in texture, layered with paint so you wouldn't even know there was hardwood underneath.

And there in the middle of the room sat Tommy, with a blank canvas two feet away. It mocked him with its pristine white slate. I wondered how many days he sat there, unmoving, the challenge set before him, but yet not accepted.

"Tommy?" I kept my voice low. "Is it okay if I come in?"

I'd learned to read the recognition in Tommy's mannerisms back then. The faint upward twitch of his brow let me know he'd like my company, so I shut the door slowly and paced over. I stooped down and reached for his hand to give it a shake.

"It's been a while. Nice to see you again."

His eyes met mine, the smile behind them sneaking through.

"Do you mind if I pull up a chair?" The wooden feet scrapped across the tacky floor and I dropped down into the seat. "There's something I'd like to talk to you about."

With his left hand, Tommy guided the wheel of his chair so that he swiveled toward me, our knees touching. He was giving me his full attention and I felt my heart quicken, my pulse a snare drum in my wrist.

"You know I loved Mallory. Your paintings perfectly illustrated what my heart felt. I saw them at Mrs. Broderick's studio. They were breathtaking, Tommy." And heartbreaking, but in the most incredible way. "I need you to know that I still love your daughter."

I tried not to startle—to not choke up—when Tommy's hand suddenly dropped to my knee with a clap. It was a moment of connection unlike any I've had with him before. It overwhelmed me.

"I know we've only recently reunited, but I plan to love her forever." I fought against the lump that balled in my throat. "I would like nothing more in this world than to make her my wife." My voice vibrated from me. Emotion rattled it out. "I don't know when I'll ask her, or if she'll even accept, but I also don't know when I'll see you again, and I wouldn't feel right asking for her hand without asking your permission first."

Tommy's eyes were a storm cloud of emotion and I couldn't decipher anything in them, couldn't read or interpret the waves that crossed through them. He wasn't expecting this conversation, though. That was extremely clear.

I cleared my throat. "So Tommy, would you allow me the honor of marrying your daughter? I promise to protect and love her until the day I die." A tear rolled down my cheek, followed by another. The fact that my love for a woman could bring me—a grown man—to tears in front of her father was startling. But the way I felt about Mallory—about Corbin—startled me, too.

I knew I wouldn't get my answer right then, and that was okay.

I would wait for it.

He would let me know.

"Hard to believe this is where it all began."

The melodic ding of the cash register, the chime of the door, and the sizzle of the fryer was a soundtrack to our first encounter and it played out again tonight. I supposed it wasn't fair to call it an encounter since it was really just me being a creepy teenager and staring at her while she ate.

"Why didn't you say anything to me when I was here? How come you waited until I was on my ass on the frozen ground?" Mallory pushed the banana split sundae forward while she popped a spoonful into her smirking mouth. The glass base slid across the glitter strewn black tabletop. It was a table that could only exist in a retro diner like this. I couldn't recall how many times my dishrag swept over these surfaces.

"You were busy with your meal and I was on the clock, I guess." I shrugged my shoulders, then finally asked the question that had been on my mind for so long. "Hey, do you mind telling me what Tuesdays at this diner meant to you?"

"Tuesdays?" She rolled the melting ice cream on her tongue, talking around the soft texture.

"Yeah, it sorta seemed like you had a routine."

"Oh." Then, looking a little embarrassed, Mallory grabbed the sundae back and drew another heaping spoonful to her lips. She took a moment to let the sting of cold subside, then swallowed, and began talking. "So my mom and I came here to eat once. I was six. She told me I could order anything on the menu—or off the menu, for that matter. So I did. Grilled cheese with mayo. Barbecue chips. Pickle and a lemonade without ice. The whole time I was reciting my order to the waiter, she smiled at me and it was the sweetest smile. She looked so pretty, even though her illness had taken the extra weight from her bones and hair from her head. When she handed the waiter her menu, she said, 'Make that two.'" Mallory was looking down at the ice cream like she could see the memory playing out in the melting scoops. "I'd asked her why she ordered the same thing and she told me she wanted our meal to be shared completely. We even ate it the same, really playing together. My mom knew how to make me feel special, even though she must've been breaking inside. She made me feel so loved in that moment, and not scared. It was a silly memory, but such a good one."

While she'd been talking, I reached my hand across the table and took hold of Mallory's free one.

"That was our last good meal together. She got really sick after that. I think she knew it would be her final real dinner with me and that's why she wanted to make it so memorable. It was on a Tuesday. She died the following Tuesday."

I was about to say how sorry I was, but Mallory looked up with tear-filled eyes and the softest smile on her lips.

"That's a good memory."

She lifted with a laugh. "Not very good food, though. Grilled cheese with mayo is not the best. But it made me think of her each time I came here and ate it. I was so young when she died. The memories that people tell you over the years, sometimes you don't know if they are actually your memories or just stories that have become real in your mind because you keep hearing them. But this," she said, glancing around the room from our corner booth. "This was real. This was something I remembered experiencing with her. I wanted to hang on to that forever."

"That's beautiful, Mallory."

She passed the sundae back to me and I took a bite. "It really is. I wish Corbin had memories and not just stories, but hey, want can you do?"

Had we not been in the diner, I would've hauled her into my arms to comfort and hold her. But comforting sometimes came in the listening moments. In the times when you offered your ear and your heart. I could tell it was good for Mallory to talk about these things and I was honored she wanted to share that with me.

"Okay, so I have another question."

Bringing a napkin to her lips, she swept it across her mouth. "Go for it."

"I know I have a lot of them, so you can tell me to stop prying."

"You're not prying, Heath. I'm doing life with you. You deserve to know anything you want."

That phrase hit me straight in my chest. I warmed all over at her words. I took a moment to compose myself before asking, "Tommy. Why do you call him Tommy instead of Dad?"

"Oh, hmm." She thought on it a moment before delivering her answer. "When he had the first stroke, we really had no idea what his mental state was. They said there was quite a bit of brain damage. For the most part, he was pretty unresponsive. Confused. It seemed as though he was off in another world more than he was present with us. The doctors suggested we call him by his name so he wouldn't be confused about his roles, or even feel pressured to have one. They just wanted him to work on regaining his strength, both mental and physical. I'm not sure how sound that advice was, but it made sense at the time."

"He knows you're his daughter, Mallory."

"I know that." She shrugged. "Part of me thinks—or at least hopes—he always has. But life hasn't been easy for him, and if I could make it easier by taking the strain of expectation off, then that was a simple sacrifice. I don't know. The name Tommy just means Dad to me, anyway, so I suppose it's all the same."

"Sacrifices are rarely simple."

She laughed again. "Yeah, I guess that's true, too. I don't know." She looked out the window, her eyes vacant with reminiscence before they refocused my way. "Any other questions? I'm serious, I'm happy to answer them."

I had one, a huge one, but it would have to wait. "Nope. That's it for now."

Waiting was something I was good at when it came to Mallory.

Thirty

Mallory

"So, how's lover boy?"

Vickie swatted my shoulder with a bundle of daisies as she sidled past. I hunkered down on the stool and dedicated my attention to the bouquet in front of me, the first official one I was putting together for an actual, paying client. I'd rearranged it many times already, but was finally content with the current grouping.

"We're not—" I stopped short, realizing Lucas was within earshot. "He's not ... It's not like that."

"Oh, please." Vickie's tone became hushed. "We're both grown-ups here. You don't travel all the way across the country with someone and not spend a little time in the sack. Am I right?" Like we were two boys in a locker room, Vickie jabbed me in the ribs with her elbow.

"In this case, you're not right. We're taking things slow."

"You mean going in reverse."

"I mean ... it's complicated."

I'd revealed something incredibly telling with that statement, it seemed, because Vickie's eyes rounded and her head bobbed in understanding. "He's impotent!" she whisper-yelled.

"No!" It was my turn to smack her with a bunch of roses. "Oops! Sorry. Thorns."

Vickie rubbed at her arm. "Whatever works for the two of you. I'm just happy that you've found some happiness. You and Corbin deserve it."

I had found my happiness. Our happiness.

And my happiness happened to be walking right through the doors of the shop at that very moment.

"Sir." Lucas tipped his head to Heath.

"Afternoon, Lucas. Mallory here?" And then he caught my eyes above the flowers that impeded my view. "Oh, hey." With two palms flattened to the metal countertop, Heath leaned over and dropped his full lips to mine. "There you are."

My body tingled, a bit from his gesture and a little from the fact that we had an audience.

"Here I am." I smiled and scooted back from the table, then reached under it to grab my purse. I flung the bag over my shoulder. "It okay if I take my lunch now?" I looked at Vickie. "I'll go wake Corbin."

She halted me with her hand firmly placed on my shoulder. "Do not—on my watch—ever, ever wake a sleeping baby. You most certainly will not go near that break room. You will leave your little guy here and enjoy your lunch date."

"That's not necessary, Vickie." I grimaced and felt thickness swell in my throat, guilty that I was always taking advantage of her good nature. She offered it so freely.

"I know it's not necessary. Not another word. Off you go."

I'd repay her somehow. For now, I just gave her a brief squeeze and followed Heath out the door. The afternoon sun burned intensely in the sky and I retrieved my sunglasses from my bag, lifting them to my face. I grabbed Heath's hand. The way our fingers fit together felt like slipping into a favorite pair of blue jeans or cozy sweater.

"Sushi sound good?"

"Always." We had found our preferred little spots around town and frequented them often. It was a three-block walk to Atomic Fish and we were promptly seated in the back of the restaurant, at our favorite table. I didn't need to glance at the menu, and neither did Heath. We had our order readied for our waiter and once he left, Heath looked at me, a seriousness contained in his strong brow.

"Everything okay?"

He pursed his lips as though to speak, and then shook it off. "Yep." Then he smiled, but only one-half of his mouth arched upward and it didn't quite reach his eyes.

I wasn't convinced. "You sure?"

"Absolutely."

It took half of our lunch for the discomfort to ease from our interactions. This was a first for us. From the first moment we saw one another, we'd reconnected in a way that was surreal. And maybe it was. Maybe this was as far as our fairytale would take us. At some point, we had to wise up and face reality.

It felt like my reality, though, to love Heath again.

As the waiter brought our check, I studied the man across from me. He was uncharacteristically silent. Where he'd usually have a quip or witty interjection, he held his tongue and ate without a word. I racked my brain and tried to call to memory anything I could have done or said to bring this about. What could have drawn in the rocky waves where we'd once had still and calm waters?

"You're making me nervous, Heathcliff McBride."

That got the faintest of smiles from his worried mouth. "Ah, my full name. I must be in big trouble." It was the first joke—albeit a small one—and I latched onto it and sucked every bit of confidence I could from it.

"Huge trouble. I might have to punish you later."

Not even a twitch of a smile.

"Okay, what's up? This isn't like you. You can tell me you're fine until you're blue in the face, but I'm calling your bluff."

I thought his face was truly going to turn blue with the breath he pent up in his chest. He blew it out too forcefully. Dragged his hand through his cropped hair. Looked everywhere in the room but at my eyes, and I wanted to grab his shoulders and shake him silly.

"Your dad sent me something."

That was not what I expected. "Yeah?"

"Yeah. I think you should see it." The words were flat and monotone. Heath wasn't allowing any room for interpretation here. "Can you come by tonight? Seven o'clock?"

"Sure let me call Sharon and Boone and see if they can watch Corbin—"

"Bring Corbin." He brought his palms against the ledge of the table and backed his chair up. Looking down after he stood, he muttered, "It won't take long."

The one thing I'd anticipated about today—the delivery of my first bouquet—didn't even register on my radar anymore. Lucas probably dropped it off and the recipient probably liked it, but I didn't care.

All my available emotions were allotted to Heath and his cryptic words and our uncomfortable lunch. It was the stutter in our relationship, this awkward interaction of ours. I should've expected it sooner or later, but I assumed it wasn't coming for us. We were easy together. So easy. I loved that the most.

Even when I'd said things were complicated, it was always the things surrounding us, never us. The emotions of divorce. The grief involved in death. Parenthood.

Employment. The things that complicated what we had were common, normal, outside complications.

Today was not normal.

I had no idea how to prepare. Had there been an entire department store's worth of clothing crammed into my closet, I still wouldn't have been able to find something suitable to wear. What did one wear for a breakup? Did you dress in your finest in a last ditch attempt to flaunt what was being given up? Or did you wear your most comfortable clothes so you could make the seamless transition from being dumped to lounging on the couch with a half-eaten box of chocolates and a full tub of ice cream, no need for a wardrobe change.

I opted for something right in the middle. The peach silk tank hung low at my neckline and I knew Heath would like it because he loved my neck. Always talked about how it was the only thing he caught a glimpse of the day I fell off my bike and landed on the pavement. I had a nice neck, I supposed, with thin collarbones and enough cleavage that I felt womanly, but not so much that I needed a sports bra for daily activities. My favorite jeans were slung on my hips and I pushed my gray leather flip-flops onto my feet. My toes needed a pedicure, but I knew he wouldn't notice.

At a quarter to seven, I stopped obsessing over my appearance, and instead obsessed over the very real possibility that I was minutes away from a breakup. As I guided my car out of the garage, I caught Corbin's eyes in the mirror that hung against the backseat. He was so obliviously unaware. I envied that—how his little boy's life was already stacked with so much pain yet unrealized, but he smiled through it all, the blissful naivety of a child.

"I understand," I recited as the car coasted down the lane. "It's okay, Heath, really. I figured this would be too much."

My words couldn't even convince myself. There's no way he'd buy any of it.

Maybe anger would be a stronger reaction. But I just couldn't muster that for him. Heath had the right to walk away from this. There was no obligation here. The memories we had could stay just that, memories. They didn't need to morph into a future, as badly as I wanted it.

My eyes were wet with the emotion that contradicted my brave face when I pulled into his driveway. I took the keys from the ignition and listened as the engine hummed until there was no noise as all. I could see my heart pulsing under my skin and thought, for a moment, that the tank top wasn't a good selection. I'd give away my nerves the instant he laid eyes on me.

I didn't care. I wasn't about hiding anymore, never really had been. I was allowed to feel scared about the possibility of tonight. Emotions were meant to be felt. That was exactly their purpose.

I wanted—more than I could express—for Heath to feel something, too. He had been a brick wall this afternoon, an impenetrable stone exterior. I planned to crack that.

After I scooped Corbin from the backseat, I walked up the steps to Heath's second-story apartment. We'd never spent much time here since he had a roommate and I had a baby. My house was always our home base. The fact that he was about to break up with me on his turf intensified the ache in my gut even more.

With two knocks, I sucked in a breath and put on my big girl panties.

"Mallory." Heath opened the door and then backed up quickly to allow me through, tripping over his feet like they'd suddenly grown two extra sizes. Instantly, out of habit and affection, Corbin reached for him. I let him. I could've been controlling and held my son to my chest, a vise grip of possession, but I allowed them their moment. Corbin deserved to have his own goodbye, too.

"I'm glad you could make it." Though he said the words, nothing about his demeanor or tone showed any ounce of gladness. It was all rote and repetition. His gaze was sidelong, not meeting mine. "Want anything to drink?"

"You said this wouldn't take long." I tried so hard to hold the snarkiness from my tongue, but it wouldn't obey.

"Right. I did." Corbin's hand repeatedly smacked Heath against his cheek, all in a playful manner, but I couldn't help but laugh. With his free hand, Heath grabbed on to the little flailing arm and secured it to his side.

"So." I looked around the room and pushed the hair from my face, letting out a breath. "What did Tommy send you?"

"You want to see it now? I was thinking we could wait a little bit."

Waiting on heartbreak was the stuff of insanity. I didn't want to drag the moment out any longer. I was not a glutton for punishment by any means. "Now would be good."

"Um." He swung around, eyes wild. Two huffs and an excessive amount of swallowing and he answered, "Okay, just give me a second. Is it okay if I hand you—?"

He started to push Corbin away from his body and I reached out to take him. "Give him here."

Then Heath was gone.

"This is so weird," I whispered against my son's forehead. "Men can be *so* weird."

Three minutes later and he was back, only to disappear again into an office just off the family room. Maybe he'd been drinking. That could explain this odd behavior. Or maybe he'd been drinking the whole time we'd been together, and only now, sobered up, did he realize the errors in his ways. In picking things right back up with me.

"Okay. All set."

Heath brought with him a parchment paper package, one unmistakably holding a painting of my father's under its protective cover. Propping it up against the wall, he stepped back like it was about to go off, some bomb under wraps. He brought his hand to his chin and tilted his head the way a dog does when you ask if it wants to go for a walk.

"Should I be doing something with this?"

"Open it." Like he could nudge me with air alone, Heath bobbed his nose in the direction of the package. "I'm curious to see what it is."

"You haven't looked yet?" This was getting increasingly bizarre by the minute. I was definitely not ruling out alcohol. Heath was all jitters, springs bound in his muscles, ready to snap.

"I wanted to open it together."

Breakups were never easy, but Heath had never been good at them, I supposed. The last time he broke up with me, he left town, never to be heard from again. At least this time we were both present. I guess I could thank him for that.

"So I just, what? Just rip it open?"

I looked over my shoulder at Heath, whose knuckles stroked against his scruffy jaw. "Yeah." He broke from his daze. His eyes refocused as they met mine. "Just go for it. I've been waiting for this answer for weeks now."

My head wobbled hesitantly. "Answer? There's some kind of answer in here?"

"I asked him a question when we were in Kentucky. I'm assuming this is finally his answer to that."

My forehead wrinkled, causing my eyes to narrow. I hooked a finger under the flap at the top of the package and balanced Corbin against my hip, over-exaggerating my stance to keep him securely there. "Do I get to know the question?"

"Depends on his answer."

"Oh, Heath, you absolutely confound me." Then, before going any further, I spun around on my heels to look him wholly in the face. "So this is not a breakup? You're not breaking up with me?"

Every muscle in Heath's body slumped, the air and strength sapped out of him. His head slunk forward and his gray eyes bulged. A tentative smile built on his lips, growing slowly like it was being pulled at the corners. "Are you serious?"

I was about to signal my answer with a nod when he propelled toward me. His arms were the pressure of a boa constrictor, bound all the way around, and it made me yelp in his embrace.

"Oh, sweet Mallory. You came here thinking I was going to break up with you tonight? How sad is that?"

"Super sad." My words slurred against his chest and Corbin continued with the face-slapping thing now that Heath was again in arm's reach. "Seriously, I was super sad over it."

"You didn't even seem sad. If anything, you seemed crazy pissed."

"Well, you seemed nervous as hell! What was that about?"

"I *am* nervous as hell! I've been staring at that package for days now."

That an inanimate object could derive so much emotion was impressive and a little intimidating. "So why didn't you just open it?"

"I wanted you here." Heath shrugged. "I want you here for everything."

That was all I needed to hear.

"Well then, without further ado, let's get to it, shall we?"

Like Christmas morning, I ripped into that package with gusto. The brown paper floated in strips to the floor. I shuffled back on my feet, my chest heavy, my hands sweaty.

I scrutinized Heath's eyes more than the painting.

The artwork was like many of Tommy's other pieces: colors spun together, brush lines crafting form from flowing and blended strokes.

"So ... what is it?"

Heath's lips lifted. "A yes." His face lit up entirely, a one-eighty from this afternoon. This looked so much better on him. "It's a definite yes."

Thirty-One

Heath

I had his blessing.
One down, one to go.

Sleep eluded me all week. I'd nailed Tommy's painting to the wall across from my bed, thinking it would serve as inspiration, but in truth, it only made me exponentially nervous each time my gaze settled on the canvas.

Without his answer, my hands were tied, and having your hands tied wasn't always a bad thing. It meant I could stall. Procrastinate. Wait on making the biggest decision I would ever make. Sure, I'd proposed before, and to say that didn't mean anything would be to rob that moment of its value. There was something valuable in my first marriage. I'd learned lessons. Learned who I was supposed to be and how I was supposed to treat others. Kayla wasn't the only one to make mistakes within our union. I'd certainly been responsible for plenty.

I didn't want to make mistakes with Mallory.

And I hoped it wasn't a mistake jumping into this, both feet first.

All I knew was that I couldn't wait another minute without making her mine. Forever this time.

Tommy's answer was so well kept within the paint that I knew without a doubt Mallory had no clue to its meaning. The image was identical to the one at the studio. The one where Mallory and I were intertwined on the hospital bed, the outline of the boat surrounding our tangled bodies. I'm sure she figured she was looking upon that same image. Only I'd noticed it, tucked away like one of those Search and Find books where the pages were cluttered with colorful objects and distractions.

There, on her fourth finger, was the shiny glint of an engagement ring.

And that's all I needed.

Well, that and one more thing.

I slouched against the leather cushion, letting the vibration of the potholed road ease out some of the apprehension wound in my chest. My arm swung out the window; my thumb drummed against the steering wheel. To the vehicles passing by, I'm sure I looked the picture of relaxation: the way my sunglasses shaded my eyes from the glare reflected through the bug-splattered windshield, the music thumping out a hypnotizing beat with too much bass, the breezy rush that ruffled my hair, grown too long with neglect.

Yeah, I looked calm and collected. Not a care in the world.

Couldn't be further from the truth.

I drove past the house one time. Then another. And another. The last swing down the street, I was forced to stop at my destination. The woman watering her plants four doors down—wearing a pink fluffy robe and leopard print slippers—she also wore the look of a person well acquainted with calling the police when a suspicious fellow happened upon her neighborhood. And I definitely looked suspicious. Gone was that carefree dude coasting down the highway. I was all shifty eyes, clammy hands, sweat laden brow.

Hiding out in the driveway wasn't an option with Nosey Neighbor eyeing me, so I engaged the truck in park and hopped out from the cab, not without flicking a friendly wave to the woman in her robe.

"Evening!" I hollered, then, two at a time, I bounded the steps to the porch, ready to knock when the door fell open before I had the opportunity.

"Heath! We've been expecting you."

They looked like most parents did. Good ones, actually. He was easily six and a half feet, and burly to boot. The handlebar mustache, flecked with gray, was a nice frame around his genial and authentic smile, and the way he kept his hand pressed to his wife's back did something to my stomach that felt like a memory. Warm and natural.

She was darling, a half-pint with a ruddy stain on the apples of her cheeks. Her blouse was the kind that all women her age wore: billowy to hide her rounded midsection, but dressed up with the glitz of a sparkly necklace she'd likely had for years but only pulled out for an occasion like tonight.

I liked them both instantly.

"Boone." I nodded toward the man. "Sharon." Rather than accept the hand I offered, she threw her arms around my waist and pulled me into the foyer, the act camouflaged in a hug.

"Oh, Heath. I can't tell you how glad we are to finally meet you." She gave my biceps the type of squeeze an aunt gives, the one that's just a little too hard to be comfortable but loving all the same.

"This is where we say things like, 'We've heard a lot about you,'" Boone interjected, popping his head around his wife to address me. "And you tease, 'All good things, I hope.' To which we answer, 'Of course! Of course!'"

"So we'll just skip over all of that?" I asked with a friendly elbow to Boone's side.

"Yup. No shooting the shit for us. Tell it like it is."

"I like your style."

"Give the boy a break, Boone. He hasn't been in the house thirty seconds and you're already laying down the law."

"Only because you wouldn't let me get it printed on the wall. Told you it would make things easier." He swiped his hand in the air in an arc as though reading a sign. "Rule number one: no bullshit. Rule number two: see rule number one." He turned to me again. "You see, we're simple people around here, Heath. Not much to remember."

The quick snap of Sharon's dishrag against her husband's backside made me jolt. I hadn't even noticed it there, draped over her shoulder.

"Leave the boy alone! I swear he'll want out of this family before he ever even joins it!"

Boone pulled straight as a pencil. I did pretty much the same, but it didn't feel quite as substantial a posture since Boone easily had six inches on me.

Rubbing the back of his neck with a paw of a hand, his mustache twitched up on the right. "How about we crack open a few cold ones before this little lady gets herself into even more trouble, running her mouth like that."

"Oh, I'll run you right out that door, Thomas Boone Quinn."

"Woman, go fetch us our beers!"

Boone tipped the neck of the amber bottle toward me. "Another?"

I waved him off. "Nah, I'm good with the one. Thanks."

I didn't want the haze of alcohol to cloud the words I needed to say. To slur my ability to get the job done.

"So you're a teacher, I hear?" He leaned back against the white Adirondack chair and crossed his legs at the ankles, his hefty boots making a thud. "High school?"

"Yes, sir. I've been at Whitney for five years now. Senior Honors English."

This was shit-shooting, but I'd take it. I'd been stalling from the moment Boone walked me through their impressive home and into the backyard. We both knew the reason I was here so I couldn't understand my hesitation in saying what needed to be said. But my upper lip beaded with sweat and my knuckles were white against the arm of the chair.

I almost excused myself to hide out in the bathroom, but that was a cowardly move.

I released the death grip on the armrest and ran my hands down the thighs of my pants.

"Sir, I have a question I'd like to ask you."

"The answer's yes, Heath." Boone studied something at the far end of the yard. A bird rustling in the tree or a squirrel chase. His head leaned forward as his eyes squinted. I followed his gaze until, out of my periphery, I saw it suddenly swing my direction. "The fact that you would even find it necessary to ask our permission is a testament to the kind of man you are." Wrapping his lips around the bottle, he pulled in a long, hearty swallow of dark beer and then released a satisfied sigh. "Mallory is our daughter, maybe not by blood, but she's our daughter all the same. When our son married her, she became family. Forever."

My chin twitched and I bit my lip, hard.

"So I guess I just need to warn you."

"Warn me, sir?"

"Warn you that, whether you like it or not, we're a packaged deal." Boone cracked the top off another longneck. "You get her, you get us." He hooked a thumb over his shoulder and nodded toward the house. "Even the crazy one in the kitchen."

I flopped back in my chair and let my head fall against the planks and smiled as I said, "I wouldn't have it any other way."

Thirty-Two

Heath

That couldn't have gone any better.

I was still on cloud nine when I hopped into my truck. Finding my phone, I cranked the music to max volume, and I used the dashboard, the steering wheel, and the brake pedal all as the instruments for my drum solo. My head bobbed to the beat, banging with the percussion. I drove for miles, a stupid grin on my face, my body buzzing.

That came to a sudden and unfortunate halt when the sirens—which, for a moment, I thought accompanied the current track playing from my phone—broke up my personal rock concert.

I reached across the cab to crank down my window. "Officer," I greeted, then was thrown by the face that came into view. "Officer Douglas?"

"Mr. McBride."

My registration was current. My insurance renewed. The paper he'd flung into my backseat last time was not a ticket, but instead a note that said, "It was nice to finally meet you," which—although a little weird—did not require payment or a court appearance.

Sure, I'd been enjoying my music more loudly than necessary, but I wasn't breaking any laws here. So I wasn't nervous this time. I was on the brink of being pissed, and it took a lot to get me there.

"Sir, I'm not sure what I'm being pulled over for, but—"

"Would you mind stepping out of the vehicle?"

Okay. Now I was nervous. I would never survive jail. I barely made it through my shave at the barbershop without passing out. The types of improvised weapons and shivs that I'd seen on cable TV prison shows made me crap my pants in fear. Jail time was not an option.

Obediently, I popped open my door and followed Officer Douglas to his cruiser. His thick boots left loud and intimidating stomps and my heart matched in time and sound. He walked to the shoulder of the road, then slouched against his car, his ankles crossed, arms tightly folded over his chest. Even under his black sunglasses, I could see the intense squint of his eyes.

"Heath, there's something I need to tell you."

"That there's a warrant out for my arrest?"

The officer's head cocked. "Should I have any reason to believe there's a warrant out for you?"

I laughed, but it was tight and forced and full of apprehension. "No. No, sir. I was only kidding."

Officer Douglas released a gruff sigh. "Heath, Officer Quinn was my best friend. Not just on the force, but in life."

I wish I could say that relinquished all my pent-up nerves, but in reality, his statement only multiplied them.

"We grew up together in Kentucky. Transferred to California at the same time. We were just kids when we both graduated from the academy and started our first year with the unit."

He was going somewhere with this, so I didn't interject.

"I was there for the accident, Heath."

"Mallory's?"

"Yeah. And I was there for all the months that followed." With his hand, he slid his glasses to his forehead. Blew out a hot breath. "You have to understand that Dylan had just come out of a really bad breakup. He'd planned to marry the girl and she just up and left for Europe. Some foreign exchange program. Met a guy while over there and eloped. Dylan was shattered. More depressed than I'd ever seen him. It was hell for him."

I scraped my hand through my hair. "I'm not sure what any of this has to do with me."

"I deleted your texts, Heath."

My mouth gaped open. "What?"

"We retrieved Mallory's phone from the accident," he said. "I saw the way Dylan looked at her. It was the first time his spark returned. He felt like he could be her hero, and that did something to him. Gave him purpose again. And I finally had my best friend back."

"Where are you going with this?"

"I read everything you wrote to Mallory." Police officers weren't usually the ones doing the confessing. The shock still hadn't fallen from my face. "How you would always love her. How sorry you were. How it wasn't over."

My hands twisted in my pockets and I gave Officer Douglas a wary glance.

"I blocked your number, Heath." His voice was stilted. "I had a high school friend of mine hack into her e-mail account and delete everything you sent her, too. She never saw any of it."

Had I not known any better, I would've thought Boone slipped something stronger into my drink. My skull pounded. I planted my feet wide and ground my teeth. "Why are you telling me this now?"

His nostrils flared, head whipping back and forth in a twitch. "I wasn't just close with Dylan. When they started dating, Mallory became a friend, too. I care about her, Heath. Watching her survive Dylan's death was awful. She was so alone. But then I pulled you over that day," he continued. "I finally put a face to the name. And it reminded me that someone else had shared his feelings for her, too."

Two minutes earlier I'd wanted to deck the guy. But there was sincerity in his tone—at the very least, vulnerability. He didn't need to share this with me. I could appreciate the humility it took to finally let the truth out.

"You were Mallory's chance at happiness again. Maybe you were supposed to be her happiness all along."

"She was happy with Dylan," I defended, feeling the strange need to interject.

"Yeah, she was. But we all know he'd made his mistakes. Things didn't work out in Europe for his ex and one weekend when Mallory was back home visiting in Kentucky, he flew her out to stay with him. Mallory found out and, Mallory being Mallory, took him back. Forgave everything."

Mallory being Mallory.

Her forgiveness—the grace she offered others for the very least of offenses to something on this horrible scale— was what I loved about her. Was what challenged me to become a better person. Daily.

"Heath—I'm so sorry for everything I did. Honestly. I thought I was doing right by my friend, but I can't shake the feeling that I intervened where fate should have led the way."

I pressed my lips flat and my arms tensed. I shook out my hands and said with more reluctance than I'd hoped to convey, "It's okay."

"It's not."

"No." My voice was tight. "No, it is. You didn't know me. You didn't know what Mallory and I had. All you saw was the potential for happiness for your buddy and hey, how can I fault you for that?"

"Because it was a shitty thing to do."

I barked out a laugh. "You're right. It was a shitty thing to do. That I won't argue with. But it would've been even shittier if you'd never told me. And for that, I have to thank you."

Officer Douglas smiled. "I wish I could give you a lifetime's worth of exemptions from parking tickets, but— being illegal and all—I can't."

"You weren't above illegal activity in the past." I winked with a grin.

"Ouch."

"Hey, man. Only pointing out the obvious." I dropped a hand to his shoulder. "But seriously, thank you for coming clean. It means a lot."

"Thank you for always being so good to Mallory. It's nice to see her have her spark back, too."

I swiveled to walk back to my truck but said, "And it's my plan to make sure she never loses it again."

"Good plan." Officer Douglas tipped his chin to me. He hollered my direction. "I'll be sure to stay out of the way this time."

"That's a good plan, too. And no offense, but I'd be perfectly happy if I never saw you again, Officer Douglas. You and those flashing lights of yours."

"Absolutely none taken."

The interruption to my drive home set me back about twenty minutes, but I was a staunch believer that everything happened for a reason. Even Officer Douglas's shenanigans twelve years ago. Whatever the motive, he felt he was doing the right thing, and who was to say that I wouldn't've done the same thing, had I been in his shoes?

All right, I wouldn't've done the same thing, but that was not the point. I figured the grief and deceit he'd harbored the last decade was punishment enough, and I wasn't about to lay it on even thicker. He deserved to move on, too.

I hopped right back onto my cloud nine and enjoyed the view, but not for long.

Pulled over on the shoulder up about a quarter of a mile ahead was a gray sedan, its hazard lights ticking out a distress warning.

With my left hand, I turned my blinker on and coasted the truck up to the back of the vehicle, slowing against the dirt on the side of the road. I stepped out of the cab and called out to the driver who was exiting her car at the same time. She appeared young—probably a college student— and pressed herself against the vehicle as a semi rolled past in the slow lane next to her.

"Everything okay?"

"Flat tire!" she yelled over the roar of cars. "Mr. McBride? Is that you?"

"Brittany Carson?" When I got closer, I recognized her as one of my students from my very first year of teaching. "How the heck are you?"

"Well …" She glanced to the offending tire, its air completely gone. "I could be better."

"Know if you have a spare?"

Brittany walked around to the trunk. "I think so. I've never had to use it, but my dad said there was one when I called him."

"He on his way over?"

She shook her head. "No, he's at work, but I'm sure I can figure it out."

"Let's see if we can figure it out together. For starters, the tire's probably going to be under the vehicle. The jack is most likely in the trunk. Let's pop it open and see what we're working with."

Brittany's face when slack with relief. "Thank you so much, Mr. McBride. I had no idea what I was doing and this isn't exactly the safest spot to pull over. I don't know why it's flat. I don't think I ran over anything."

I located the jack and dropped it to the ground. "Probably a nail or something, but we'll take a look. I hate to say it, but I'm glad I just got pulled over, otherwise I wouldn't have been driving down the road at this time of night to find you."

"You got pulled over?" she asked. "That totally sucks."

"It wasn't so bad. It was actually really great, to be honest." Brittany gave me a look like maybe I'd just fallen from a tree, but I shrugged it off. I grabbed a crowbar from the toolbox in the trunk and rapped it against my palm. "Let's see what we can do about turning your evening around, too."

Thirty-Three

Mallory

The cruiser drove up to the house at 8:36 p.m.

I fell apart at 8:37.

"I can take you down there."

I sat on the edge of the leather armchair, elbows digging sharply into the fleshy part of my knees.

"Mallory?"

My body rocked forward and back, forward and back.

"Mallory."

I'd avoided looking at him by cradling my face in my palms, but the tears and the snot and the sweat made them slick against my cheeks. My hands slipped with each rocking motion.

"Mallory—I need to know what you want to do."

"I don't know what I want to do." I flinched at the hand he placed on my back—at the flimsy offer of comfort that drew my shoulders to my ears. "I'm sorry, Scott. I just don't know what I'm supposed to do."

He was still in his highway patrolman's uniform but had fidgeted loose the top button on his shirt. "I can drive you there. Or I can stay with Corbin if you want to drive yourself."

"I can't drive." I couldn't see two inches in front of me. The room swam in my vision. "I can't drive right now."

"Is there someone you'd like me to call?"

I croaked out a laugh. "How awful is it that the only person I want to call right now is Heath?"

"Mallory. God. I'm so sorry."

"I know." My mouth hinted at a small smile. "Of course I know, Scott."

He waited like he said he would and when Vickie and Lucas arrived, Scott held me against his chest for a solid, wordless minute. It felt like it might've been more for his sake than mine, but I was okay with that. We could console each other; we'd done it before.

"Go." Vickie shoved at me with her duffle bag the instant she walked into the entryway. Her eyes blinked rapidly but didn't conceal the reddened veins that webbed them. "*Go*. I'll be fine here with Corbin. I brought my things for overnight."

After finding my phone, I reached for my house keys and then turned to follow Lucas out the front door to his Jeep. His mother caught his elbow and meant for it to be a conversation between for the two of them, but the stern volume was easily overheard.

"You *do not* fall apart in there. You understand me?"

"Yes, ma'am."

She gritted through her teeth. "I mean it, Lucas. You keep it together … for her."

Another nod from her son and we were down the walkway and in the car.

Lucas fiddled with the radio, never really landing on any station for more than half a song. It didn't matter. I couldn't use the distraction of music to temper my distraught mind. Everything was worn out, all emotion exhausted.

I'd lived this before.

Maybe at some point, you ran out of tears. My heart broke at the possibility that there weren't any left for Heath.

When I saw him, though, I saw through that lie.

Each loss was a fresh wound, even if the pain occurred in a similar way. Some hurts just dug into the old scars. But it could cut them, too. Rip open the healed-over flesh to expose the same ache, same throb, just in a new and sharp way.

Lucas and I waited six hours in a room designated for that task. Where we'd get one answer from a particular nurse, another would come by with a completely contradictory statement or update. I didn't know what information to let my heart rest in. Hope seemed like a foolish thing to chase.

Despite the confusion, two things were clear: he never saw it coming and he wouldn't likely walk anytime soon.

My emotion bled out of me when I ambled into the hospital room and finally laid eyes on Heath, the man I loved—had always loved—as broken on the outside as I felt on the inside. My scars split wide open.

"He's in an induced coma," a young brunette nurse said to us before leading us all the way in. Machines beeped steadily near Heath's hospital bed and monitors flashed out a regulated pulse. "He had some swelling to his brain and large amounts of internal bleeding. He's lost a lot of blood, along with the lower portion of his left leg.

He won't be responsive, so don't expect that from him. But you are welcome to stay until family arrives."

Heath's parents, along with Hattie and her husband and children, had left two days earlier for a summer trip to Cancun. I spoke with Anthony on the phone just three hours ago when they were about to board their return flights, which would put them in town right around dawn.

Tomorrow he could be with family, but tonight he would be with me.

"I'll wait in the hall, Miss Quinn."

"Thank you, Lucas." I squeezed his hand.

There had been an empty feeling in the hollow of my stomach—an ache that bent me in half. The sort of despair that heartache shares with the rest of your body making you physically ill. Seeing Heath—finally being in the same room as him—took that away.

I only felt one thing. Gratitude. Not for what had happened, but for the fact that he'd survived it. That he wasn't completely taken from me. His act of kindness had a horrific result, but he was still here.

Heath was still here.

As I stepped closer, taking in the tubes that threaded in and out of his body, studying the new marks on his skin that were crudely sewn together, watching the steady rise and fall of his chest, I felt something else.

"You are such a good, good man, Heath," I whispered against his cool forehead, my lips lighting on his bruised skin. "Always doing the right thing."

He really was good. When it came down to it, Heath was the kind of man I hoped Corbin would grow up to be, and that realization struck me in the gut even harder than the news of the accident. Where that brought shock, this brought peace.

Heath was the man I wanted to raise my son with. He wasn't Dylan's replacement. Of course not. People couldn't replace others. And our life together would be different, it had to be. But circumstance took Dylan from me and gave Heath to me. It took my mom and gave me Nana. It took pieces of my dad but gave me the gift of his talent in his paintings and our new way to communicate. It didn't replace the person or cover up the memories, but it filled in the void with something different. A different kind of love.

Love was the healer that poured into the cracks of heartbreak.

Heath's hospital room was dark, only the light directly above his bed turned on. It contoured the cuts on his face dramatically. I examined each one, reminding myself to be thankful that they weren't worse. As gruesome as it was, this was not the worst-case scenario. There were other families in this very hospital living out that horror right now. I'd lived it out before. There was thankfulness to be found in each scar that would mar his face, in the time it would take to heal, in the recovery and the physical therapy and the process of regaining his strength.

What started as a well-meaning stop on the shoulder of the road resulted in a gruesome hit and run. A hit and run that sideswiped Heath, leaving him trapped under the stalled vehicle, his leg pinned under the tire, his body a heap of unconscious flesh and muscle pocked with gravel and asphalt.

Scott was the first on the scene, as he had been at my accident so long ago.

It must've felt like déjà vu.

When he came to my house shortly after, he was rambling about texts and secrets and how sorry he was and if I could ever forgive him. I couldn't process any of it at the time though I later pieced together what he was trying to reveal. I understood his involvement, and I forgave him, of course I did. It was something we would need to talk through, but I saw the regret in his eyes and tears and heard it in his voice. Maybe he felt like he'd upended my life back then, but he was sincere in trying to make it right now, and that was all I could ask out of anyone.

261

The thing I could process immediately, though, was the fact that Heath had been hurt, that he was suffering. But now, looking at him under the thin blue hospital sheet, his eyelids shut, his body stilled, he looked almost peaceful.

I smoothed his hair with my palm and brought my face close. "This is going to put a damper on those ballroom dancing lessons I just signed us up for." Maybe it was morose, but to joke felt better than to cry. "You'd said that you were two left feet, but now you don't even have the one."

With a twisted laugh, I cupped my hand to my mouth. Had anyone heard me, they would've thought it insensitive, but if there was any chance that Heath could hear—could understand what I was saying—it would be worth it. It was the sort of thing he would say to me, I knew it.

"I love you." I dropped my head to the empty side of his bed, the space between his body and the rail. I closed my tear-stung eyes. "With all the heart that I have left, I love you, Heath."

Exhaustion must've set in because the next thing I remembered was feeling Hattie's delicate hand on my shoulder, her palm rubbing slow circles to wake me. I startled and rushed to my feet. The room spun, black circling in at the edges of my vision.

"Shhhh," she shushed, her finger brought to her lips. "It's okay. You don't have to go. Sit for a few minutes. Stay."

I rubbed at my neck. "No, no. I should go home to Corbin. Is everyone else here?"

"Mom and Dad are getting briefed by the staff." Hattie tilted her head toward the hallway. Through the window, I could see Heath's parents deep in discussion with one of the doctors. His mother had both hands to her mouth; his father had both hands on his wife's shoulders. They were doing an excessive amount nodding, but that's what you did when hearing news like this. Like bobbing your head would somehow rattle the words into your brain in a way that made them easier to understand.

"The nurses said he had a good night. That they expected him to be much more restless. Having you here calmed him, Mallory." Hattie gave my wrists a squeeze. "Thank you for being here when we couldn't. We can't thank you enough."

I didn't have words that would be able to come out alone. Any I tried to utter would have tears attached, so I just bobbed my head and hugged her back before I reached for my purse.

"Lucas is in the waiting room and said he's ready to drive you home whenever you like."

"He's still here?" My stomach tightened with guilt. "He didn't have to stay."

"He loves Heath, too, Mallory."

Of course he did. Heath was an incredibly easy guy to love.

"Will you call me if anything changes?" I asked before turning to go. "Or even if things don't change? Just … just keep me updated?"

Hattie smiled as she took a seat in the empty chair next to her younger brother. "Of course. But for now, go home and love on that baby of yours. Take a nap. Get a shower and some food. We'll be here and you're welcome to come back at any time."

"Is it bad that I don't ever want to leave?"

Hattie's eyes crinkled with another grin and she gave me the sweetest of looks when she said, "I know for a fact that my brother feels exactly the same way about you."

Thirty-Four

Heath

Someone had crammed a hundred cotton balls into my mouth, beaten me within an inch of my life with a sledgehammer, and then vomited flowers all over the room.

I was about 99 percent sure that's what happened, at least.

My tongue scraped my throat with a gritty swallow. My dry lips tightened. My eyelids had weights attached to them, which made opening them a herculean effort. I groaned.

"Heath!" Hattie shuffled to my side. Her hand found my arm, right where a needle jabbed into my flesh like I was a human pincushion. I groaned once more. "Oh my God, I'm so sorry!" Then she whipped her head away from me and shouted, "Mom! Dad! Anthony!"

Her voice grew fingers that wrapped around my brain and squeezed it like a vise. I groaned again.

"Sorry," she whispered this time. "Sorry."

"Why does this room look like a wedding aisle?" I turned my head as best I could to observe the table to my left, overflowing with petals and greenery.

"Because your girlfriend is a florist. That, and all of the Whitney kids get a discount there."

"Got it." I was incapable of doing anything but groan; even my words were pained. "What happened?"

"I think I should wait for a doctor—" Hattie started to say, but it was too late.

I wiggled my toes. On the right side of the bed, underneath the starchy blue drape, my foot twitched. On the left, nothing. Bile crept into my throat, burning my nose and eyes.

"Hattie …" The volume of my voice rose at the end. Panic lifted it an octave higher when I said it again. "Hattie!"

"Shhhh, Heath." Her hand flew to my forehead and raked through my greasy hair. "It's okay. It's going to be okay."

"Oh, God."

There, in a hospital room with only my older sister to witness, I lost it. Sobbed like a baby. At one point a doctor halted in the doorway, but I think Hattie shook him off because he nodded and turned away. My lips were slick and drool pooled in the corner of my mouth. Hattie held my face to her chest and dragged her hands against my scalp, rocking me against the thin mattress. Each movement of my jumping shoulders stabbed me with agony.

And then, as quickly as I fell apart, I pulled myself together. "Can you get the doctor?" I sniffed against my hand as I wiped my face. "I have a few questions."

"Of course." Hattie raced out the door like she was sprinting at a track meet. When she returned, she had the sleeve of someone who I assumed was on the medical staff in her hand.

"You didn't have to physically drag him in here." I laughed, but it hurt my ribs and my brain to do so.

"Heath." The doctor lowered a hand to the bedrail. "I'm Dr. Callahan."

"Good to meet you." I winced when I tried to stretch out my palm for a shake.

He denied my offer and trapped my hand to lower it to the bed. "Just rest, Heath. You've sustained some pretty significant injuries last night. Do you remember what happened at all?"

I remembered being pulled over, then finding an old student of mine stranded on the side of the road. I recalled hauling the old tire to the trunk, skirting around the side of the car with the spare in hand, and then crouching down to fit it on the wheel hub. But that was it.

"I don't remember a lot. Just changing a tire and then nothing. Just blank."

"You were struck by a passing vehicle that swerved out of its lane going about forty miles an hour. We're guessing the driver was distracted by something. Their vehicle dragged you forward five feet and wedged you under the car you were attempting to fix." The doctor's light blue eyes squinted behind his thin, round spectacles. "Heath, you lost part of your left leg in the incident. Just below the knee. The bone was so badly crushed and muscle mangled that all efforts to reattach it were lost. I'm so sorry."

My head wobbled unsteadily. "Okay." I hissed the painful words. "Okay."

"You are lucky to be alive."

It seemed trite for him to say, but I understood his intentions. "Don't I know it." And I honestly did. I was lucky. Maybe a little unlucky, too, but I could see the good and how it possibly outweighed the bad in this scenario. "How long before I can walk again?"

"First things first, Heath. Your body has a significant amount of healing to do."

"I understand that, but timeline-wise, what are we talking?"

Dr. Callahan grimaced. "I hate to give any projected amount of time for this kind of recovery."

That did not satisfy me. "If everything goes smoothly, what the best-case scenario?"

The doctor rubbed at his jaw. "You're not going to let me out of this room without an answer, are you?"

"Not a chance." I smiled, but my lip cracked at the side, opening up some cut I must've had. I brought my thumb to my mouth to swipe at the blood but the doctor retrieved some gauze from a nearby cupboard and handed it to me. "Six months? A year? Two years?"

"Definitely not two years. Best case—and I mean *best* case—is that you can leave the hospital in a week or so. And that's just leaving the hospital. The real work begins after that."

I nodded to keep him talking.

"If the site of the amputation heals without problem, you could be fitted for a prosthetic as soon as two to three weeks. But the average fitting time is usually two to six months post-surgery."

"Well, I'm not really satisfied with being just an average guy, so I'm shooting for weeks rather than months."

"All of that will depend on how things mend, Heath. Attitude is often more than half of the battle, but your body physically needs time to recover."

"Understood." I did, at least mentally. My heart had more hope in it than my brain, though. "So walking. When will that happen?"

"With hours and hours of physical therapy and the help of a rehabilitation team—and if all things happen as quickly as you hope—I would say anywhere from four months to a year."

"So by November."

"*Possibly.*" Dr. Callahan leaned forward. "I don't want to set any false expectations here, Heath. This is going to be a long road to recovery. Prosthetics are expensive. Rehab takes time. There are more variables than I can even list at the moment."

"But there's a chance that by Thanksgiving, I'll be walking again."

The doctor relinquished a sigh. "There's always a chance."

Life had a strange way of giving me second chances. This was one I was banking on getting.

Thirty-Five

Mallory

I tightened my black jacket around my waist as I walked through the hospital parking lot. Though only August, the sharp chill in the air required the extra layer, and I was thankful for it. Plus, hospital rooms always seemed to be several degrees cooler than other establishments. Maybe germs didn't survive well when the temperature dropped. Whatever the reason, the lightweight overcoat was a necessary addition tonight, and I adjusted the fabric while I traipsed through the automatic entrance doors that spread open wide.

Heath had been in the hospital for a week and a half, which was a week and a half longer than he'd hoped. If it were up to him, he'd be at home, recuperating while he prepared lesson plans. But not at his home. There was no way he'd be able to navigate those stairs to his second story apartment.

His roommate, Paul, had been surprisingly incredible this week, helping Boone and me move the majority of Heath's belongings into my spare bedroom at the other end of the house. Maybe we weren't at that stage in our relationship yet—the one where our lives intertwined right down to waking and sleeping—but this was the only reasonable solution I could come up with. He would need someone to take care of him, and I was more than willing to be that person.

I passed familiar faces in the hall as I rounded the corner to the elevators. Spending any prolonged amount of time in a hospital made you realize that this was, in fact, home for many people. While it was looking fairly good that Heath might be discharged in a few days, there were others who would be here for months at a time. There were also some who would never leave.

Blessings were constantly showing up for us, just waiting to be counted.

I rode the elevator to his fifth floor and my favorite nurse at the front buzzed me in through the locked double doors.

"Hey, Mallory. Here to see the hottie in 23?"

Even under all the injury, Heath was still one incredibly good looking man and the nursing staff didn't hesitate to appreciate that.

I flashed a smile. "He's not sleeping, is he?"

"Even if he is, I'm sure he'll wake right up once he finds out you're here. Seriously, that man does not stop talking about you."

Well then, let's give him something to talk about.

The halls were quiet this late in the evening. While still visiting hours, it was close enough to dusk that most people had gone home to give the patients a little time for rest. Sharon and Boone had only been available to watch Corbin after a dinner they had planned with friends. I figured Heath would be surprised to see me so late, especially considering both Corbin and I had spent most of the morning by his side, reading board books and watching baby television programs. Nothing brought a contented gleam to Heath's eyes like being around Corbin, who he had recently affectionately dubbed his "best little buddy."

I was quickly falling in love with the way he loved him.

My heart swelled with that thought as I rounded the corner to Heath's room. The blinds on the window were slanted at a degree that made peering into them impossible, but the low light slipping through hinted that he might be awake. I knew that Nico and Natalie were supposed to come by for dinner like they did nearly every day, and it looked like they'd already left for the evening. My fingers lighted on the door and tapped softly.

"Knock, knock?"

He cleared his throat before calling out, "Yeah? Come on in."

When I toed the door open, the look on Heath's face was enough to make me melt.

"Mallory!" The sheets rustled around him as he fought to sit up in the inclined bed. "You're back!" He held out his arms as if to ask for a hug and said, "I thought I didn't get you again until tomorrow."

"You know I couldn't wait that long to see you."

"Come on over here." He flapped his hands impatiently. "But first, press that button for me, would you?"

"The one to call the nurse?"

"Yep."

I knew he tried to stifle it in an effort mask the pain, but Heath groaned as he adjusted his position in the bed. I pressed my finger into the red call button and didn't let on that I could hear his discomfort.

"Nurse's station," a tinny voice echoed through the speaker.

"Hey, I, uh, just wanted to check to see if I need any vitals read anytime soon or if the doctor was going to be making his rounds or anything like that. Because if not, I'd like to rest for a bit without any interruptions."

"Sure thing, Mr. McBride. You're all current on your medications and the doctor just finished up his shift. The next one won't be on for a little while. We'll leave you alone."

With a coy wink and smirk that dimpled his cheek, Heath gave me a thumbs-up.

"What do you have planned that needs so much privacy?" I lifted my leg up and over the railing and wedged my body into the space next to Heath on the bed, careful to slide his tubes and IV out of the way.

"Oh, gee, I don't know."

Slowly, Heath drew his face nearer to mine and lowered his mouth to my lips. He kissed me tenderly. Brought his hands to my jaw and brushed my cheek with his knuckles. I shivered all the way to my toes and pressed my body to his as much as the bandages and machines and monitors would let me. It wasn't easy to make out with someone who was hooked up to so many different things. The only way to kiss was with caution. The aggressive build that seemed to come so naturally when we touched was something I fought against each time our lips connected. As badly as I knew he wanted me, the last thing I wanted was to physically hurt him.

While his body was fragile, I figured his eyes were fair game.

I pushed up to prop on my elbow and pulled out of our kiss. With one hand, I tugged at the belt around my waist and loosened it. A nervous blush heated my skin, fluttered my belly.

Heath stilled. His lips parted. "You got something under there for me?" His voice was throaty and raw.

"Maybe." My heart rammed inside my chest. I pinched my eyes shut, like that might miraculously calm my nerves, but they still floated around in my stomach like a swarm of butterflies. "Please don't laugh."

Then, in one movement, I opened the front of my coat and slipped it from my shoulders, letting it fall to the bed. I couldn't open my eyes. I couldn't face the disappointment I figured his expression would convey. I shook with anxiety.

"You little thief." Heath's finger bopping against my nose made my unwilling eyes spring open. "I told you that was mine!"

My gaze dropped to the pink lace negligée that clung to my trembling body. "Oh yeah? You wear it often?"

"Only when I'm vacuuming. Housework is always more fun when you feel pretty."

I pushed Heath's shoulder and felt horrible when he grimaced in pain. "I'm so sorry!" I gasped. "I forgot."

"It's okay." The words gritted through strained teeth. "But seriously, Mallory. You have to remember, I'm hooked up to all kinds of machines, and what you're doing to my blood pressure and heart rate by wearing that thing is going to shoot it all off the charts. They'll have the whole nursing staff in here in no time."

"Oh." I fumbled for the coat.

"Hey! What are you doing?" Heath pulled the jacket from my hands and threw it to the foot of the hospital bed. "All I said was that we'd set off some alarms. I'm definitely not opposed to that." Then, scooting as much as he could without falling off the bed completely, Heath lifted the thin sheet and motioned me closer. "Come in here with me, would ya?"

I shuffled over and found the warmth of Heath's body trapped under the covers.

"Good thing they're not monitoring you, too, because I know this gown is doing all kinds of things to your heart rate. Nothing sexier than a man in a skirt."

"Hey, don't joke. Those Scottish men in kilts are actually pretty hot."

"True. True." He nodded his head at the observation. "But the ones with two legs tend to be hotter than the pogo sticks."

My heart dropped. "Heath. Stop."

"Mallory. It's okay. I've come to terms with it." His eyes tightened. "Sort of."

"This is going to be a huge transition for you, Heath. It's okay to grieve over it a little."

"Oh, I've done my share of grieving these past couple of weeks, but it hasn't been over my leg." Leaning to me so his chin was pressed to the crown of my head, he kissed me softly there and said, "I've been grieving that fact that you have been here for me each and every day, Mallory. You've been by my side each moment." His voice vibrated and he coughed to clear it. "I left you. I left you when you were in just as bad of shape. Probably worse. You woke up and I wasn't there."

My chest constricted. I took a breath to speak, but Heath talked over me.

"When I woke up and only Hattie was here, I figured it was my turn. My turn to suffer alone. It would only be right." It stung to hear him speak those words, to think that payback on this sort of level even existed. I didn't work that way. *We* didn't work that way. "But then she'd said that you were the first person here. That you stayed with me until they pretty much forced you to go home and get some rest. Spend time with my little buddy." I felt his warm tears drop onto my forehead but didn't wipe them away. He sniffed and said, "I should've fought my parents harder. I should've *made* them let me stay. They, of all people, should've known how much you needed me during that time."

"We were kids." It had become a mantra, a way to excuse our broken history.

"I'm sick of saying that. I loved you then like I love you now, Mallory. And you deserved to feel loved by me. I left you."

If he'd been in better shape, I would've punched him in the gut. Knocked some sense into him. I supposed it would've been the same as beating a dead horse, though, all the times we'd gone over this. "We need to stop bringing up the past. We've moved on from that. It's fine. We're fine."

"I never moved on. Maybe in my actions, but never in my heart." His thumb played on my bare shoulder with gentle strokes while he spoke. "I can't thank you enough for sticking with me, Mallory. I think it's going to get a lot worse before it gets any better, and I'll probably be a dick and take out my frustrations on the people who least deserve it, but I need you to know that you being by my side is what makes all of this bearable. I can deal with not having a leg. It sucks, it's going to be a bitch trying to get around school those first few weeks, it'll be painful and awful, but I cannot—I absolutely cannot—deal without you."

"You won't have to."

"But I would understand if, at some point, I do."

My words weren't sinking in, weren't providing any confidence where he lacked it, so I took another approach. I moved in closer to Heath. Pushed my chest to his so the silk fabric of my nightie rippled against his skin. Trailed kisses along his strong jaw, dropping my lips to every cut and scrape that blemished him. His lips touched down on mine and we nipped back and forth, shifted forward and back on the thin mattress and squeaky bed frame.

Every movement was slow motion, the way I hiked my leg over his hip and tugged gently at his blond hair. I took caution with every step. His body had been so badly cracked, torn, and abused. I needed my body to heal him, to piece him back together and love him to health.

Had we not been in the hospital, I would have given Heath every part of me, right there. But I could wait on that. He had my heart, my life. Someday he would have all of me. I was his and forever would be.

All he had to do was ask.

Thirty-Six

Heath

I'd been scared shitless for this day.

"See you Monday, Mr. McBride!" one of my students—I hadn't yet memorized his name, but he was in my third-period class—yelled down the hallway crowded with scurrying bodies that raced to the parking lot to get a head start on their weekends. Navigating the halls of Whitney High was not made any easier when crutches were involved. Three times this week I'd crashed to the ground when a crutch got wedged against a locker or landed wrong on the slick linoleum or tripped over the foot of a passing student. My messenger bag also swung at my side like a pendulum and further pushed me off balance. Each time, a throng of kids rushed to help me up.

Today had been a manageable one pain-wise, and all I had left to do was successfully get down the fifteen daunting brick steps at the front of the building. School had been back in session for three weeks already. Each day I could feel my strength and coordination picking up. I'd developed a routine. Mallory had also learned to wrap my leg which helped with the edema that I'd experienced the first few days back home.

Well, back at Mallory's home. Moving in with her should've been the highlight of my year—in reality, my life—but these weren't the circumstances under which I'd hoped to take that leap. It felt like it was more out of necessity than excitement. Sure, she was genuinely happy to have me there, and I would be lost without her help and care, but this was a step that I doubted we'd be taking had the accident never occurred.

But it had, and these were our cards.

I purposefully hung out in the lobby a few extra moments to converse with students that lingered after the bell in an effort to wait out the crowds. It was all flurried and frantic for about five minutes before the chaos settled. That was the best time to try to scale down the Mount Everest in front of me.

"Need a hand, Heath?" Paul stopped short when he saw my struggle with the large door, how I switched both crunches under my left armpit and pushed against the handle with my hip. "Here, buddy, I got that."

"Thanks, man." I smiled. Humility—even when forced—was a good and necessary thing for me to experience. "I appreciate it."

"No worries." He held the door wide and waited as I repositioned my crutches to hobble forward. "How're things going at the new place? Mallory taking good care of you?"

"She is." Even though I wanted to be the one taking care of her. "It's not very romantic, wrapping your boyfriend's stump and all, but she's a trooper."

"I doubt she's being a trooper, Heath. I'm sure she enjoys every moment she gets to lay hands on that sexy body of yours," Paul jeered. I knew he was waiting for me to scale down the steps. He didn't have to, and I certainly didn't ask, but I appreciated how he slowed his pace and followed just a few steps behind me.

"Oh, you know it." Finally, with a huge release of breath, I made it to the sidewalk. Hattie grinned at me from her minivan that was pulled close to the curb, waiting to pick me up. She waved excitedly. "Have a good weekend, Paul."

"You too, Heath. Is today the big day?"

My stomach flopped at his words. "Sure is."

He dropped a hand to my shoulder. "It'll be great. Excited for you, buddy."

"How does that feel?"

I pinched my lips together and fought the grimace that wanted to form. "A little tight. Uh, I don't know. Maybe not. Is that normal?"

The young blond woman kneeling on the ground in front of me, who had just told me her name was Heather, nodded. "That's likely from the swelling. We'll provide you with another shrinker sock that you can wear at night and that should cut down on it a little. But you've been wrapping it, yeah?" I nodded. She shifted the liner, turning it just slightly on my skin. "That any better?"

"Lots, actually." I ran my fingers over the joint where the prosthetic met my skin. "That feels pretty good."

She reached for a set of thin boards just off to the left on the gray tufted carpet. "I'm going to have you stand now, Heath. Use the arms of the chair, if necessary, to hold you up at first."

I hadn't, in over a month and a half, stood on two feet. My stomach churned and my mouth went dry. Then, more easily than I had anticipated, I pushed up from the seat. Wobbled a little. Regained my balance, and held my breath, as though breathing would be that extra push to force me back down into the chair.

"Relax, Heath. You're doing great." Heather scooted back and eyed my stance with scrutiny. "How do your hips feel? Out of alignment at all? Or pretty even?" Before I could answer, she brought a tool to my waist that had a level in the middle, and she strained her eyes as she studied the bubble of air that floated a little off center. Reaching for a white pen, she drew two dots on the prosthetic. "I'm going to have you sit so I can adjust that and we'll try again. You're doing just great, Heath."

I had to admit, I did feel great. I was on schedule with Dr. Callahan's projections and my personal goals. There'd been a hiccup a while back when I'd developed an infection in the site of the amputation, but that was tackled quickly and mended without much setback. I couldn't even count the hours I'd put in with physical therapy already, and all the strengthening exercises they had me doing. The uphill battle didn't feel so uphill anymore.

"Okay, let's try this again."

For the second time, I rose to my feet, and this transition was much more natural than the first.

"Good. Good." She lifted the tool to my waist again. "This looks really great, Heath. Can you try to take a few steps forward?"

I didn't know why the panic flooded in. I didn't figure the fitting for my new leg would only involve standing and sitting, but I hadn't let myself mentally prepare for walking. For even setting one foot in front of the other. My fingers tensed. I clamped them into my palms.

Heather stood and walked backward, away from me. "Just a couple steps forward. You can do it, Heath. This is a great fit on you. Trust that it's going to support you."

With my head angled to the ceiling and with the utter of a silent prayer, I put my new left foot in front of my right and pressed down. I felt the pressure in my knee as the prosthetic held my weight. *Held my weight.* I didn't collapse to the floor. I didn't fall flat on my face. I only took four small and hesitant steps before reaching out for Heather's arms for safety, but I did it. I could do this.

Heather guided me back into the chair where I released a few clarifying breaths. I rubbed at my jaw with my hands and then dropped my face into my palms. I tried so hard not to lose it in front of Mallory that I often found myself losing it in front of complete strangers instead.

Poor strangers like Heather.

"I'm sorry." I took the Kleenex she fluttered at me and blew my nose loudly. "This is really embarrassing."

"This is not embarrassing, Heath. This is why I do my job. For overwhelming reactions of joy like this. Has anyone—other than your mom—ever witnessed you taking your very first steps? It's a privilege to be here for it. Cry away. I'm choking up over here, too."

Heather's words brought more tears to my eyes. "I'm just glad I didn't fall on you."

"Wouldn't've been the first time. But you will fall, Heath. That's inevitable. Just be sure to always get up. That's all it comes down to. Getting back up."

Thirty-Seven

Mallory

"He walked today!" My voice screamed excitedly into the receiver. That news had been trapped in my head all day long and I'd been bursting to tell someone. "He *walked*! How unreal is that?"

"Crazy unreal," Heath responded. "That's awesome, babe. I can't wait to see when I get home."

"I'm not sure he'll do it again soon, but you never know. He's all clumsy and awkward, but he's so, so proud. It's even cuter than crawling if you can believe that."

"I can't believe that. Baby army crawl was my favorite."

The red bell peppers sizzled in the pan on the stove and I added the onions to the mix, moving them around with the spatula. Smoke curled in wispy coils and I flipped on the vent to suck them up. Fajitas were Heath's favorite and I knew he'd had a trying week at school and deserved a good meal. Friday night fajitas had quickly become a little tradition for us.

"How long 'til you're home?"

"Not long at all." When his voice echoed not only through the phone, but also the kitchen, I jumped out of my skin, which sent the wooden utensil soaring across the kitchen and left me shaking in surprise.

"Heath! You scared the crap out of me!"

With the help of his left crutch, he walked across the room and hooked me into his body with his free arm. His nose nuzzled against my hair. "Mmmm, you smell like food."

"Is that a compliment?"

"Most definitely. I'm starved." Heath glanced around the room like he was searching for something. "So, where's our little walker?"

"Just finishing up his nap." I bent down to grab the spatula from the floor and chucked it into the sink. I pointed to the flickering baby monitor across the room. "I was going to get him as soon as I finished up here."

Picking at the mound of shredded cheese on the cutting board and popping a handful into his mouth, Heath shook his head. "Nah, let me. I see you've got a good thing going here. I wouldn't want to get in the way of that."

"I swear, the more time you spend with Boone, the more you're starting to sounding like him."

"That's not really a bad thing, is it?"

"It's not a bad thing at all." I grinned. "And yes, it would be super helpful if you could get Corbin ready for dinner. I've got a bit left to do here."

Thirty-Eight

Heath

I propped my crutch against the wall and hopped over to Corbin's crib, mostly because it was easier to handle a one-year-old without hanging on to a crutch, but also because it also made him burst into the cutest fit of giggles every time.

"Hey, my favorite little buddy."

Corbin grasped the rail of the white crib and used it to help him jump wildly up and down. His smile gaped so large that drool dripped right out from it. It soaked the neckline of his cotton onesie.

"I hear you had a pretty epic day." Reaching down, I hoisted Corbin from his bed and hauled him over to the rocker near the window. I needed to steady myself with a hand on the wall, but once in the chair, we settled in for a snuggle. "Walking already, huh? That's huge!"

Corbin babbled something incoherent and I pressed a kiss to his forehead.

"Super impressive, buddy. Not to steal your thunder or anything, but I gotta let you in on a little secret."

Leaning close, I brought my mouth to his ear. "I walked today, too."

As if he could comprehend what I'd said, Corbin let out an excited squeal.

"I know, right? Big day for the men in this household."

There was a collection of board books stacked like pancakes on the low table next to the rocker, and I picked up the top one to flip it open. It was one of Corbin's favorites with fuzzy farm animals and noises that chimed with each turn of the page.

We were on the pig page, his little hand under mine as I guided it over the soft texture when he looked up me with his huge baby eyes and stopped my whole world from spinning.

"Dada."

It was a mistake, of course it was. I shook it out of my head with a jerk.

"No, buddy. That's a piggy." I pressed his hand to the book. "See? Oink, oink."

"Dada."

I closed the book shut and placed it back on the table. Then I saw her.

"How long have you been standing there?"

Mallory fidgeted uneasily with her apron and glanced to the monitor on the table next to me. She slumped against the doorframe. "You walked today?" Her eyes were wet, her cheeks pale. "Why didn't you tell me?"

"Corbin's super confused about his farm animals. I think we need to take a field trip to sort it out—"

"Why wouldn't you tell me?"

My feet planted under me and I pushed back in the rocker and sighed. "I didn't want to steal Corbin's thunder. This is a big day for him. For you both. Like 'going in the baby book' kind of day. I've walked before."

"It's not the same, Heath. This is a really big deal."

"This is a moderately big deal."

"This is a big deal and you should have shared it with me."

I huffed out my air. "I'm sharing it with you now. I walked today. Four steps, but that's it. I was scared shitless and worried I wouldn't remember how to do it, but I did it. Maybe I'll do it again tomorrow."

Her tears streamed down her face. "I'm proud of you, Heath."

"Yeah … I am, too." Now I was crying. I found it a little ironic that the only one not crying was the actual baby. "I didn't want to tell you about the appointment in case it went badly. In case I ended up sprawled out on the floor in a heap of shame."

"There would be absolutely no shame in that." Her mouth was downturned. "None."

"It's cute and adorable when babies fall down when they're learning to walk. It's a whole lot less adorable when a grown man eats it." I scratched at my neck. "The faces on those poor kids at school this week—you should've seen them. It was like they were horrified and sad for me and embarrassed for themselves and it made me sick."

"Do you think my father never fell down?" Her voice shook out of her in a way I'd never heard before. "Do you think I never had to come rushing into his room when he'd crashed to the floor, the paint and the brushes splattered and scattered around him? And do you think— ever for one moment—that I was *embarrassed* by it? That I'd lost respect for him or something? Heath—" Mallory shifted her weight and her eyes narrowed. "I love you. Good or bad. Walking or not. No matter what, I'm here. I'm not going anywhere. So you sure as hell better *let* me be there for you."

She said them as vows and my heart became a kick drum, thundering uncontrollably in my chest. "Mallory—"

"By the way, he knows what a pig is," she said before turning to leave to head back to the kitchen. "And he knows who you are, too."

289

Thirty-Nine

Mallory

"Lucas is delivering the last of them. I've got things taken care of here if you want to take off a little early."

"No, Vickie. Let me help you close up shop." I shut the door to the glass case and pressed my hands to my green apron. "I'm happy to help."

"Nope. Head home to lover boy. I'll be fine here."

I rolled my eyes dramatically but blushed at the phrase she so commonly used when it came to Heath. I'd been working for Vickie long enough now to know that she wouldn't put up with my protest, so I gathered my purse and keys after giving her a hug goodbye and headed to the lot where my car was parked.

Heath had been at home with Corbin all day. He'd had the day off from school and for the last week, he'd left little hints that he wanted to watch him when I went to work. I'd brushed it off, nonchalantly saying I was happy to bring Corbin to the shop with me, but I could tell Heath was sincere in his ask.

So I let him. I would be lying if I said I wasn't nervous. Of course I was apprehensive. Not that I thought

Heath couldn't handle it—that wasn't it at all. I was just in the baby routine and it wasn't something you could easily fall into. I knew when Corbin's cry rose at the end, it meant he was hungry. And when he would rub his tummy, he wanted his pacifier. A flapping hand meant he needed his blankie and a pouty lip indicated he was ready for a nap. I'd cracked his baby code and didn't want to give Heath any additional challenges. He'd overcome so many already.

That being said, it did something to my heart to know that he wanted to spend the day with my son, without me around. It didn't feel like Corbin was the extra part of me anymore. This plus one. This little person that came along when Heath had agreed to be mine. He wasn't baggage. He was a bonus, a huge and wonderful bonus.

I found my heart feeling so much fuller than it ever had with each mile I drew closer to our home. I couldn't wait to hear about their day. I knew a zoo trip and frozen yogurt was on the agenda and around noon, Heath had sent me an adorable selfie that documented their day. The giraffe in the background made me laugh and the ice cream cone with more toppings than I would ever allow made my mouth burst into a smile.

It was an image of a father and son. Maybe not officially in title, but definitely in love.

I'd saved it instantly as the new wallpaper for my phone.

The door was unlocked when I reach the house and my keys clanged against the entryway table as I set them down next to my purse.

"Heath?" I called out like I did every day. He was often home from school several hours before Corbin and I were finished at the flower shop. "Heath? You home?"

"In here!"

His voice resonated down the long hall. I tried to place it and it sounded like maybe they were in Corbin's room. That would make sense. I looked at my wristwatch and realized it was just after Corbin's nap. The breath in my lungs released. Heath had made it through the entire day, following my son's schedule like a pro. This was the closest feeling I'd had to family in the past two years, and part of me wanted to burst into tears while the other couldn't contain the happiness that brought about.

I toed off my shoes and left them in the hall. I couldn't wait to see both of my boys. I picked up my stride and when I got to Corbin's room, only to find it darkened and empty, I stopped in my steps.

"Heath?"

His voice was a bit further off when he answered, "In your room."

I rounded the corner and froze.

"Oh my God, Heath."

I immediately recognized so many of the arrangements I'd crafted just this week. There was the gerbera daisy bouquet I'd arranged yesterday placed on the nightstand, and the calla lily basket I'd worked on earlier in the morning now sitting on the dresser. At least two dozen more sprays of floral arrangements were decorated around the room, and where flowers were lacking, petals were strewn in their place.

And there, among the colorful display, was Heath, Corbin held firmly against his side.

"Hey, you." Heath's smile was soft, just like his voice. "Come on in."

I couldn't keep the tears from forming, and they blurred my ability to walk without bumping into the maze of arrangements. "Heath, what is all of this?"

He motioned me forward until his hand fell into mine. "Did you have a good day at work?"

"Yeah." I warily glanced around the room, at the scene before me. "Did everything go okay with Corbin?"

"It was the best day." Heath's eyes hadn't diverted, even when Corbin arched backward, trying to be free from his grip. "We had the best day."

I wouldn't allow my heart to guess where this was going. I couldn't be let down in that way. Instead, I dragged out our conversation and tried to fill in the quiet gaps. "I'm glad to hear it."

"How about yours?"

I laughed. "Well, I'd say half of what kept me busy today is in this room. And I wondered why we had so many orders last night."

Biting his bottom lip, which left the most adorable dimple in his right cheek, Heath winked at me. "Yeah, I might've had a little something to do with that."

"Looks like."

That was the extent of my procrastinating. I couldn't draw this out any more than I'd already done. There was a next step here, and the air around us vibrated with anticipation.

"Mallory." Heath's neck pulled tight with a swallow. "There's something the two of us wanted to ask you."

Forty

Heath

My stomach had been in knots all day. Twisted and churned. It helped to have Corbin as a distraction today, though. His needs trumped my nerves.

But now, seeing her standing in front of me, feeling the quickened pulse in Mallory's wrist as I held her small hand in mine—this is where the real anxiety settled in and cradled my heart. There was not an inch of my body that didn't buzz with the expectation of what I was about to do.

"Mallory?" Her light eyes impaled me. Her mouth fought a smile she so badly wanted to wear. "You know how when you first meet someone, you instantly fall in love with everything they love?" She nodded, though I didn't need her to. I'd keep talking even if she didn't encourage the words from me. "Like, I cannot tell you how many grilled cheese sandwiches I ate back when we first met. As silly as it was, I'd associated them with you."

"Well." Her voice was timidly quiet. "I am a little cheesy."

"Only a little." I smirked. "But you know what I mean, right? How suddenly, anything that reminds you of that person—that's what you want. That's what you want to surround yourself with."

Her gaze would not let go of mine; her lips would not relinquish the grin they spread into.

"Flowers remind me of you now. I doubt you realize it, but when you come home from work, you smell like them. Like this totally natural bouquet. I can't look at a flower without thinking of you. But you've always been a flower to me. This stunning, delicate thing that blossoms with beauty."

"Heath, that's so sweet."

Maybe she felt like an answer or recognition was needed here, but I kept talking.

"But those are just things. Sure, I felt closer to you, liking the things you liked, but I felt a part of you when I loved the people you loved." My mouth was tacky, my throat dry. I inhaled a breath that could burst my lungs and kept talking. "Boone and Sharon—they're wonderful. Seriously. I adore them. They've welcomed me with the biggest, warmest open arms I could ever imagine." The mist in Mallory's eyes couldn't be ignored, but I let her tears form. Let her emotion well in her eyes just as it did in mine. "And Tommy and Nana. From that first day at the dinner table back in high school, I knew they were something special. The love they have for you is so evident."

Mallory's hands trembled. I gripped on tighter, but the shake in mine just magnified hers.

"Each and every one of those people are amazing, Mallory, but this little guy?" I bounced Corbin up on my hip. "This guy means everything to me."

The hiccup that slipped through Mallory's lips made my heart clench, and when she cupped her mouth and let the tears stream, I was right there with her.

"I love your son, Mallory. The fact that you would think highly enough of me to even let me into his life is a blessing I'll never understand how I ever deserved," I said, readying my balance and my resolve. "All of those things and all of those other people, sure I can love them to the extent I know how, but this guy? He's a part of you. In loving him, I get to love even more of you."

Her shoulders racked with sobs and I wanted to take her so badly into my arms but I couldn't. Not just yet.

"Mallory." Then, with all the strength I could muster, I grasped firmly to Corbin and steadily lowered myself, one slow inch at a time. This was what we'd been working on the past two weeks during physical therapy. Not on taking steps forward. Not on one foot in front of the other. But on kneeling down, dropping to one knee.

I'd fallen many times during my rehab. Stumbled painfully before my knee touched the ground. Flattened out and completely bailed. I had bruised shins and a bruised ego, but I kept at it, always forcing myself to do more than was comfortable or more than what felt possible.

She was the reason I got up. Mallory was the reason I always got back up.

She was the reason after my failed marriage. The reason after the accident. Mallory was now, and forever would be, my reason to persevere.

"More than I want you to be my wife, I want you to be my family. I want you and I want Corbin and I want us. When I lost you all those years ago, the pain I experienced was more than I thought I could ever bear. But I was wrong. I could bear that a million times over if it came down to it again." Her mouth dropped open and she brought both of her hands to my shoulders. I shook nervously back and forth and I suppressed the pain and the strain on my leg, but she trapped me in her grip to steady me. Calm me. I reached for her hand and gave it a squeeze, and then lifted Corbin from my hip to hand

Mallory her son. "What I can't bear is losing both of you. Life has given me more second chances than I deserve, but I don't need another chance to do what I should've done so long ago."

Reaching into my back pocket, I pulled out the black velvet box Tommy had sent me. I cracked it open and held it out for Mallory, who swayed softly back and forth with her child in her arms. "Mallory and Corbin Quinn, will you allow me the honor of loving you both until the day I die. Will you let me protect and cherish and treasure you every day forward? Will you let me be the man you need in your lives, the one who will lead passionately, love faithfully, and never, ever forget the huge blessing it is to call you mine?"

Mallory dropped to her knees. Maybe from my words. Maybe from the sight of the ring that had adorned her own mother's finger so many years ago, but she knelt down with me on the carpet in the middle of her bedroom and reached for my face, grabbing hold of it.

"Yes, Heath." Her mouth found mine and after a kiss that stole my breath, she pulled back, her thumb running across my bottom lip as she said, "We both say yes."

I ignored the throb in my leg as I took the quaint diamond from the box and slipped it on her finger. It was the most beautiful thing I'd ever seen, the way it sparkled just like her eyes.

"I love you, Mallory." Another kiss pressed to her lips. "I've always loved you."

"I know." She smiled and Corbin pressed his cheek against my cheek. "We know. And we love you, too."

Forty-One

Mallory

The two bands on my finger felt like home. That was the only way to describe it. I'd worn rings before, and there was a familiar comfort in them, but this time, when I glanced at my fourth finger and saw my mom's engagement ring, and the diamond-encrusted band that Heath had chosen to match, I couldn't imagine my hand without it.

With that, I was instantly comfortable.

With the white lace nightie and matching panties, not so much.

We'd decided on a date that was close to our engagement. Like four weeks close. Heath had reasoned that we'd waited a dozen years already and that waiting wasn't something we needed to exercise anymore. We were experts in it.

But there were things to do and affairs to get in order. The first was selling my house. As much as I'd loved that place, it was the backdrop for my life with Dylan. It wasn't a new life that I was embarking on, I knew that, but it was okay to let go of pieces of the past when stepping into the future. Plus, we'd found the perfect little cottage three blocks down from *Grow* where I'd be able to walk to work. It was also fifteen minutes closer to Whitney High, so that was another huge selling point.

We'd spent the last couple of weeks packing and unpacking, but tonight was the first official night our new place. It was also our first night as husband and wife.

Heath and Mallory McBride.

The ceremony had been small—only fifty of our closest friends and relatives—and Boone had joyfully agreed to officiate. Heath nearly busted a gut when I'd told him that Boone was an ordained minister. Apparently a burly, three-hundred-pound hulk of a man did not fit his idea of a pastor. But even with his gruff exterior and occasional misplaced remarks, Boone did a beautiful job. I wouldn't have wanted anyone else to marry us. It was the perfect day from the guests to the flowers to the celebration.

Everything related to us getting hitched went off without a hitch.

But I didn't have that same confidence when I looked into the full-length mirror hung on the back of the bathroom door. I'd been working out this past month like all engaged women seemed to do, and though I noticed a bit more muscle where I'd been softer, I doubted Heath would recognize the improvements. It was a subtle and less than impressive difference.

I pushed my hand to my stomach to cover my belly when I heard him call out from the bedroom. "You okay in there? I'm ready whenever you are."

Of course he was. The poor guy had been waiting our entire relationship for this moment, and it would be a lie to say I didn't share that same anticipation, too. I grabbed my wineglass from the counter near the sink and threw back the last swallow that remained.

"Coming."

With a wink at my reflection in the mirror for a boost of confidence, I pushed open the door. Right away, I noticed the candles that dotted the furniture, their amber glow flickering against dark walls. Quiet, instrumental music filtered from the surround sound speakers.

And there, leaning against the foot of our new queen-size bed, was my husband.

He was gorgeous. He wore gray drawstring pants low on his hips, and the strong V that trailed into his waistband made my heart ram into my throat. He was all muscle and man and strength bound in this incredible body that was all mine. *Mine.*

I smirked to myself.

"What are you smiling at, Mrs. McBride?" Heath took a step toward me and dropped his large hands possessively to my bare hips. He nipped at my neck. "Hmm?"

"Nothing." I smiled against his skin, arching my head back to allow his mouth to continue its greedy exploration of my body.

"You sure about that?" His breath was hot. I shivered when it hit my chilled and pebbled skin. "You looked pretty damn amused."

"Did I?" The words became harder to form. My brain was suddenly working in short and choppy sentences, unable to string anything more significant together.

"Mmm hmmm," was all he responded before swinging his arm around my back and spinning me in one motion. With one move forward, Heath pressed his leg between mine and forced me softly back so the backs of my knees hit the mattress. My breath trembled from my lips and panted out. "You okay?" Heath's eyes searched mine. His brow quirked up.

"More than okay," I assured him with my mouth on his neck, his chest, his shoulder that I was, indeed, very okay.

"All right," he said through a convincing smile.

Then Heath hauled over me, gentle and tender though everything from the sheen of sweat on his bare chest to the way it rose rapidly with his shaking breath showed the enormous restraint that took. I backed myself up on the bed, scooting along the mattress as Heath crawled above me, his arms on either side of my head.

Everything buzzed as his full mouth explored each inch of me that now belonged to him and no one else. Every piece that was forever his. Heath slipped my straps from my shoulders and eased the garment from my body and every place his fingers touched, his lips eagerly followed.

My breath quivered and my chest followed its shaky rhythm. The nerves I'd harbored were instantly replaced with a new hunger for Heath. To explore his body. To discover the pieces of him that, only now, were mine. He brought his lips back to mine and he slipped his tongue into my mouth and I grasped onto his shoulders as our mouths moved against one another in the same rhythm as our bodies and our souls.

I'd had sex so many times in my life. I'd even made love before. But what Heath and I were doing wasn't on that same scale. This was where they'd said two became one. I'd never understood it before, how in marriage and in love that could ever happen, but this was it.

I no longer belonged to myself, and Heath was not his own.

We were one in flesh and body and life and love.

As I tugged at his waistband and found a place for my hands to fall, every hesitant emotion that I'd clung to before dissipated immediately. I was safe with Heath. He was my protector and now my world. My former anxiety that wound tight in my chest was replaced with the intense need to be with this remarkable, astonishing man. To surrender my insecurities and my worries and to trust him with my heart, with my body.

He'd had his own hang-ups, too. More than once he'd apologized for his leg and expressed his worry that it would be a turn off for me. In that moment, I understood the anger he'd felt when I'd apologized for my body before—for the stretch marks and the changes that being pregnant had brought about. In my eyes, there was nothing about Heath that wasn't perfect. I finally understood that he felt exactly the same when it came to me.

And there was nothing about the two of us that wasn't perfect together.

We found our connection almost instantly, the slow build that graduated into a rhythm that surged with the need our bodies knew exactly how to achieve. I trusted him fully and he reciprocated that surrender with each kiss and intense look in my eyes that fluttered my belly and threw my heartbeats off course. Our clothes, the sheets, our hands, and legs all tangled together as we chased our desire and our longing. Only when he pulled back to ask if I was okay did we stop or pause to let our breath catch up with our racing hearts.

"You are incredible, Mallory," Heath said as he ran his hands over my body, his eyes dragging down with them. "This is incredible." His words sighed against my feverish skin. "I'm seriously the luckiest guy in the entire world."

Maybe we were both lucky, though. Lucky that life allowed us just one more chance.

We spent all night in one another's arms, our bodies and hearts connected in the most intimate ways. I fell asleep there in the safety of his embrace.

We'd had our rocky start, our choppy seas when the storms came, but Heath would forever be my safe and constant place. He was more than just my boat now. He was my heart's vessel. Maybe he always had been. Maybe he'd been keeping it safe for me all this time and finally, now as one, our hearts could beat together.

All I knew was that from now on, until the day it stopped, mine would forever beat for Heath, the first— and last—love of my life.

Epilogue

Heath

"Look what's here!" I flung open the front door and the pewter handle smashed into the drywall. I cringed. "Sorry—I'll fix that, but did you see what the mailman left on the porch?"

Mallory was sitting cross-legged on the floor in a flowing purple dress while Corbin ran circles around her. The dizzying scene made my head spin and I raced as quickly as I could to interrupt his current lap, scooping him up in my arms. I'd been walking for nearly a year now, but I still wasn't as proficient as I'd hoped to be. Mallory said I was being too hard on myself, but sometimes I figured it was her job to talk me down. It was a job she was infinitely good at.

"What are you all excited about?" I said to my son, who tried hard to wriggle free from my grasp. "Hmm?"

"I could ask you the same," Mallory grunted as she pushed off the ground, using her belly as momentum with a hand to her arched back. "What's in the package?"

I'd written him only a week ago and did not expect such a quick response, or even one at all. That it had just been a few days was insanely impressive. I was dying to rip it open.

"Just a little surprise for you."

"Heath." Mallory smiled and it pushed her full cheeks to her eyes. "You know it's not a good idea to surprise a pregnant woman, right? You want to send me into early labor? How comfortable are you with home births?"

"This is one you're really going to like. Much better than the last one."

"Why you would think an obscenely pregnant would want a striped magenta bikini is beyond me."

"Because, umm, have you *seen* your preggo boobs?" I scratched at the back of my neck and smirked. "And yeah, because boobs."

Mallory swatted me with her hand. "You are too much, you know that?"

"Back to my surprise." I brought the package from where I'd settled it in the entryway and propped it up against the family room wall. I stared at it for a moment, wanting to savor the anticipation a bit longer. This was going to be so good.

"Are we going to open it, or just admire the wrapping?"

"Admire." My fingers rubbed my chin and then I let out a satisfied sigh. "Okay, done admiring. Have at it."

Her brow raised. "You want *me* to open it?"

"Yep. Go for it. Just rip right in."

Waddling adorably to the package, Mallory tossed a wary glance over her shoulder before taking the edge of the paper into her hands. With a synchronized *one, two, three,* she peeled back the parchment and let out the loudest, sharpest squeal. "Oh my God, Heath! We're having a girl?"

There, on the canvas, was a smattering of pink paint, strokes and splatters of peaches and corals.

"I thought you wanted to wait to find out?"

I shrugged and came up behind my wife, wrapping my hands under her belly and bringing my chin to her shoulder. "In case you haven't caught on yet, I'm really bad at waiting."

"I think there are plenty of people who would disagree with you on that. Remember those twelve, long years?"

"I'm good at waiting when I have no other choice. But we had a choice here. I honestly couldn't wait any longer to find out more about that baby of mine growing in your belly, so I sent your dad the envelope with the ultrasound and asked him to let us know the verdict." I pressed a slow kiss to Mallory's neck. "I want to know everything there is to know about our baby. Her likes, her dislikes. The sound of her voice. The way her tiny hand is going to fit in mine. Would you hurry up and finish with this whole pregnancy thing so I can finally meet her?"

Mallory's round stomach tightened with the laugh. "Only a few more months. You'll just have to be patient with this."

"If I have to," I relented. "But only because you asked so nicely."

"Oh really?" I loved that even though we'd been married ten months and pregnant for six, Mallory still had the energy and desire to flirt. It was a huge turn-on, though everything she did turned me on. "Only because I asked nicely?"

"Mallory, have you not realized that you can ask me for anything and it's yours? This really isn't a big secret, you know."

"I don't need to ask for anything else. I have you and Corbin, and now our daughter." Her eyes rounded and she turned in my arms to look at me with an awestruck expression. "Wow. We're having a *daughter*, Heath."

"I know." I was still processing it; how incredible our lives had turned out to be. "It's pretty damn amazing, right?"

She rested her head on my chest, turning her belly sideways to fit deeper into my arms. "Did you ever think way back when you stood on my front porch that this is where we'd end up?"

I nodded my head and my chin pressed into her soft, red hair. "Yes. This is exactly where I wanted to end up. Remember when you asked how on earth we weren't a thing already and I said that I was working on it?"

"Yeah."

"Well, it took me over a decade to get there, but that was me working on it."

"Determined." She laughed.

"I'd say." I pulled her closer. "It wasn't easy, but it was so unbelievably worth the wait." I rubbed circles on her stomach and said, "And this little one is going to be worth the long wait, too."

"Good things come to those who wait," Mallory recited, fitting her small hand over mine.

"Great things," I agreed. "Letting my heart wait on you was the best decision I ever made. I'm not even sure it was an actual decision. I could never let go of you, no matter how hard I'd tried. I just couldn't shake my love for you, Mallory."

"I'm glad." She held me tighter. "And I love that we were able to pick up right where we left off."

"There was no doubt in my mind that we wouldn't. We just had to wait for life to give us another chance," I said. "But remember, you *are* the girl that does seem to love everything, so of course you would love that fact."

With her lips pressed to mine, Mallory kissed me tenderly. Our gaze connected as she said, "I might love everything, Heath, but I love you more than anything, and there's a difference."

I just smiled down at the woman who so wholly possessed me it made it hard to breathe. "I know there is, Mallory. I feel it. I've always felt that difference with you."

It was the reason that—after all those years, and for all the years to come—Mallory would forever own my heart.

She made all the difference, and I wouldn't have had it happen in any different way.

THE END

Megan Squires is a writer and a photographer and loves to photograph based on what she writes and write based on what she photographs. She's fueled by Diet Coke and an overactive imagination and can't do without the San Francisco Giants, her romance novel-filled kindle, and her cowgirl boots.

And she loves *love*. Like seriously adores those butterflies you get when you think about that first kiss or reminisce about holding hands with someone you'd been crushing on for years. Even if it was cringe-worthy and terrible, there's just nothing like connecting with another human being on that nervous, hesitant level. Relationships are complex and wonderful and scary, and Megan gets a rush each time she has a chance to write about them and all of their layers. This is why young and new adult literature are her genres of choice.

A graduate from the University of California, Davis, with an international relations degree, Megan currently resides in Sacramento with her husband, two children, two golden retrievers and two horses. She's practically building an ark. She documents her dreams with both her keyboard and camera and has enough characters in her head to keep her busy for years.

You can visit Megan online at
www.megansquiresauthor.com.

Made in the USA
Columbia, SC
13 October 2020